# MY HEART WENT WALKING

## SALLY HANAN

 FIRE DRINKERS PUBLISHING

Lines quoted from "Be Melting Snow," "Desire and the Importance of Failing," and "#1369" by Rumi, Jalal al-Din. *Kolliyaat-e Shams-e Tabrizi. Public Domain.* Translated by Coleman Barks and John Moyne as *The Essential Rumi, New Expanded Edition* (HarperOne; reprint edition, 2004).

Interior design by Inksnatcher
Cover design by Vanessa Mendozzi

Printed in the United States of America

Library of Congress Cataloging-in-Publication Data
Names: Hanan, Sally, author
Title: My Heart Went Walking: An Irish tale of love, loss, and redemption/Sally Hanan
Subjects: | BISAC: FICTION/Women's Literature and Fiction. FICTION/Sisters. FICTION/British and Irish Literary Fiction. FICTION/Historical Irish Fiction.

Description: First e-book edition. | Austin, Texas: Fire Drinkers Publishing, 2022. | Summary: "Runaway Una returns to her Irish hometown to save her dying sister and face her sister's boyfriend, the love she left behind." — Provided by publisher.
Identifiers: LCCN 2021911369 | ISBN 978-1-7333330-3-0 (hardback) | ISBN 978-1-7333330-4-7 (paperback) | ISBN 978-1-7333330-5-4 (e-book)

LC record available at https://lccn.loc.gov/

For information about special discounts for bulk purchases, or if you'd like the author to speak at your event, please contact Sally via www.sallyhanan.com.

*To Gerry, my forever home*

# TABLE OF CONTENTS

# NAME AND PLACE PRONUNCIATIONS

Ashlinn – **ash**-lin

Bríd - **bree**dge

Cavan – **ka**-vun

Connor – **con**-er

Cullen – **cull**-un

Dalkey – **dawk**-y

Donegal – **dun**-ee-**gawl**

Dunfanaghy – dun-**fan**-ah-he

Dylan – **dill**-un

Enniskillen – **enn**is-**kill**-un

Gallagher – **gal**-ah-her

Gillian – **Jill**ian

Kieran – **keer**-on

Kilmacud – **kill**-ma-**cud**

McLaughlin – ma-**glock**-lin

Navan – **nav**-un

Seamus – **shay**-mus

Sinéad – shin-**aid**

Una – **oon**-ah

# GLOSSARY

banjaxed – ruined

banshee – a wailing ghost

bedsit – studio apartment

biscuits – cookies

boot of the car – trunk

bricking (about something) – very scared

buggy – stroller

candy floss – cotton candy

cooker – stove

crèche – day care/nursery

crisps – chips

cross – angry

debs – prom

eejit – fool

fadó, fadó – long, long ago

flapjack – a thick soft biscuit made from oats, butter, sugar, and syrup

flats – apartments

floozy in the jacuzzi – statue of an implied naked women in a fountain

fringe – bangs

gaff – house or flat

gander (take a) – have a look at

git (awful) – a stupid or unpleasant person

give it a lash – try to do something, give it a shot

give someone a lift – give someone a ride

gobshite – terrible person

gobsmacked – very surprised

goohing – having a goo or look at

grinds – tutoring

guard/ Gardaí – policeman/the police

hack it – handle it

half term – a short break in the middle of a school semester

hot press – a shelved cupboard the water heater sits in, usually used for storing sheets

hussy – a girl or woman who people judge to behave badly

icing – frosting

immersion – water heater

Jaffa Cakes – a small round cake/cookie topped with orange spread and chocolate

janey mackers – oh my gosh

jumper – sweater

knackered – exhausted

knickers – undies

lay into someone – to attack somebody violently with hard hits or words

Leaving (the) – government final high school exams

lino – linoleum

locked – drunk

loo or the jacks – toilet

lorry – truck

mad about – likes someone a lot

manky – filthy, rotten

midge – no-see-um

mitch school – play hooky

mot – girlfriend

nappy – diaper

national school – elementary school

not on your nelly – not on your life

on the tear – out drinking

penknife – pocketknife

petrol – gasoline

porridge – oatmeal

poxy – lousy

rag order – hungover, sick, or disorganized

rashers – bacon

runners – sneakers

sixth year – 12th grade/senior year

snog – French kiss

sod (lucky sod, sod it all) – a person, a difficult thing, feck it all

spazz out – to act in a silly way

Sudocrem – a brand of diaper cream

taking the mickey (out of someone) – getting someone to believe something that isn't true

Terry Wogan – a famous Irish singer and show host

trolley – cart

the day that's in it – the special day it is

up the pole – pregnant

wains – children

weir – a dam in a stream or river to raise the water level or divert its flow

windscreen – windshield

yoke – a word that replaces "thing"

# 1983

*You know how it is. Sometimes we plan a trip to one place, but something takes us to another.*
—Rumi

# 1

## Una

### Donegal, Ireland

### September
### Wednesday

You stupid, stupid girl!"

I back my way to the door. Mam's finger is pointing right at my heart. I turn and run.

I have no idea where to run though. Our woods? Cullen's house is down the road, but that's the first place she'd come looking for me, probably to call me more names the nuns would put us in detention for at school. Mam's never called me that before, never shouted at me like that before.

I need to hide for a while until she calms down. I split out the back door and breathe in the view for a minute while I sort myself out: the lofty fir trees along the road, blowing their arms around like priests with holy water; the vast garden of bulbous winter vegetables

Frank Jones has growing next door; and the fields embraced by haphazard stone walls and hedges slowly rising all the way to the mountains.

I spy a place to hide, even if it's really lame and she'd find me in a second—the car. Why did I tell Mam at all? Why, why, why? I open the back door and curl up on the soft seat.

MY TIMEX SAYS IT'S SIX. The two brothers' heads sparkle past the car window in response to Mam's call to dinner, oblivious to my scrunched-up body in the back. Ellie's probably helping Mam get dinner on the table and getting little Ruthie into the high chair.

My stomach is in rag order now. I can smell the shepherd's pie I helped Mam make earlier, before I told her I was pregnant, before she called me things Father Barry tells us will condemn us to hell forever.

Jesus, Mary, and Joseph, if you're up there, help me now. I haven't a clue what to do.

Forty minutes later and I'm starting to feel like I want to puke and I can't open the car door fast enough, but Mam put a child lock on the back door and I can't get out and I puke all over the green back seat of her Honda Civic. Can life get any worse?

Holding my breath isn't working. I reckon dinner's over and Ellie's skedaddled to the bathroom with little Ruthie. I flump onto the front seat to get out and sneak along the hedge of prickly holly leaves to the bathroom window, its dull light weaving through the gloaming onto my feet. My tights aren't much use against the sweep of wind that's blowing in through every thread of them. I hope to God Ellie's in there. Sure enough, the joint blur of one big and one tiny body moves behind the pocked

4

glass, along with the low murmur of Ellie's voice. She always talks to Ruthie when they're in there. She always talks to everyone, but Ruthie's her best listener ... when she's got her trapped like that. I bang my knuckles against the icy glass and wait with a fist under each armpit to ward off the wind.

Ellie's coffee-colored hair appears first, followed by her Brigette Bardot face—according to every boy in town. "What the hell are you doing out there? Are you trying to get in the window?"

"Not right now; I just need a wet towel." I dangle an arm through the open space.

Ellie sticks a towel in the bathwater and rinses it out a bit. Ruthie starts to cry and stands with her half-naked body on the bath mat with her arms reaching up to the window. She always wants to be with the sister she can't have.

"Thanks." Ellie stares at me for a second before I hunker back down and head for the car.

Wiping the wet towel over the seat is only making this worse. It's spreading my puke, not mopping it up, and despite the awful stink of it all, I really want some dinner. Maybe Ellie can get me some later, or maybe I can get back into the house when they've all gone to bed. Or I could go to Tanya's house and help myself to her fridge. Best friends and all that.

I do my best with what's left of the rank, lumpy mess on the seat and wave my hand to fan the air, much good it'll do my nose.

Ellie's left the window open a smidgen and she helps me wriggle my hips through and plant my feet on the toilet seat lid. Lucky for me, Ruthie's out of the bath now, but she's got her fat little leg trying to reach up and over the edge of it, back into the bubbles. I throw the towel into the water that's on its way down the drain and swish it around.

Ellie's acting as if nothing weird is going on at all. That's how the Gallaghers do things. We pretend everything is normal, no matter what kind of shite is happening, until someone says it isn't.

"God, what have you done to your hair, Una?" She reaches up and pats a bit against my ear. "You never could get it straight. Someone should invent something for that."

I suppose puking your guts up all over your mam's car would set the hair dancing.

Ruthie plays with the mess of it while Ellie puts her nappy on. "Here we go, Ruthie," she says. "First, I fold in each side of the nappy, like this, and then I put the liner in it, like this." She grabs Ruthie's feet in one hand and dips her fingers into the Sudocrem I just opened for her. "And now I'm going to put it on your bum bum, like this, until your bum looks like an ice cream." She smiles, but I don't know if I have it in me. She sticks the big nappy pins in *very* carefully, clicks down the pink cap on them, and then stands Ruthie to her feet. We're like her other mothers.

Ellie looks up at me, into my eyes, and I wonder if she knows, if Mam told her; but Mam's probably mortified, wondering what everyone's going to say. It'll be all over town in hours if she says anything. Father Barry'll probably use me as an example of Mary Magdalene in his next sermon. Oh God, I'll be kicked out of St. Joseph's! What am I going to say? I haven't told Cullen I have his baby in this deep part of my body, and I don't plan on telling him either. I'm scared stupid and I have no idea how he'll react. But if Mam tells?

But I had to tell her. She's my mam, for God's sake. I'd kept it in for so long and I knew she'd notice it soon. She's always gone on at us about telling the truth. I felt evil for not telling her. Do I feel better now?

No. Not at all.

"Upsadaisy, Ruthie," says Ellie. "Give me your foot so we can get your jammies on." I hold Ruthie's little body so she won't fall over. Ellie's the nice one. I'd trust her, but I don't want her to have to keep secrets. It wouldn't be fair on her. But here's what I didn't tell Mam. If I had a choice to do it all over again, I would, only with a Durex this time and no drink.

There. I've said it. I liked it, and Father Barry and all the nuns at St. Joseph's can stay in their miserable, sadistic, single lives because they don't know what they're missing. No wonder Mam keeps having babies. It's the only time she's allowed to do it.

*"The A-Team* is on at eight, and I want to be sure Ruthie is fast asleep by then so I don't miss any of it. Can I get you anything?" Ah, Ellie, always thinking of everyone else.

My tummy growls. "Do you think you can get me some dinner?"

"Cornflakes?"

I nod and lock the bathroom door after her. I can't face anyone else right now and pretend I'm okay. Thank God the rest of them are in watching the telly. After a few minutes she knocks on the door.

"Thanks." I grab the sloshing bowl of milk and cardboard flakes. She forgot the sugar. I chomp it all down but then have to make my teeth-brushing time longer than usual. It takes a bit to get rid of the scraps of soggy cornflakes in my teeth and that manky taste of sick, and each brush feels like it'll never get this level of yuck off them. I'm staring at my reflection in the wet mirror, looking at this face with my white skin and my red eyes.

"Your face is shaped like a heart because everything in your heart comes out of your mouth." That's what Cullen told me once. Cullen…. I hiccup.

I make sure no one is in the hallway, other than that picture of Jesus pointing to his glowing heart that kind of gives me the creeps, and place my feet, heel, toes on different spots of the carpet where I know the floor won't squeak. My hands keep me steady, fingers splayed on the wallpaper's embossed ferns and crowns that lord over every step. I let out a big breath when I finally get to shut the bedroom door. I won't be reading tonight. My current book lands on the pile of other library books in the back of the bedside locker. *Click,* and the bedside light is off. *Swoosh,* and my icy toes can't fight through the flannel sheets to reach the hot water bottle fast enough. My cheek sinks into the pillow like quicksand, along with my thoughts. What am I going to do?

I thought about leaving Donegal, leaving these mountains and beaches that feed my soul, and going over to England on the boat. I've heard they'll do you know what over there. I don't know anyone who's done it though. I can't imagine what it would feel like to have something go up inside me and take away the tiny, beating heart that Cullen Breslin put in there. It sounds too hard. I just can't do that. I'm not that kind of girl. Mam's sat us down so many times and, smiling, told us she's going to have another one, and then comes a tiny, squirmy, curled-up ball of eyes and hands and love.

I've already thought about it. I want to hold this baby in my arms. I want to bend my face down to hers and kiss her forehead and smell her baby smell. I want to have her tiny eyes look for me. I want to hold her heart close to mine.

She'll look just like Cullen, of course. She'll have his soft lips, his blue eyes the color of that hand lotion in the Body Shop—I think it's called Sea Green, but it's really blue, I swear. She'll have a big smile like Cullen's too, and a dimple on her right cheek, and her hair will be the color of a Cadbury's chocolate flake.

Mam's all about us making our own decisions and living with them, like it or lump it. This isn't something I can like or lump. Maybe Mam will come around and pretend the baby is hers and I can be a big sister to my own child. Maybe everything will be all right ... except Mam warned me that day after Mass when we saw Ciara Brady show up with her huge bump. "I'm so glad you're not like that Ciara. I feel sorry for her mother, but I don't know why she didn't send her away," she said. And then she said, "I will never raise a bastard of a grandchild." But I've seen her with her Ruthie. I think that once she holds my baby in her arms, she'll change her mind. She has to.

The noise of the telly thumps through the walls. Dad's probably in his chair watching the football, with his hand moving back and forth from his mouth to the tin of biscuits, using his belly as a table, the boys watching every stir of the hand to see if he'll pass the tin over.

Ellie tiptoes into our room. Her clothes fall to the floor before her static nightie crackles in the darkness. It must be bad out there if she's not watching the football with Dad—their ritual. I hear her footsteps crossing the carpet between us and feel a fat wad of toilet paper planted next to my face. She must have heard me sniffling. My fingers curl around it. I can see her outline hovering before she moves back to her side. I know she wants to ask me exactly what the deal is, but we don't do that here, even though we're almost twins with just the eighteen months between us. We just don't ask.

Her sheets swish. "Una?"

"Huh?"

"Are you all right?"

I keep my face to the wall, and it takes me a second to get my wits back with the shock of her asking. "No. Not really." I smooth the pillowcase crease by my nose. "But thanks, Ellie."

The noises in the house trickle to a halt. Ellie's little snores ripple through the blanket she always pulls up halfway over her face.

I haven't a clue what to do next. All I could think about earlier was what to tell Mam, and that wasn't much of a mouthful of words. All I said was "Mam, I'm pregnant," before she laid into me. Now I'm lying here like a bag of wet cement and no brains at all. Funny how I can always try and fix everyone else's problems but when it comes to me, all I can do is hit myself for not thinking and for being so stupid.

I was stupid. I had this stupid idea that she'd sit with me and talk about it. But we don't talk about things. Ever. I knew better. How can I look Mam in the face in the morning? What'll Dad say? When will she tell him?

Mam came in a bit ago, but when she looked over at me, she said nothing. She kissed Ellie good night, but then she left and closed the door. Is that her saying she's never going to talk to me again, or does it mean she's still thinking about what she wants to say?

# 2

## Una

### Thursday

Mam's tires chomp into the gravel going out the driveway. Ellie is in the kitchen in the blue dressing gown she made in Home Ec. The braiding on the edges is coming loose. She turns from the high chair, the spoonful of porridge in her hand. "Mam left you a letter." She nods to the table.

Stomach revolting again, I get the bread knife and slice the envelope right on its edge.

> Una,
>
> I haven't told your dad yet. To be honest, I don't know what to tell him. Do I tell him that his oldest isn't headed for college? He was so proud. Neither of us ever made it that far, and we were so sure …
>
> What the hell were you thinking? What the hell was that boy thinking? You haven't

*even told me who it was. Do you even know???*

*You'll have to go to a doctor. Maybe you're not even pregnant.*

*I love my kids, but I have no intention of rearing yours too. How are you going to look after a baby? You're only sixteen, for God's sake! Will you even do your Leaving? Will what the government gives you be enough to have a place to live and put food on the table? Can you go to college if you can't get a babysitter half the time? How will you ever have any future? Sure look at my life. I wanted this once. I wouldn't change any of it, but sometimes I wish I hadn't married quite so young. I'd love to have waited a bit and trained up in something and had a decent job. I wanted that for you. I want that for all my kids.*

*Remember the day you brought that mug home? "Mirror, mirror on the wall, I am my mother after all" is written around it. We both laughed that day. You said, "You always say I'm just like you, Mam, as stubborn as they come. When you drink your tea, maybe it'll calm you down enough to forgive me for whatever I've not done that day." Well, Una, there's not a whole lot I can say about the sorry state you're in today. Forgiveness won't help you much. You've taken on a lifetime of everything for a few seconds of sex, and I hope to God you can handle it. This is all in your hands now.*

*I'm going to see the nuns and ask them to take you in. Then you can put the baby up for adoption once he's born. Please don't embarrass the family by doing anything stupid.*

*Mammy*

My whole chest feels like it's in a nutcracker being squeezed tighter and tighter. That's when the tears start to track down my face.

"Una?"

I put my hand up to stop Ellie talking. Every part of me feels like dissolving jelly.

So there's no point even talking about it. When Mam sets her mind on something, she never budges; there's no arguing with her. If she says this baby inside me has to be given up for adoption, then that's what's going to happen, no matter how much I fight her. But you don't think about those things when you're after living scared stupid for weeks. You have to tell and hope for the best.

Could I get Dad on my side? But that might start them fighting and him drinking again, like they did when he lost his job and was on the dole for so long. I hated those years. I don't want that for the wains. He was disappointed in himself then. Would telling Dad make him go back to the drink because he'd be so disappointed in me?

Forget breakfast. I have to protect this baby. I have to. I walk slowly to the hot press, one foot in front of

the other. Breathe, breathe. I have to get away from here.
I get a bag down. I need to pack. What do I even pack?
My hand's on the zip, but I can't pull it back. No. I have
to talk to Cullen. He's the only one who understands me.
I have to tell him.

He'll know what to do.

The wind has picked up something fierce outside;
even the grass looks like it's ready for liftoff. I put on a
jumper and run out the back door and across the fields
of wet grass to Cullen's house, my capris flapping against
my thighs as my runners squish grass and dandelions and
kick their spores free from their inner circle.

Every step has a picture that flashes into my mind
with it.

Cullen leaving school before he does his Leaving.

Cullen asking me to marry him because it's the right
thing to do.

Cullen starting a shitty job, maybe even two, just so
I can stay at home with our baby.

Cullen slowly dying inside because anything he's ever
wanted in life is locked behind a death sentence ...
because of me.

And that's when I know what I have to do. 1. Keep
my baby. 2. Never use this baby to glue Cullen to me,
even though I would love nothing more than to be with
him forever because it's not his fault.

I stop in the middle of the field, push my hands
against my head until it hurts, scream into the wind. I
can almost feel physical pain in my chest as it starts to
freeze over. My mind continues to war with my heart.

*You could stay, you know. Tell Cullen the truth, ignore the
gossip and the stares in town, tell your mam to go feck herself, let
Cullen take care of you both. You could let him make the decision*

*instead of you making it for him.*

*No! He's too kind, too generous, too good. He won't choose what's best for him!*

*And you will?*

*I know him well. I know what he'll choose. And I can't let him ruin his life. I can't saddle him with us. He needs to be with someone sweet and kind and lovely. I'm none of those things. No, this is not even an option.*

My hand turns his back door handle, instantly slippery with the fear from my palms. Mrs. Breslin's at work, always at work. I push door after door until I burst into his room. He's lying on his crumpled duvet, staring at the ceiling.

"So you're talking to me now?" he says, his eyes still on the flat white above him.

I stand there, lungs expanding, shrinking. "Yes."

He rolls onto his side and looks into my eyes, the sea green of his own rich and wild. I want to plant myself in him. This is what I was afraid of. This is what I ran from.

"Yes," I say again. "I need your help."

He sits up and pats the duvet beside him. Runs a hand through his curls. Puts it back down on his lap to meet the other one.

I can't look at his face right now, his legs … those hands … but I sit down. Swallow. And begin story time. The one I thought up as I ran through the dandelions and set them free.

It's not as hard as I thought it would be—lying to Cullen—especially while I'm talking to the door of his bedroom instead of to his face. It's like I'm walking through foggy woods and all I have to do is keep coming up to the next tree trunk to find my way out.

"So after that party where we, you know … it took

me a few days to try and understand what happened. *I've been in love with you since I was thirteen. I wanted all of you. I will always want all of you.* And after about a week, I decided that I was just really drunk and I used you to see what sex was really like. I'm really sorry about that. Using you." My hands are jittering like mad and I can't hold them tightly enough.

"But then I did something even worse." I can't look at him at all. I know already what his face will say. The pedestal he's always had me on will crack and I'll fall through the broken trapdoor.

"I'd been talking to Dylan for a few weeks at the caravan park—that fella whose parents left him there for the summer, and whenever I went for a walk on the beach, he always ended up walking with me. I told him about what I'd done, and he said ..." *Here we go.* "... he said I should have done it sober, and how would I like to see what it's like when your brain can enjoy it too?"

I can see this grand story that never was in my mind, and it almost feels real apart from the sound of Cullen's wobbly breathing. *The fog. Find the next tree.*

"And then he kissed me and took me back to his caravan and we had sex." *And now for the coup d'état.* "And he was right. It's much better sober."

Silence.

I can hear the birds chirrup near his window.

The wind surging against the walls.

The RTE radio jingle fading in and out in the kitchen.

But silence.

"And I know you always thought I was so wise, but it's even worse than that." My hand reaches up to my tummy and rests on my scarlet jumper. "I'm pregnant, and I think it's Dylan's, and I'm going to Dublin to tell him because Mam wants me to give the baby to the nuns and there's no flipping way in hell I'm going to let her, so all I can do is go and hope for the best."

It's only now that I look at him, look at his curls flattened by the pillow he was on a few minutes ago, look at the fists he's made of his hands, look at the way he's pushed his knees tightly together. His words trip over each other, frostbitten.

"Are you sure it's Dylan's?"

*No, Cullen, I know it's yours because yours is the only skin I ever wanted next to mine.* "Yeah, because I had my period right after the party." *I didn't. I finished it the day before I put my lips on yours and watched my brain cells dance away.*

"It looks like you've decided then. Was there anything else you needed me for?"

My heart might as well stop beating. "Well, no." I stand up. Pull my jumper down over my bum. "Thanks for listening." I turn around to face him. His head is still down. "I'll let you know how it goes."

"Yeah," he says. "You do that."

I can almost hear the bolts shrieking *bitch, bitch, bitch* as he locks off our friendship behind me and determines to never let me back in, and I run to get as far away from the agony as I can, even though I will never get far enough.

Now I know why they call it crying buckets. I've never lied to him before, never hidden part of myself away. It's always been my whole heart with him. I can't bear to keep walking.

ELLIE MUST HAVE SEEN ME get the bag down. Her fingers shove something into my back pocket. I feel it with my fingertips. Money. Straightaway, I know where she got it from. As soon as she turned fourteen, she got a job babysitting, and she's been saving up her money for over a year to get a puppy. Mam said she could have it if she paid for everything herself. She nearly had enough, and now she's giving it to me.

"You want to turn me into a basket case?"

"I don't know what's going on," she says softly, "but you look like you're going somewhere and I want you to have it." She leaves me in the hallway with the picture of Jesus's illuminated heart, but I turn it to face the wall and follow her into the kitchen. She lifts the porridge pot off the cooker and walks with it to the sink.

"Ellie, something happened and I have to leave for a bit. Mam's really angry with me and she said some things that make me think I'd be safer if I wasn't here."

She stares at me like I've gone off my rocker. "Why wouldn't you be safe?"

I make fists out of my hands and knock them together. Do I tell her? I look at the floor, noticing the part where I dropped a plate on the tile when I was five. I'm always reminded of that when we bring up everyone's stupid stuff they've done. "I'm sorry, Ellie. And tell Mam I'm sorry too."

Ellie reaches out to put a hand on my arm, but I pull back. She holds her arms to her chest, stung by my rejection. "Why don't you wait until she gets home so you can talk to her? Is it that bad?"

I have to lie, again, but I can still add the truth. "I'm just sick to the teeth of Mam always telling me what I'm doing wrong and what I should be doing and how I should be doing it. I'm exhausted trying to make her happy. I'm fed up of always having to be home at ten

19

and her going ballistic if I'm a minute past." I take in another gulp of air. "I have to get out of here, Ellie. I have to be treated like I'm old enough to know how to live my life my way."

I turn before she can see my tears start up again and walk out of the kitchen. She doesn't follow. I put a few things in the bag on the bed—some jeans, a pair of boots, all my knickers and socks, warm jumpers. I can't make it too heavy. The thought of leaving her and all the family stabs me in my chest, but I can't cry now, not now. I breathe in the smell of home, kiss my worn teddy's missing ear stitches, give him one last hug, and put him on Ellie's pillow. She'll know what it means.

She's standing at the front door with Ruthie on her hip. I kiss Ruthie's curls for the last time. "Tell Mam I'm going somewhere safe and not to be worried." Ellie nods and I walk away without turning my head, each step farther and farther from the only home I've ever known.

It's only half eight and I'm out on the road with my thumb in the air. The cold is clawing into my cheeks, but I'm well wrapped for it. I stay as close as I can to the side of the road, past O'Leary's colorless two-story house with the big brick posts and the gate—taking on airs, said Dad, past the Walshes' place with the grass I swear she cuts with nail scissors every day, past the national school with its twenty-five windows lined up like a ruler.

A friend of Mam's stops for me. She loves a good bit of gossip. I'm not going to give it to her. "Well, hello there, Miss Gallagher. Why the big bag?" I can see her nose sniffing already under the coil of her imaginary crown.

"I have some old sets of Ellie's football clothes and

I'm going to give them to a friend's sister in the town."

She seems happy enough with that, nosy cow. I try to notice everything I can in this last look of what's become so familiar. Down, down the hill into town, the Four Masters bookshop and Magee's on the right, the Abbey Hotel with its brick front straight ahead, and the flat face of the Central Hotel two doors to its right. The sky has stretched out gray clouds like a roll of cloth above us.

Mam's friend drops me off at the Diamond in the middle of town and I wave goodbye until she can't see where I'm going. The Dublin bus should get here sometime in the next few hours, and I can hide in the doorway of the hotel until it does.

I wish I could have told Cullen the truth, but if I had he would have done everything to stop me. And then his big grand future would be over trying to save mine. He was always too good for me anyway. I'm doing him a favor. This is the way it has to be.

I'm glad the bus comes quickly. It doesn't give me time to think about what I'm doing, where I'm going. I put my one-way ticket in the driver's hand and make my way from cloth-covered seat to seat until I find one with only a few other people nearby. Mam's made it more than clear what she'll make me do if I ever go back. My heart crawls up my throat when I think this through. To never see Ellie and the boys again? To never hold Ruthie on my knee? To never laugh with Cullen and feel him so close to me?

The tears fill up my eyes and erupt into steady streams that plop off my chin onto my lap. We're driving over the Pettigo Mountains now, and all I can see is a blur of tears between my eyes and the window. What are they all going to think? What's Cullen going to think? No wonder hell is for people who have sex before they get married. Too many people get hurt, and I'm scared. I deserve to burn forever.

I could have stopped. I could have stopped right after that first drink, but we were having fun and I never thought I'd get to the point where I'd be lying in the back garden of the party with my knickers down and Cullen …

I knew. I knew, but I wanted it to happen too. It was like every part of me I've ever been able to close off before was wide open, and every piece of me cried out for Cullen to be more than just a friend. I wanted him to be part of me.

It wasn't even like I thought it would be. I thought if I ever did "it" with someone, we'd be sober and stare into each other's eyes the whole time, saying lovely things to each other. After it was over, I turned my head to one side. He just lay there staring at the stars, like a statue. Even if he'd said something right then, I really don't think I'd have remembered it.

Would things be different now if I hadn't acted like I remembered nothing about that night for weeks, like he was someone who was still my best friend and I had done nothing to change that? I pulled him outside that night. I walked him back through the grass until I stopped and kissed him. Our first kiss.

"Una—"

I put my drunk hand over his mouth and pulled him closer to me. I pushed my whole body up against his and kissed him harder until he stopped pushing back. I've always been the determined one.

Oh God, what have I done?

I still remember the strange look on his face the next day. We were both standing outside the church, waiting for the rest of the family to be done with Mass, and he was just staring at me.

"What?" I said, laughing. What? What kind of dumb girl pretends like nothing's happened? Me, that's who. I was so scared I'd lose him, so scared that if we talked about it, he'd tell me that it was an awkward one-night thing he regretted, so scared we'd lose everything. I've had a glass or two before, but this night was different. My whole body felt like some kind of mist I couldn't control, and every thought I can usually put in the right box in my head disappeared. The only thought left screaming was *Cullen, Cullen, Cullen*. He went along with it. My guess is he was just as bothered by it and is glad it's going to be an unmentionable from now on. But it's not unmentionable anymore, is it? I have a few inches of his living baby inside me, and he has no idea it's his. It all seems so stupid really. Like me on this bus leaving Cullen and everyone I love behind. Stupid.

But I'm not going back. I can't. There's no way I'm going to let the nuns take my baby ... our baby. I can do this all right, on my own, with no one telling me what I have to do, not even Cullen. I'm not going to have some quick wedding where we all smile and pretend I'm not pregnant and he's standing there trying to be happy when I've ruined everything for him. We weren't even going out together. That'd just be cruel.

I close my eyes and lean my head against the cold glass. Sleep would be welcome, but sinners don't sleep. They just keep going over their sins in the hopes that they won't sin so badly the next time around.

# 3

## Cullen

Una wouldn't talk to me for weeks, then she throws her grenades and now she's gone? I missed her *so much*—her random singing, her inappropriate comments, the way she sees the world so black and white. I just wanted to be with her, to listen to her talk, to watch her expressions when her excitement takes over. I still do. I love being a part of that *life* in her. She's the one who pulled me outside. She's the one who asked for more. I've been wanting more ever since. Then she went and had sex with someone a week later like it counted for nothing.

It counted to me.

I lie on the bed and stare at the U2 poster she gave me back when we were talking. "Two Hearts Beat as One" is playing on my boombox. I can't concentrate on anything. Every day I went over and over that night and the way she treated me after, and for the life of me, I didn't get it. Twelve years. Those greedy kisses. She said she was my best friend. The feel of her waist under my hands. I thought I knew her. The oneness I'd hungered

24

for for so many years finally reached. And now this.

Mam's yelling that the phone's for me. I get off the bed and head for the hallway.

"Yeah?" I say into the phone.

Some girl's crying on the other end. "Cullen?" she says.

"Yeah?" It sounds bad, whoever it is.

"Um, Cullen? This is Ellie. Una's gone. Is she with you?"

My stomach turns into bits of string. So she's done it. "No. What do you mean, gone?"

"Mam and her had a fight and then Una packed a bag and left ... she left this morning and we don't know where she went. She said she was tired of Mam bossing her around all the time and she needed to get away. Mam went looking for her in the car, but she hasn't come back yet. I thought maybe she'd gone over to your house, like she always does."

I press the phone harder to my ear, as if I can get her to say it a different way. "I'll go and look for her. Don't worry, Ellie. I think I know where she might be." I can hear Ellie letting all her breath out now.

"I hope so, Cullen. I'm really worried about her this time. She's ... she's not been herself these days."

I can see Ellie on the phone, her lips stuck into the receiver, her huge eyes blinking away tears, her hand pushing her dark hair out of her face. She was always a bit soft. Una's the daredevil.

"Don't worry, Ellie, I'll find her. I'll call you when I get back with her, okay?"

"Okay, Cullen. Don't forget."

The phone goes dead and I stare at it in my hand. I promised Una I'd keep her secret. Now I have to play

25

along.

"Mam? I have to go and look for Una. Her mam needs her." I run out the door before Mam can answer. I should have put an end to this shite when she came over. I should have told her what I think about that night. I should have asked her to go out with me. I don't want to just be her friend anymore. But do I? Do I want to be Dylan's leftovers? She said it was better sober. Why wasn't I the one to show her that? Why couldn't I kiss her sober? Feck. Feck, feck, feck.

Where would she go in Dublin? I have to pretend to look for her. I promised I wouldn't let on. Maybe the woods. I'll go there first. Say she's not there, that maybe Tanya knows something because isn't that what best friends are for—to tell them all your secret stuff?

When did she plan all this? Why didn't she tell me sooner? Although I hadn't even talked to her for weeks, or maybe I should say she hadn't talked to me. It's not like I hadn't tried at Mass, or when she walked by my house so many times and I ran out on the road, but she was up ahead like a train, pretending she couldn't hear me shouting her name. I sort of gave up then. If she didn't want to talk to me or hang out, then I was going to let her be and wait until she changed her mind about talking. That's always the way it's been before—whenever she was pissed at me, she'd give me the cold shoulder for a while, but she'd never gone weeks without talking. Although I suppose having sex with Dylan made her feel awkward around me. Maybe they've been having sex every chance they got ever since. Or talking. Right.

I take a gander out the window and throw on a jacket and grab one of the hats Mam knitted me last year, then pull the back door shut behind me.

She always told me what she was thinking about. I'd go on about a new football move, the lighting in the videos on *Top of the Pops*, a book I was reading, the way I found out what was wrong with the cooker and how I fixed it.

"How come, when I ask you what you're thinking, all the things you think about are so boring? You should be thinking about 'thinking' kinds of stuff, like why people you love get angry and why the grass is the exact green it is." We were staring at the sky together that time.

"Well, I was born a fella and that's the way fellas think." Made sense to me.

She threw her sandal at me, like I was making it all up. I wasn't.

"Why is it girls always expect fellas to think like they do and then they get upset when we don't, and then when we start to think we understand what they're going on about, they get bored explaining?"

She laughed at that one and didn't have an answer for me.

And now she's flipping up the pole because of some gobshite who wasn't scared of his own words.

The rain falls around me in tiny droplets. The sky looks like it has a grudge to see through to its fulfillment, but I have to go. I walk into the woods at the back of the house 'cause that's where we went all the time, her climbing the trees and gawking at everything for ages, me climbing up with her, and us lying back if the branch was thick enough and just listening. We never really needed to talk up there. I'll always like that about Una. She knows when to say nothing. When she has an opinion, she'll let you know, though, that's for sure. And all her questions!

It's not the same here without her. I walk on to the stream where we jumped banks and balanced from rock to rock. I jog up to the top of the hill where we looked down and picked people and made up stories about their lives. Then I find my way out to the road and up to the weir where the water disappears around a corner. Of course she's nowhere. Story of my life since the party.

I sit there by the water for ages, willing her to come back and sit by me. The water is as smooth as Dad's headstone, but some hidden power underneath it keeps pushing it forward and into its downward turn. Sometimes I sit here and she just appears, like she knew where I'd be. We have that kind of connection.

Well, I can't sit here forever. I need to talk to Ellie.

"UNA'S MAM AND THEN THE GARDAÍ called in," says Mam, talking to my back on her way to the loo.

Do they all think I have something to do with Una gone missing? She decided. She left. She was my best friend, but she hasn't been since the party, since ... I'm not going to tell them that. "No, Mam, she's been acting strange for a few weeks and no, I don't know what's going on, and no, I don't know where she might be." Pants on fire.

I'm sad. I'm worried.

Oh God, what if ... but I let that thought run out of my head as fast as it runs in. Una's never *not* told me things. She always blabs it out in the end. But if she hadn't had her period, would she ...? No, she never would. But in the moment? No. That's not my girl. She never lies, hates lies, gets so angry when someone does. She doesn't have it in her. She was always going on about wanting to get away and really live, but I never thought she'd do it this way, without me. But what if Dylan is this really great guy and she knows he'll look after her now?

I don't know what to do, but I'll keep up with the act and give her time to get away. I've looked in the woods. I'm asking her friends tomorrow. I'll ask Ellie exactly what she said again, pretend to see if I missed something. Maybe she's still here anyway and never left, couldn't face the thought of leaving us all. Not likely. When Una says she'll do something, she bloody well does it.

ALL THE TIGHTNESS IN ELLIE'S FACE relaxes when she opens the door to me.

"Thank God you're here. Mam's face is like a bag of daggers with all her marching around the house."

I follow her into the kitchen and she leans forward so no one else can hear. "Mam told Dad Una ran away after them having a big fight. Said it was over her coming home later now she's older. Mam drove to the Diamond to see if she was waiting on a bus and then went to the guards, but she's bricking about Sean McGee telling his wife and then it'll be all over town that Una Gallagher's on the run. You know what people say about you when you run away; they make up all sorts of shite. And she's scared stupid Dad'll go back to the drink over it all."

She wrings the kitchen cloth and wipes the table crumbs into her hand before shaking them into the bin.

"Mam says Sean's a good lad, but you know, Cullen, he has an awful mouth about him, and he's a bit of a one for the ladies too; but sure isn't he married now with a little one on the way? No more time for that, sure there isn't." She rinses out the cloth and hangs it over the edge of the cooker.

"Sean was asking if there was a fella she liked she might have gone to see. So you remember that one fella Una wasn't all that mad about? That's the only one I could think of—that one she kind of liked from Dublin. Maybe she went to see him? I can't remember his name."

"Dylan."

She eyes me sideways. "Yeah, Dylan. Did you ever meet him? Anyway, Una said Mam didn't even know the half of why she was leaving. She's had plenty of fights with Mam before and they just didn't talk to each other for a bit, and here she is gone, maybe for a long time." Her mouth droops and she blinks a few times. "Will you stay for dinner?"

"I will, aye."

She pulls a box from the freezer and starts ripping it open before nodding her head towards the back door. "Potatoes are out the back."

NO ONE'S TALKING at the dinner table. Ellie's pushing her fish fingers around the plate. Mrs. G's eyelids are a bit of a fuchsia color from rubbing. The rest of the wains' barometers for getting away with murder are on high alert. Charlie's trying to make Owen laugh, but Owen's kicking him under the table to make him stop and making angry faces at him.

Ellie pulls on Charlie's arm when she thinks no one's looking and he freaks out, getting a look from Mrs. G before she gets up from the table and runs into the sitting room. I hear a snort into a tissue, then another. Mr. G just sits there and gives me the nod to put on the kettle for the tea. Are they just not going to talk about this? Are they going to pretend everything's fine like she's gone off to Tenerife on a holiday or something?

Ellie pushes the chair back so hard it scrapes the floor and then yanks Ruthie out of her high chair. Ruthie's chubby leg catches on the plastic and she yells. More tears.

The phone rings. Mrs. G runs out of the sitting room to get it and we're all looking to see who it is. "Thanks, Sean, thanks very much." She sticks her head back in and yells at us all: "Sean McGee says that was her on the Dublin bus. The driver said it was her from her photo." The phone handle slaps back down and she waits out there, as if Una'll call if she has enough brainpower to make it happen. No such luck though. If I know Una, it'll be a while before she calls. I wish she could see us all sitting here, hoping she's okay, sick with fear about what might happen to her, sick with guilt that I'm not telling them the truth. How could she ask me to lie like this?

All I can hear is my breathing, until I open my mouth. "Do you think it'd do any good for me to go to Dublin after her? Ellie said something about how maybe she's gone after that fella Dylan who was in that caravan park for the summer. Maybe I could find out where he lives and go to the house at least, see if he knows anything." I need to find her. I need to tell her how I really feel before she signs up for a death sentence with someone who doesn't care about her, someone who was happy enough to get his feckin' hands all over her and then disappear. Dylan. I don't even know his last name and I already hate him. "I could try and get his name from the caravan park owner—that fella Jim McLaughlin with the big beard whose ma runs the Christmas sale every year."

31

"Ah, Cullen," says Mr. G. He puts his napkin on the table. "Where would you stay? What would your mam say?"

"I could call Tony, remember him? He went to live with his granny after his mam and dad died in that accident last year on the main road."

A faint light brushes across his face and lifts every crease. "Ask your mam then. I'd go with you meself if it weren't for this gammy leg."

I send my plate up the table and stand up. "I'll best be off then. I'll need to plan this out a bit."

Ellie stands up too. "I'll see you out." She stands by the open front door and scratches her nails up and down her teeth. Una does that too. "Bring her home, Cullen, where she belongs." She takes my hand in hers for a moment and puts her other hand over it, keeps it there until it feels a bit weird.

"I'll do my best." Sure what else can I say? Her eyes are looking straight into mine like a doctor's torch. All seeing. I want to tell her the truth so badly. She has a face that needs the truth. But no. Instead I step out and she shuts the door softly behind me.

# 4

## Una

I went to Dublin on the bus once with Mam. She took me to get presents for everyone for Christmas 'cause I was the "big girl." Ellie was all upset, but on the way down Mam told me she wasn't in the mood for Ellie rambling in her ear for five hours there and back. She must have felt guilty for telling me that because she gave Ellie one of those big makeup sets they were selling at Dunne's Stores. Ellie painted us girls with that stuff for the next two years. She really liked the Blondie look, and once she got the crimper, she was unstoppable.

Ellie never said anything about going to Dublin after that. I suppose she knows that asking is like making Mam say no, just because you asked.

I shouldn't have told Mam about the baby, but then, what could I do? It's not like I could walk around town telling everyone who stared, "No, you nosy cow, I have a cushion stuck up my shirt." Even if I hadn't told her, she would have figured it out. She always does.

I get off the bus in Cavan because I'm half starved, but the minute I stand in the doorway of the café, the smell of the sausages makes me want to throw up again. It's such a shame 'cause I was always a bit fond of the sausages. I hope this doesn't mean our relationship has come to a bitter end. Mashed potatoes and butter, carrots, and two sausages sliced into it ... *Oh God!* I'm lucky enough to find a hawthorn bush around the corner before it all comes back up—by the wall of someone's front garden, but whatever—and I make it back to the bus in time. Someone sits in beside me this time, so I pretend I'm asleep the rest of the way, but I can't sleep at all, and there's a masochist in my brain singing a U2 song over and over.

I read a bit of a book in The Four Masters last week about being pregnant. It says that all the puking should stop by fourteen weeks, and that it normally starts at about seven weeks. I don't need to count up how pregnant I am by being sick though; I can count it from the night of the party, the one where Cullen changed my life forever. I'm about ten weeks by now, and she's about the size of three-quarters of my thumb. She might be born on the fourteenth of March. Just as well it's not the fourteenth of February. Now that'd be funny.

I look at my watch. About another hour and a half to go before we get there.

IT'S ALMOST DARK on the last leg of the journey, but I can make out the tall houses from another time lined up in rows. People are walking quickly, and iron railings are everywhere—around the bits of green grass, around the houses. All the buildings are like twice the height of the ones at home. We turn a corner, and when I look out the front window of the bus, I can see O'Connell Street spitting people and cars all the way down to the river in the fading light.

"Last stop." The driver pulls close to the pavement, right outside a cinema. I have no idea what to do. The lady beside me gets up wheezing, like Dad after the combine harvesters spread the wheat chaff over half of Donegal, and off the bus, along with everybody else.

The bus driver looks back at me in the mirror, his nose wider than his mustache. "This is the last stop." He has a voice like Terry Wogan's. He should really be on the radio, not driving people like me up to the big smoke every day. He hasn't a face for the telly, that's for sure. I want to ask him if he can tell me where to go to ask for help, but can anyone really help me now? I just walk down the steps and out into the capital city of Ireland.

It feels a little warmer down here, but I'm still shaking a bit. I stand outside the cinema and stare at the posters, pretending I'm reading every word. This isn't like home, where everybody knows each other and they stop and chat. This is a place where you have somewhere to go. I walk down the street a bit and then I look back up it, edged by a few parked double-decker buses in one spot. I see one old lady staring out the window, looking so alone.

Everything is so gray and dreary, but the view opens up a bit the closer I get to the river. The air is smoky, and I could swear the pavement is mixed with soot. It's a far cry from home.

I SHOULD HAVE THOUGHT this through. I've been walking around Eason's bookshop for hours now, and there's a man staring at me from behind the cash register on the second floor. I think he thinks I'm stealing or something, probably because of this elephant of a bag

I'm trying to carry around with me and because I'm now sitting on some broken lino in the corner. I've counted every ragged edge in it, so much so that I know I could get a maths prize for it, although God knows I never won one in school. That was Tanya's kingdom of stars. I've gone to the toilet four times. And now it looks like they're closing.

The man starts walking towards me, but I'm up and off the floor before he can come close. This was my safety for the last few hours, and as I walk past the smells of books and stationery and out the door, my heart sinks and sinks and sinks into an ocean of nothingness.

But I keep walking. Across the O'Connell Street Bridge and its probably manky water, with a few dead bodies to boot, down a street, past the big old doors of Trinity College, and on to another street. Mam brought me to the McDonald's here last time we came, and I don't know how I remembered the way, but I did and here I am. It's almost singing to me.

A very nice lad says, "Here, let me help you with your bag." He reminds me of Cullen, he's that thoughtful. He orders his food after me and then carries my bag for me while I bring my tray to the table by the window, but then he disappears. I sit there and stare out, chewing each bite of this hamburger until all the flavor is sucked out of it and it's like there's dirt in my mouth.

I should have been going back to school next week. I was going to study really hard and make Mam and Dad so proud, and next year I was supposed to have it all waiting for me—my big chance to do something brilliant with my life. And I shut the door to all that. But sure what the feck else could I do?

And now McDonald's is closing too.

I stand outside the doors breathing in and out, in and out, trying so, so hard to think of what to do next. Maybe there's a corner somewhere, a space away from everything that I can curl into, and I hope and pray that our Blessed Lady will have pity on me, even though she probably can't bear to look at me right now. I turn right, then left, and then I see it—a church. I hang around until no one is looking, throw my bag over the metal prongs of a fence, and then climb over after it. I'll stay the night here. At least it's better than sleeping in some doorway. I hide behind the best bushes so no one can see me from the street, make a sort of sleeping bag for myself with my clothes, and wait for sleep to fill my head. Me and my baby. Cullen's baby.

I don't care how hard this is. This baby and me, we're in this together.

## Friday

MY SHIVERING BODY wakes me up. I can just about see the outline of my hands, and I'm near starved. I take the bag and set it on top of my body to try and add another layer of warmth to this pathetic bed I've made myself, but it's no use. I can't get back to sleep. I peek out past the clumped leaves and through the railings to the street. All's quiet but for a bird in the tree above me. He seems to think it's a great day to be alive. Well ... we'll see. I watch him, dancing from foot to foot on the tree branch, red chest sticking out proudly. He turns his head sideways and casts his bright eye on me. Yeah, I know, Mr. Robin. If it's going to be a great day to be alive, I'm going to have to act like it and start looking for a job.

I have about twenty-five pounds and some pennies

left over from the bus and McDonald's. That's not going to last long here in town. But there's nowhere open yet, so I lie there, staring at the warm little bundle of feathers and chirps and planning out my day.

AT SEVEN THE DOORS of McDonald's open and I'm the first one in. I head straight for the toilets so I can wash my hair in the sink, and then I try and dry it off a bit on the roller towel. The smell of breakfast is too much for my stomach, though, and I rush to the toilet and let go of whatever was left from last night's meal. Not a great start to the day, but now I'm hungry again and I think it's safe to eat. I go back to my people-watching window from the night before and wait. Eight o'clock comes and goes until I'm standing at the counter asking for a job.

The woman's voice rasps in the back of her throat, and her yellow-stained fingers are pressed on the counter in front of me. "Sorry, luv, but I get people asking all the time. I have nothing ta give you right now."

Probably just as well. The smell of hamburgers is starting to make me feel sick again.

The rest of the day is worthless. Door to door, cash register to cash register, and no one wants help. No one wants me.

"Have you ever worked a cash register before?"

"What sort of customer experience do you have?"

"Can you type more than sixty words a minute?"

The only experience I have is in looking after the wains, listening to the nuns while they teach, and doing all my homework on time. Not a whole lot of work experience in that unless someone is looking for a minion. I could probably babysit, but when I did that at

38

home, it was always for friends of Mam.

My back feels like the lawn mower ran over me; my feet hurt like I've walked on nails. I just want to lie down on a stuffed sofa somewhere and watch TV. And I can't. I have nothing. Maybe that means I am nothing.

# 5

## Cullen

### Friday

It doesn't look like Una talked to anyone but me. Tanya's as gobsmacked as the rest of them.

The guards say the bus driver remembered Una's face. It's been stamped on mine, that's for sure—her fringe always poking her in the eyes, unless she was flattening it back on her head while she talked. Her gray-blue eyes looking straight into mine when she was all serious. Her dimples and what she called her "chunky" cheeks when she was laughing. All five foot two of her getting on that bus and running to Dublin to Dylan?

Why did she never talk to me about the party? Could she not handle what I did, what we did? Why would she act all weird after, when she was the one who started it? She'll tell me when I find her, the eejit. And then why would she try to find out what it was like sober with a stranger? She's never been that weird before.

I went to the caravan park and got the name of the fella. Dylan Byrne. Jim didn't want to give me the address, but I told him my girl had been two-timing me with Dylan and I was going down to give him what for. He practically handed me the keys to the house.

I pack the last few things into the football bag and walk into the kitchen to say goodbye to Mam. She pushes her *Women's Weekly* to the middle of the table, open on the romantic story pages, and lifts her glasses off her nose.

"Did you pack your knickers? And your toothbrush?"

"Yes, Mam."

"Do you have enough money, do you think? Maybe I should give you some for your food while you're at Tony's?"

"Yeah, twenty should do it."

She smooths my hair down, brushes some imaginary specks off my shirt, and goes off to find her purse while I run back to the bedroom for an extra pair of jocks. I can hear her at the door with her car keys.

"Hurry up! Don't want to be late."

"Mam, the bus doesn't come for another hour!"

She purses her lips. "You can never be early enough, ya big lump. Remember that, Cullen, when some poor eejit decides to marry you and it's your wedding day. Never early enough."

We get to the Diamond and park the car across from the Abbey Hotel. "Now, Cullen, 'tis a great thing you're doing here. Find that silly girl. I don't know what's got into her, running off like this. Bring her home and I'll sit her down and give her what for. All right? Now behave yourself, watch your pockets, and I'll pick you up on Sunday night, God willing, unless you call and tell me you're on another bus."

I get out of the car and open the boot. She sticks her

head out the window.

"And tell Tony's gran thanks for putting up with you."

"I will, Mam, I will. And thanks for the lift."

She gives me a hug that'll last a few days and watches me cross over to the Abbey Hotel's bus stop. She'll sit there until the bus comes if I let her get away with it, but I wave at her and she gets the hint. As always, she has to say just one more thing through the open window as she drives past me.

"Be good!"

Yeah, it's a bit late for that now.

THE BUS HEADS UP through the mountains, past all the piles and piles of peat me and the lads ran through that one time Tom got a loan of his mam's car. Then we move real slow-like through Enniskillen, past that big bottle-green wall and all the British soldiers with their rifles hanging off their shoulders—always a bit scary— but sure doesn't it cut half an hour off the trip to go through the North?

I think back to that time Una and me had just read *Harriet the Spy,* back in sixth class, and we wanted to be just like her, so we wore matching outfits—dirty jeans, a sweatshirt, and a torch we hooked onto our belts with pieces of wire we found in Una's dad's shed. We had to have a notebook on us at all times, and we wrote loads of notes in them about everyone we knew—just like Harriet. We'd sneak around the school and people's windows and listen in on conversations in the supermarket to try and find out all the local secrets and maybe solve a mystery or two. Mac, the old fisherman down the road, caught me one time outside his window, and Dad threatened to beat the tar out of me if I ever did that again. We never did solve any mysteries. Maybe if I'd spent more time reading more serious stuff, I'd have known more about motorbikes and how many people die on them. It was right after that when Dad died. I could have told him.

I start talking to the woman beside me. It turns out she's Tom's sister's mother-in-law, so we have a grand old time talking about Tom's family and the grandbaby on the way. She could have been an auctioneer, the way she can pack that many words into a minute, but it's a great way to pass the time and not think about losing Una.

THE BUS DROPS ME OFF at the cinema on O'Connell Street and Tony's waiting for me there.

"God, Cullen, your mammy's been feeding you well!"

I pat my stomach affectionately. Tony was never one to mince his words. We walk down the street a bit to another bus stop and wait until it lets us on. We sit on top, right at the front, and watch while it curves around the city in stops and starts until we cruise down along the Strand Road to the last stop and jump off. Tony's grandparents live in a big house off the beach. It's all very posh.

I just tell him the bones of it—she ran away, God knows why, but I have a name and address and I think she might be there.

"You want to go to Dundrum today?" Tony's eyebrows are almost as high as his hairline.

"Yeah, she's been gone a few days already, and the more I look now, the more chance we have of finding her."

"I didn't think you were this into her, to be honest. Coming all the way down here to find her and all. Don't get me wrong, it's great to see you, but ..."

"Yeah, we're just friends, but I'm close to the family." I can feel my heartbeat speeding up, and my cheeks, I'm sure, are flaming red, but I keep going. He's turned to pick up his jumper off the bed and put it over his head, thank God. "I was always over there," I say to his back, "and they're gutted. I want to do my part, ya know?"

He nods, pulling the jumper down past his belt. "Let's eat and go, so."

Tony's granny walks us to the door after a massive lunch and slips Tony a tenner and some change. "For the chipper."

An hour later Tony shifts the gears of his granny's car into park on a side street in Dundrum. "Right," he says. "Where do we go next?"

I'm a bit nervous, to be honest. Neither of us knows Dundrum at all, and I have the address marked on a big map that fills up the two front seats. I have a photo of her that Gail, her mam, gave me, so I do all I can do. I start giving Tony directions.

A few grinding gears and bad turns later, we're standing outside a white, two-story, semidetached house on a street full of them. They all have low white walls around a patch of grass and a tree or two in the middle of it. A fella about our age opens the door, short, big fuzz on top of his head.

"Dylan?"

"Yeah." His eyes drop on Tony, then me, and he folds his arms before he leans against the doorframe.

*This is what Una signed up for?!*

I hold up the photo of Una. "A friend of mine ran away a few days ago and we think she might have come to your house, so I was wondering if she was here."

"Una? Japers no." He scratches his nose. "Why would she come here?"

"Well, um, she sort of said you two, um ..." I switch from one foot to the other, sizing him up, imagining her kissing him, him touching her. It makes no sense. I've seen her posters in her bedroom. This fella is the opposite.

"God no, haven't seen or heard a peep from her since we got back last week."

I stand there, my feet glued to his welcome mat, my fists feeling tighter and tighter, imagining them landing on his face over and over. I look at Tony. He looks back at me. Shrugs. I breathe.

"Well, thanks then. Sorry to bother you."

We sit outside in the car, Tony filling it with the last fumes of his cigarette. "I thought you were going to punch his lights out," he says.

"I was."

"So what stopped you?"

I shift my body around to face his. "Do you think he's telling the truth?" I say.

"Looked like he was." He rolls down the window and I watch the smoke do a runner up the telephone pole.

"What the feck do I do now?"

"Case the joint?"

I nod and start folding up the map while Tony parks the car down the street a bit, and there we wait. I still want to beat the fecker to a pulp, but what if she never told him?

I want her to be safe in Dylan's house with a cup of

tea in one hand and a good book in the other. That's what she always did when she was at our house when we had the telly on. What would she be doing here if she never confronted Dylan? What if she's slept with a whole bunch of fellas and I was just one of them and she has no idea who the father is? Una? No. What if I never find her? I can't swallow. I have to find her. I have to find my Una and make sure she's okay, no matter what she's done.

The trees have started to turn into silhouettes against the streetlights in the cul-de-sac. Tony puts a hand on my arm. "Cullen, it's half nine. We're going to have to come back tomorrow."

What if she's lying in an alley somewhere? No one else is out looking for her. But I nod, click on the light on the sun visor, and open up the map again.

Tomorrow I'll find her. I know it.

## Saturday

WE'RE BACK IN THE CUL-DE-SAC again, stocked up on Fanta and crisps. It's ten o'clock, and people are starting to walk around with their umbrellas up. Tony's face is stuck in the pages of Stephen King's latest book while I'm on lookout. We stay like that for the whole morning, Tony occasionally muttering things like "ugh," and "gross," and one time he digs his nails into my arm and has to close the book for a minute. And not a single person opens the front door of Dylan Byrne's house. Until one does.

It's Dylan coming out into the drizzle. He looks at the clouds, pulls his hood over his head, and starts walking to the main street with his shoulders reaching almost as far as his feet with each step. I slap Tony on the knee and we're off, wipers squeaking. The 48 bus comes almost straightaway, and we follow its stops and starts all the way in to Dublin. We see him get off at Stephen's Green, so I hop out of the car while Tony parks. Lucky for us, Dylan walks into the shopping center and gives Tony time to find me.

But then we lose him.

I'm freaking out, but we go into all the shops in case she got a job in town and he was just in telling her we showed up.

Nothing.

Tony stands in front of me, hands in his pockets and waiting for directions.

"What if Una isn't with Dylan at all? What if she did go to his house and he told her to bugger off?"

"Sure wouldn't she go back home then?"

No, not Una. Stubborn as a goat. I hope she's dry. Today's a real pisser, and I highly doubt she's got an umbrella on her. Ah, sure it's only a bit of water, she'd say.

Tony and me walk down Grafton Street as far as a newsagent near Trinity, looking, looking for her face and her Doc Martens. We stop for lunch in the McDonald's on Grafton Street and show one of the women working there her photo. She runs a finger over it, shakes her head.

"She looks familiar, but sorry, I can't remember from where."

With a bit of a spring in my step, we head out again, moving back on up to St. Stephen's Green. Maybe she's feeding the ducks in the rain, waiting for Dylan, and he's just been lying the whole time.

Because the rain's stopped for a bit, we head into the

park and eat the sandwiches Tony's granny made us. It's Saturday afternoon and we still have nothing, apart from that woman at McD's. We hovered outside it for ages, and nothing. My gut tells me she never went to Dylan's and we're not going to find her. And it breaks my heart.

We walk up and down Grafton Street one more time, feet following the pavement like it's the yellow brick road. They found their magician. The tin man found his heart. My head is turning from right to left the whole time, hoping and praying I'll see her. *And then what, Cullen? She cries and hugs you and kisses you, tells you she's sorry and that she wants to come home? Eejit.* And my lead-filled shoes somehow follow Tony's lighter walk while I try and think of the right words to give Una's mam and dad tomorrow.

## Sunday

WE'RE BACK AT TONY'S after another few hours at Dylan's place. We watched him come home and stared at his door after that until a guard knocked on our window and asked us to move on, that we were scaring the neighbors. I can't hack this. I can't help feeling all this is my fault.

School starts the day after tomorrow. Sixth year was supposed to be brilliant, the year we're treated with a bit more respect and our freedom is just nine months away. Una was excited about it. She had big plans. Sometimes I thought they might include me. The way she came on to me that night ...

I can feel the anger burning into my fists now—at myself. I wasn't as important to her as I thought I was. Everyone is relying on me to find her, and I've failed them all. Just like I failed Una.

I lash up the stairs and throw my bag against the wall. The entire contents fall onto the floor and the bag lies limp beside them.

The bus home to Donegal takes its sweet time coming, but finally I climb up the stairs and sit in the front so I can put my feet up and send some blood back to my heart.

MAM LETS ME DRIVE after she picks me up off the bus. I drop her off at home before going on to the Gallaghers' place.

Mrs. G—Gail—has her face in a tea towel. Mr. G—Seamus—is quiet. They knew I'd call if I found her, but there was always that feather of hope floating from side to side, until it landed in the quicksand.

Mrs. G walks over to me and holds me close for just a minute. "Thank you for helping."

Ellie's still staring at the floor when Gail and Seamus move to the sitting room, her mam's hand wiping at her eye before she turns the corner. "So this is it," Ellie murmurs. "This is when we're supposed to forget about her and keep living?"

I run my fingers over the back of a kitchen chair and stare at the floor as well. White lino with blue lines, just like at Tom's house.

Ellie takes a deep sigh. "I'm going to call a friend and tell her I'm coming over. I don't want to be here in this poxy misery."

"I'll give you a lift."

ELLIE STARES OUT THE WINDSCREEN. "Mam went to the school today to tell the nuns she's missing. They said they'd light a candle for her. I don't know how

49

much good that'll do. Una can be a stubborn old goat.

"No one's talking. Dad's shouting at Mam that she's her mother's daughter, whatever that's supposed to mean. Mam's cleaning the house like there's no tomorrow. I'm trying to help Mam as much as I can. Every time I say something, she sighs, like I'm using up her air. You know?

"It's like part of me is missing that I didn't know I'd miss. I even miss her arguing with me about how to do stuff, and she's only gone a few days."

I can't hold my face together. Bits of it keep going in different directions.

"Sorry, Ellie. I'm really sorry I couldn't find her."

"It's not your fault she's gone, Cullen. You were great to go down." She sticks her head back in the car window when I'm dropping her off. "Don't blame yourself at all. She'll be back before you know it."

I pretend to smile. Yeah. Before I know it.

I'm backing out of the driveway very slowly, to avoid the tabby, when I know what I have to do. I have to talk to her mam after school tomorrow and tell her exactly what went down.


WE'RE IN THE ABBEY HOTEL in the farthest corner of the bar, whispering so no one can hear us say what's really going on with Una. Well, they'll hear one thing and turn it into something else altogether. Gossip is like petrol in this town; it runs a lot of motors, starts a lot of fires. I trace a scratch on the sticky table, my half pint growing bubbles of water on the glass by the second.

Mrs. G wipes her mouth with a serviette and ducks her head forward again like a penguin climbing a hill. "Oh," she says. "So you know." She takes another sip of tea. "I told Seamus about the baby. He wants to go after whoever it is who did this to her. Is it that Dylan fellow's?"

"That's what she said." No point in adding any conjecture to her words.

Her mouth starts trembling, and her eyes fill up as she asks, "Do you think she's okay?"

I run my finger around the teacup. "To be totally honest, Mrs. G, I don't know."

# 6

## Una

### Sunday—one week later

I wake up feeling like I'm a sponge that's after sitting in dishwater all night, and the tap keeps pouring in more water. The bushes, the trees, there's nothing to protect me from this rush of venom across the city. My hair, my knickers, my bag of stuff—there isn't a dry piece of anything on me or around me. I'd lie here and cry, but what good'll that do anyone? Not me, that's for sure.

I try and find a place for my bag that's higher than the pools of mud and sticks, and my search takes me around the edge of the church to a place that's cemented. There are no hidden corners here, though, so I don't know what to do. I trudge back to where I was, put the bag on the spot that's the least muddy, and hope for the best. I can't go looking for jobs now. If I was back in English class talking about analogies, I'd look like an unbaked cake. I feel like a puddle in a pothole ... but I'm not going there. Nope, I won't let my mind go there.

So what can I do? How can I get dry and make myself

look decent? The roller towel in McD's won't dry out my shoes, and with my clothes clinging to me like a baby monkey, I can't see how to dry them out properly.

I would have been back at school Monday before last, sitting at a wooden desk near the heater, but I'm still bloody well here, aren't I, in the godforsaken bushes. I've been gone over a week now, and every day gets worse. It's been bucketing rain all week. I have nothing left to wear, I have nowhere to shower, and McD's is my only food, if it stays down. I'm down to my last pound and fifty pence. I'm petrified. And to top it all off, it's my birthday. One year past the sweet-sixteen-and-never-been-kissed year. Ha! There's no celebrating this one. I just need to survive here.

I've heard of shelters, but if I go to one, they'll find out my name and I'll be put on the next bus home. I can't let that happen. No bloody way. I pull some branches together and set my bag on top of them and think about heading to McDonald's again. They're starting to look at me funny, probably 'cause I smell by now. I've been trying to clean up in the sinks there, but it's hard to do it when your clothes are stuck to you from six days of rain. Oh shite, they're closed on Sundays!

That's when I look up to see this man standing over me with an umbrella.

"Can I help you?"

And the tears I've been holding up inside begin to match the downpour around us. Four little words. Four little words no one else has bothered to ask.

"Come on inside and I'll make you a cup of tea. You look drenched. Here, let me carry your bag."

I follow him to a building attached to the church and go through into a small kitchen. It's dry, and he has the electric heater on.

"I'd like to introduce myself. I'm the rector here at St. Andrew's, and my name is John Abercrombie. You can call me John. Tea?"

I nod, and he plugs in the kettle and pulls a mug off the mug tree every house in Ireland got with their Green Shield stamps. "Now, you don't have to answer," he says gently, "but you look like a drowned rat about to face the guillotine, and I'd like to help you, if I may. What's the best thing I could do for you?"

He has a kind face. He's about thirty, and he's wearing sensible clothes—a shirt under a woolly jumper and trousers with a crease down the front. His hair is starting to go already too. The kind of man your gran would want you to marry because he dresses like your grandad. He sits down a few feet away, puts his hands between his knees, and waits for my answers.

I move the chair a bit closer to the heater and sit down too. How much do I tell him? Can I trust him? My gut tells me I can. Can I trust my gut? I let it all fall out of my mouth anyway.

"My name is Una. I'm pregnant and my mam wants the nuns to take my baby, so I ran away. I've been sleeping in the bushes here since last week, and I'd really like a safe place to stay, if you can help me with that. I don't want my mam and dad to know where I am though. I want to keep my baby." I look around. "And I'm Catholic. I shouldn't even be in here. The priest says we can go to hell for even standing on the steps of a Proddy church."

John nods. "Ah yes. Milk and sugar?" He doesn't wait for my answer and brings over the bottle of milk and a bag of sugar. "Oh, I'm sorry, you're probably starving, but all I have is some cans of beans and a sliced pan. Can I make you some beans on toast?"

I wipe away a few more tears. "Yes please."

He sticks four slices of bread in the toaster and pulls a saucepan out of the cupboard. "Now, Una, I'm going to have to ask you to do something you might be really uncomfortable with, and I hate to do it to you, but I'm about to do the ten o'clock service and I can't leave you here on your own when I don't know you well enough."

I jump up. "It's fine. I'm fine. I'll leave, thanks."

John, Rector John, Father John, whatever the hell he calls himself, stops what he's doing and looks me straight in the eyes. "Una, from what you've just told me, nothing's fine. I want to help you, but I need you to help me first. I know you've probably never been in a Protestant church before, but if you want my help, you're going to have to come in. I'll only take about thirty minutes." He stands there waiting.

I can't move. I can feel my heart going *badaboom, badaboom.* Inside my head a jumbled mess of fear and shame and hope and loss pile together. I've made so many horrible choices already. Would this be another one? I look away, look at the toaster with my toast that's already popped up, look at the saucepan waiting for the beans, look at anything but him. I quit. It can't get any worse than this. I'm already in a kind of hell. I'll go to the Proddy church, hell be damned.

"All right."

"Great. I'm running a bit late on things, so would you mind?" He holds up the can of beans and the can opener. "I have to go into the study and get my sermon notes, and the heaters aren't even on yet in the church. Mrs. Reid is going to kill me!" He explains: "She's the organist, and the cold gets into her bones a bit."

I take the can from him and clamp the can opener into it on the countertop, squeaking my way around it until I can pry it open. He disappears for a few minutes, which I'm fine with, and reappears with a shirt and jumper.

"Sorry I can't give you anything else, but at least your top half will be dry." I change out of my soggy stuff in the toilet and am soon back in the kitchen with the arms of both his shirt and jumper rolled up three times. It's great to feel drier.

Soon I have a right feast in front of me, which I eat much too quickly. I add some more water to the tea bag and wait. It's nice to be able to breathe again and to have something warm inside me, even if it's only for a little while.

Eventually John comes back into the kitchen wearing a long black smock thing and a white collar at the front of his neck. "Ready for church?"

No, I'm not, but whatever. I follow him to the back door of the church and into a small room, and then on into the main part.

"Mrs. Reid, this is Una, the girl I told you about."

Mrs. Reid looks like she's about to stand by someone's coffin and lower it, except for the hot pink jacket—probably worn in the hope of meeting someone. Something tells me she's not going to meet him here. She gives me one of those looks—the one that starts at your neck and goes to your feet and back up again to your hair—and sniffs. He must have told her about the baby.

"Okay, Una, if you sit there by Mrs. Reid, we'll get started soon."

The wooden pews are hard and worn, with long

cushions on them that feel like they're stuffed with horsehair. I sit back on mine, back ramrod straight like a nun is standing over me with a ruler. A few old people come in behind me. I don't want to look around more than once. I know they're already staring at my back. It's so bloody cold in here. For a second I feel sorry for Mrs. Reid, coming here every Sunday and having to sit in the frozen tundra of boredom. Because that's what this is. It's about thirty minutes of hymns, reading from a prayer book, and listening to John talk about Jesus and his disciples being brotherly. Little do I know that I'm about to be mortified.

John leans forward in his pulpit, hands on the edge, and looks at the few faces before him. "And in the spirit of brotherly love, I have an unusual request to ask of you all. As I'm sure you've noticed, we have a visitor with us today."

Oh God, he's talking about me. I shrivel into myself and look at my hands.

"She's in a bit of a predicament and needs somewhere to stay for the next few weeks. If any of you have a spare bed you could give Una here, I think you'd be more than emulating the kind of love Jesus talked about so many years ago."

I'm still hiding, feeling the eyes on my back.

John walks back down the little stairs and says a few more words before Mrs. Reid pounds the keys with more gusto than I saw in the first two hymns, probably because she'll be home soon in front of her fire with her slippers on.

I sort of stand up with the rest of them while John walks down to the front door, and then I don't know where to look, so I stare at my rain-sodden shoes until I feel a tap on my shoulder. An old man with single hairs standing in every direction on his head holds out a liver-spotted hand.

"Welcome to St. Andrew's. I wish I could help you, but I hope you find somewhere. It's lovely to see a young face here."

Mrs. Reid busies herself with her bag of music sheets and I study the swelling that bulges out and over her Sunday shoes. No wonder she needs her feet up. I see another old couple talking to John and looking over at me as he talks. People stand around in different pews, probably asking about gardening tips and talking about how much rain we're getting. The old couple comes towards me. He's tall with broad shoulders, gray hair that's almost waving at everyone; she's about my height with a squishy, grandma-level figure, gray curls rippling as she walks. Kindness shines out of their eyes, almost like a lamp in the middle of my storm. My heart leans in to their next words.

"Hello, em ..."

"Una."

"Hello, Una. I'm Catherine Pringle, and this is my husband, Des. We'd like to help you out. Would you like to come back to our house for a bite, and we can get to know you a little better?"

John says to let him know what they decide. He's given me a phone number for his rectory, and says that while it wouldn't be a good idea for me to sleep there, he'll figure something out if the Pringles change their minds. He pats me on the back as we walk back into the church. He reminds me of Dad a bit, the way he's just *there*.

John gives Mr. Pringle my bag. It's embarrassing,

seeing him hold such a dirty, sodden thing next to his fancy smock, but there you have it. Mr. Pringle lifts it onto his now-coated shoulder and waits for his wife and me to walk in front, out into the newly revealed sunshine.

Mrs. Pringle walks like a nurse, and we follow her flat shoes and navy wool coat around a few corners until we're standing in front of a small shop framed in fire brick red, with the words *Pringle Leather Works* painted in white letters above the window. She disappears inside and Mr. Pringle gestures for me to go in before him. The smell of leather is rich, pouring off the shelves of handbags, belts, and other accessories. I stop to inhale it before we walk on into the back of the shop through a small doorway. The room is about twice the size of our living room at home, with two long tables lining the walls, holding up all kinds of pots and coffee mugs filled with leather tools with bulbous wooden handles. In the far corner to the right is what's probably the most expensive piece in the room, and it looks like an industrial sewing machine. There's what looks like a wooden clamp beside it, and rolls of leather sitting atop each other on long shelves in the middle of the room. An old sink is in the other corner with a kettle, some mugs, and a box of tea bags on a shelf beside it.

Mrs. Pringle heads up the stairs along the left wall, and we follow her up the carpeted staircase, through the door into a hallway, and turn right into a kitchen. Mr. Pringle leaves my drenched bag on the kitchen floor and walks away, leaving me staring at Mrs. Pringle's back while she fusses about, putting bread and jam on the table. I watch her walk to one of the cupboards and when I see the plates in it, I go over and reach out for her to put them in my hands. A tiny smile appears at the corner of her mouth before she turns around to take some cutlery out of the drawer, every piece with a pearl handle. I fill the kettle, plug it in, and move three mugs from the draining board to the counter while Mrs. Pringle takes some things out of the fridge and adds them to the growing meal.

"Desmond, lunch is ready," she shouts out the kitchen door. "Una, why don't you sit there? Des usually makes himself a sandwich with all this ham, cheese, and tomatoes, while I prefer to eat the bread separately. Feel free to eat yours any way you'd like."

We wait for Des—until his sheepskin slippers move softly across the floor and he's sitting down—before I put some mayonnaise on two slices of soda bread and create the best sandwich I've had in weeks.

"That's the way." Des nods in my direction, and we munch in silence for a while before the questions begin. But they don't pour on the questions thick. Not like Cullen's mam would have asked. She would have been getting the right story ready for the rest of the town.

"How long have you been in Dublin? Do you have a place to go if we were only to give you a bed for a few weeks? John let us know about the baby. How far along are you?" And that was that.

"Well ... I've been here a few weeks, but I had nowhere to stay, so I slept on the church grounds."

Des pushes his big, brown-rimmed glasses back up his nose and sends Catherine a meaningful glance across the table. I can't help but stare at his wild gray hair. It's like the waves on the Donegal shore.

I turn back to Catherine. "Whatever you can do for me would be great, to be honest. I don't want to impose.

I think the baby should be here in March, if I counted right."

Des grins at me. "You're welcome to stay with us for a bit," he says. "We don't want you and the baby out on the streets like that. And in all that rain!" He shakes his head.

I let out a sigh of relief. Catherine chips in. "We're glad to help. I'll show you your room after lunch, and we'll have to get you to a doctor as soon as we can to make sure everything's okay in there."

It's the box room, with the walls painted a pretty lemon color and a wardrobe with some drawers at the bottom of it in the corner. The bed has one of those white spongy headboards with buttons in it, and the duvet is white with little white ducks on a line of yellow ribbon at the end. There's even a small window with matching white and yellow curtains. With wet eyes, I turn and give her a shaky smile. She hugs me, which I wasn't expecting at all. We don't hug much at home. Or at all.

"Glad to help, Una. We'll have dinner at about six thirty. I'm sure you'll want to have a shower and wash some of your clothes. The washing machine you'll have seen in the kitchen. We can hang your clothes on the drying rack by the heater in the living room. The bathroom is right outside your door, and I've turned on the emersion for you. It should be nice and hot in about twenty minutes. And right beside the bathroom is a hot press, where you'll find a towel and an extra blanket for tonight, if you think you'll be cold. Let me know if you need anything else."

And just like that, I have a room of my own, and very soon I'll have clean clothes and clean skin. I scream inside and then kneel on the floor so I can start to sort my washing piles and thank Jesus, Mary, and Joseph all in one happy prayer. Baby and me are just grand, at least for the next few weeks. Unless Mam finds me.

I need to call her, let her know I'm okay. She gets mad worried about us all, and even though I'm really pissed at her, she needs to know. I should have called days ago. What daughter doesn't tell her own mother she's okay? I have to.

I let Catherine know what I'm doing and run down the stairs and out the door to the nearest phone box; line up my 10ps and 50ps; lift my shaky finger; turn the dial down to the marker, let it go, down to the marker, let it go. Will I always know this number off by heart?

"Hello?"

My heart stops for a few seconds until I feel the artery thud in my neck. *Ba-boom, ba-boom, ba-boom.* "Ellie, it's me, Una." I suck in air. "Don't say anything. I'm just calling to let you all know that I'm okay, and I'll be staying down here for a bit. Sorry, but I can't say anything else. I miss you all!" A massive sob escapes my mouth before I hang up. I sob all the way back to the shop. What. Have. I. Done?

# 7

## Cullen

I think about Una. Like when I'm on the way to school in the back of the car. Or when school is over for the day. Or when I'm lying in bed staring at the wall and the phone rings. She could always get a laugh out of me.

She knew life could suck sometimes, but she'd get on with it instead of sinking into herself, and she was always up for an adventure. One time when Mam was away, we mitched school and drove to Dunfanaghy Beach.

"Your dad must miss all of this gorgeousness." She swept her arm from one stretch of the beach to the other while we sat like theater watchers in the sand dunes. "We'll just have to do his seeing for him." We walked that whole length of beach. "Here, have a sandwich. Peanut butter for me, ham and cheese for you," with the ham and cheese slices lined up perfectly.

It was moments like that, listening to the waves burst onto the sand and watching her hair blow around her face like fireworks. Her presence was a feast.

That's one of the other times she jumps into my head now—whenever I eat a ham and cheese sandwich. My stomach gurgles in response, so I get on my hands and knees and pull out my stash from under the bed. You can't go wrong with Tayto and Twix, and I have to hide them from Mam or she'd eat them all in one go. Right when I have the first crisp in my mouth, the phone rings.

"Cullen!" Mam yells. "Ellie on the phone."

I finish crunching and lick the evidence off my fingers before I get to the phone. "Hi, Ellie."

"Hi, Cullen. I wanted to let you know that Una called. She says she's okay and has a place to live, and she'll be staying down there for a bit. And then she hung up before I could ask her anything!"

"Did she sound all right?"

"Honestly, she was so quick to get off the phone, I couldn't say, but at least she's okay. Anyway, I thought you'd want to know. I have to run. We're all spazzing out here with the news. Mam cried when I told her. Me too, to be honest."

I say thanks, but she's already hung up. My hands are a bit shaky putting the phone back on its base myself. I rub at the greasy spot my hand left with my sleeve. Thank God she's okay. I should have known she would be. My get-up-and-go girl.

IT'S SUNDAY AFTERNOON and Mam's in watching *Glenroe* when the phone rings.

"Cullen? It's Ellie. Can I come over for a bit? I need to talk to you about Una."

I can't think of anything else I have to say to her. We've gone around and around what Una said and did that day she left, and all the days leading up to it, but whatever. "Yeah. Come in the back way. I'll be in the kitchen."

About fifteen minutes later I hear a bicycle grinding up the gravel before she taps timidly on the door. Una would have barged in, all matron-like. I'd smile, only it still hurts. I put my book down and open the door to her sixteen-year-old sister, her wild hair stuck to her chin and her cheeks the color of red jelly.

"Thanks for letting me come over. No one else understands, and I thought that maybe if I talked to you, I'd be able to make some sense of it all in my head." She helps herself to one of Mam's flapjacks from the counter and then licks her finger to pick up the crumbs that dropped onto the table. "I miss you coming over all the time, by the way. It's like you're part of the house one minute and then you're gone too. You don't need to stop just because Una's gone, you know. I thought you liked being at our place because your mam's always working or out gadding about with her friends," she says, examining her fingertips for more crumbs.

"Anyway, here's the thing, Cullen. Why did Una run away? Mam won't say anything. I think she knows why, but it makes no sense at all! One minute Una's just being Una and the next minute she's gone living somewhere else instead of going to school. It's so weird. I want to do something, but I can't think of anything. We've told the Gardaí, you went down to Dublin, and there's nothing else we can do to get her back home? That's poxy, Cullen. What if she's not okay and her kidnapper made her phone? What happens if she was hitchhiking and she made the call and now she's lying in a ditch somewhere? What if ...?" She snorts up some tears. "What if we never see her again?" She looks up at me, her lips quivering and her face like a flooding river, and I just look at her like a dumb fool.

"Can I get you some more tea?" Una always told me I was a bit useless when she was upset. *Yes, Your Honor, I sat there like a gombeen. Guilty as charged.*

"You know, Ellie, Una always did whatever she set her mind to. She's probably fine right now, sitting in some bookshop and trying to finish reading before the shop closes at six and delighted she doesn't have to listen to the nuns all day every day."

Ellie laughs a little. "Yeah, but more likely she has a job in a bookshop so she can read them all."

"It makes sense. Can you really see her *not* being okay, Ellie? You and I both know she'll find a way to get what she wants." I scratch the back of my head. "The thing is, what *does* Una want?"

Ellie makes a face and grabs her bag before heading towards the back door. I follow her outside. "Here, give these to your mam." I shake a few crabapples off one of the trees in the garden and put them in an old shopping bag for her. She gets back on her bike and freewheels off down the road while I sit back down with my reading homework—*Great Gatsby*, about a fella always wanting what he can't have.

I'm glad she came over. It makes me feel like I'm not the only one a little bit lost.

## Thursday

THE SCHOOL BELL RINGS and I head over to Una's house now that Ellie's invited me back proper-like. I'm wondering if they've heard anything more. I know her mam would tell me an' all, but just in case. Ellie opens the door and then leaves it open for me because one of the kids is screaming blue murder. Go in, walk up the three steps, turn left, and go into the kitchen. The kettle's only warm, so I turn it back on and help myself to a tea bag and a mug off the sink. And then I just sit there as if Una is going to walk in and pull out her homework. The steam starts puffing until the kettle whistle blows, and I go back to my spot with the big mug, watching the spirals of wet air curl upwards from the brown liquid.

Ellie comes in and pulls a few books out of her schoolbag, just like Una used to do, and gets to work.

"Any news?" I say.

She points her pencil at the paper. "Wouldn't we have told you?"

"Yeah, I know, but ..."

She sticks the end of her pencil between her teeth and twirls it in her mouth for a few minutes and stares at me. "If I didn't know any better, I'd think you were soft on her."

I can feel my ears starting to go pink, so I put my hand on one as if I'm leaning on it. "Ah, Ellie. You know we were best friends. I miss her. I don't know what to do with myself with her gone."

"Yeah." She takes the pencil out of her mouth for a moment to scribble something in her exercise book. "You were good friends. Sometimes I wish I had a guy friend, but then I don't. Girls are easier to talk to."

"What do you mean?" I lean down to the top of my mug and blow the steam in her direction.

"Oh, you know, we're always talking about stuff girls like, like clothes and who fancies who and what a cow one of our teachers is, and then we cry and hug and say we're going to gang up on the teacher next time and give her what for. Guys don't do that."

"You're nothing like Una, are you? She was always in

her head and you're ... you're here."

Ellie pushes her hair back from her face, pulls up a few bits from the sides, and ties it all on top of her head. "Here?" She's small like Una, but with more red in her hair, a rounder face, and bigger brown eyes. Una was always jealous of how great she looked in photos. "Stop staring, ya eejit." She throws her book at me.

"Sorry. I was thinking that you and Una don't look like each other much."

"Are you sure you're not soft on her?" She's looking into my eyes now, searching for truth. "Do you know something you haven't been telling us?"

My heart starts thumping faster and faster. *Yes, yes, I know something. I know that the girl I wanted to be with left with an unborn baby, and now I don't know if she'll ever come back. And even if she comes back, I don't know if she'll ever want me like that again. And I want that again.* "Don't be stupid. Jeepers, Ellie." And I get up, pour my almost-full cup of tea into the sink, and walk out the back door as the steam disappears into thin air forever.

# 8

## Una

I've been here a few days now, and I'm in my room folding the wash after bringing it in from the line. It smells of new beginnings. Catherine slides in beside me and starts to fold as well, her lined fingers pinning exact corners together, hands pushing out the wrinkles until everything is smooth as the layer of cream I used to pour over Ruthie's porridge. A rush of grief mixed with happiness fills me, and the tears fill up my eyes. I can't stay silent.

"Catherine, I love my little room! Thank you so much for saving me. Us."

She lifts my hand with hers and looks into my eyes. "Nothing makes me happier than to see you in it, making use of it." She falters. "It was for our daughter ..." She stops to breathe and looks out the window. "... but the only few breaths of life she ever took were in the hour after her birth. It was a long time ago, but sometimes ..." She gulps in more air. "She'd be about your age now."

I want to hug her so badly, but I just can't. I'm just

not a hugger. It makes me feel so vulnerable, opening up my arms to someone I don't know very well. But I link my fingers with hers instead.

Her gray eyes are sharp yet tender. "You're a real treasure already, Una, a real gift to us both the way you always see the best in what you've got. My mood picks up every time you start humming to the radio. And you throw yourself into everything, ready to help and learn what you can. It means a lot to us old folk." And then we both sniffle a bit. She reminds me of my gran a little, God rest her soul, with all the smiley lines around her eyes and the way she spools her curly hair in rolls back from her face.

I love this growing confidence, the *pzing* of the cash register, the way Des enters numbers in the tiny columns in his big red book, the peacefulness of Des and Catherine working together—stitching, drawing, cutting—the smell of leather. It smells like safety.

I'm part of something bigger now, part of a business, part of the grown-up world. I can breathe here. Even the thought of going home with this little one inside gives me goose bumps. I put my hand on my stretching skin and keep it there. This baby is part of who I am too.

The bell on the door rings while I'm in the back room filling the kettle, and from what I can make out, it's a woman who's about my mam's age. I turn back to the tea I'm making, at peace with my world, until I hear her talking.

"I'd like to place an early Christmas order, if you can do that for me. It's for McGee's—not sure if you've heard of it, but it's a shop in Donegal Town."

With my back still turned to her, heart thumping at twice the normal rate, I shuffle sideways until I'm at the bottom of the stairs and she can't see me. Des gives me a strange look until he hears her too, and he moves to the front of the shop to join Catherine. I head on up the stairs, just in case, but I stay sitting on one of the steps to make sure I'm still safe, that Mam hasn't sent someone to come and get me and make me come home.

The woman must have stayed for about forty-five minutes examining belts and handbags, but she eventually left after putting down a large order, and I was able to show my trembling face again.

"Are you okay, Una? Come on, love, let's go on upstairs. I'll make you a cuppa. You don't look right." Catherine cups my elbow and guides me back up the stairs to the kitchen, where I take some deep breaths and study my outspread fingers on the plastic tablecloth.

"Do you need to talk about anything?" She puts her hand over mine, making me recall her words about my being like a daughter already, and my tears threaten to run out of both eyes.

"That woman. She had a Donegal accent. I was afraid she might know my mam and that then they'd know where to find me. I was so scared!"

"Tell me, Una, tell me what happened to make you come to Dublin and leave home, and you only barely pregnant. Why would it be so awful to have someone from home recognize you? Is it the baby?"

I look at her one more time to reassure myself I can trust her and tell her the skeleton version—not too much detail into the whys and wherefores—but by the end of it, she has a pretty good idea of it all.

"Una, I think you'll be a great mother, but, you know, have you ever thought any more of letting this boy know? You said he's only seventeen and doing his

Leaving this year, but ..."

I shake my head sadly. "It wouldn't be fair. We weren't even going out. Everyone'd be talking about us behind our backs and laughing at how stupid we were. It wasn't even his fault! No. I'm not going to do that to him." I can see his face now. I'm back in the garden at the party. We've just done it, and the half-light coming from the window is on his face while the dark night surrounds everything else. I didn't want to look closer, and I was so far gone, I don't know if I would have seen it right anyway, but I'd swear he was smiling right then. But that's probably my imagination talking. We were good friends. He was a good friend. A best friend. Who got me pregnant. And it's all my fault.

Una, the stupid eejit who messes everything up.

"Well, all right then. You probably know best." I can hear it in her voice. She doesn't think it's the best thing at all. But I can hear something else in her voice too—she believes in me. And right there in her kitchen among the drying plates and used tea bags, peace fills my soul. My own mam might think I'm a slut, but this woman knows how I came to be here, and I'm still safe and this baby is still safe.

"Thanks."

Des is shouting up the stairs. "Come on now, ladies, enough with the McVities and tea. I know your sort. Anything to shirk this heavy workload onto poor Des."

We both laugh. He's great. And we go downstairs and I think it's time to get back to work, but it looks like someone has other plans.

"Right," says Catherine. She walks over to the long table with the tools on it and waves me over. "It's time you learned the names of the main tools we use here. It'll take a while, seeing as there are hundreds, but these three"—she pulls two out of a mug and picks a ruler off the table—"are a good start: the ruler, scratch awl, and leather knife. We'll start with you using them to make a belt." She pulls a small roll of thick, finished leather off a shelf and sets it on the table. "You'll need to learn how to stitch and finish edges on things later, but this'll be good practice for starters."

We sit side by side as the sun drops into the streets and sends rivulets of orange and pink through the front window, one finger of it reaching into the back room. I sit back in the chair proud of my first bit of work. Now I'm stuck on which belt buckle to choose because apparently this belt will be mine.

# 9

## Una

### December

It's Christmas Day. There's no stocking at the end of my bed this morning. Mam always did that for us because Dad was usually too far gone by the time we went to bed, it being Christmas Eve n' all. Then we'd all jump onto their bed in the morning and show them what we got. We all played along. But today I just get dressed in one of the massive preggers dresses Catherine brought home from Oxfam and sludge my socked feet into the kitchen to see what I'm supposed to do. Everyone has a tradition, right?

I find Catherine cooking Des some Christmas kippers, and boiled eggs are on the table. So different.

"I got some fresh bread from the country market yesterday, and look! A honeycomb." There's already a chunk of it missing, and the opened cells pour out their tawny sweetness onto the plate below. Des gives me a conspiratorial wink. Catherine must have driven to the market specially for the day that's in it. She's almost dancing around the cooker, with the spatula keeping the beat to the FM radio.

"I got a turkey from a farmer down that way too. Have a look in the fridge."

I open the door to see this huge thing sitting all chuffed-looking on the fridge shelf, along with a right feast beside it.

It's still Christmas morning two hours later, and we're standing together in the Pringles' pew singing Christmas carols. The angel at the top of the Christmas tree stares down at me like I'm some sort of traitor. She's right. I should be at home with my family right now. We'd have gone to midnight Mass together and then Mam would have rushed us all to bed so that we'd be asleep for Santa. This morning we'd have all been in the kitchen watching Mam and Dad eat their toast slowly on purpose, and the little ones would be watching each torturous bite before Dad gave the word to head on into the living room so we could open presents.

It's just me here—me and two old people and this six-month something.

> *Oh, raise, raise a song on high,*
> *His mother sings her lullaby.*
> *Joy, oh joy for Christ is born,*
> *The Babe, the Son of Mary.*

So much happiness over a little baby. So much went into his arrival. It was all planned out perfectly by God, apparently, so perfectly that Mary never expected to be lying on her back in dirty straw with a load of animals watching Jesus pop out of her. That must have been quite the sight. And poor Joseph. I bet that back then the women usually shoved the men out of the room and then took over, but Joseph was likely stuck standing at Mary's open thighs wondering what to do next. Sounds like it all worked out though.

I haven't even talked to Catherine about what's next for me. I'm too scared to ask. I'm pretty sure it's not going to turn out like it did for Mary.

We sit down on the cushioned wooden pew after another carol and listen to John talk to the children— yeah, turns out that once in a blue moon, whole families show up at this little church. I suppose it *is* Christmas, birth of our blessed Lord, so they feel obliged to make an appearance and say hello.

Des and I walk together to the front door while Catherine stops to chat with a friend. Everyone's in Sunday best, with some of the children fiercely pressing their favorite presents to their chests. John's standing there ready to shake hands and to see how we liked the sermon.

"Good job there, John, with keeping it short for the children. It's great the way you keep their attention."

"Thanks, Des, and happy Christmas. And how are you three doing? I know I ask every Sunday, but can I help you with anything at all?"

His smile is so real, his face so kind. He reminds me of Cullen. It's flashes like these that are the worst. Cullen laughing, smiling, caring. I left that, and here I am in a Protestant church on Christmas morning, six months pregnant and a family at home that has an empty space at the table. Maybe Mam's told them all what I did. Maybe Cullen's glad I ran because he has better things to do with his life than look after a pregnant friend. Maybe I could call again....

I picture myself dialing the number, Mam trying to grab the phone from one of the kids quickly in case I hang up, Dad standing in the corner watching, Ellie shushing them all. What would I say? What should I say? I walk back to the shop in silence while Catherine's verbal list of things to still do flies up and over Des's head.

Des turns on the big radio as soon as we've climbed the stairs and I've positioned myself in the middle of the kitchen, awaiting commands from a jittery Catherine. Renee and Renato are singing about saving their love. It all sounds so ... possible. I doubt Cullen's even thinking about me these days. I've been gone for too long, and his mad eejits of friends are probably already planning their next night on the tear. Did I really want to be that close to him at all? Was it just the drink talking? It makes me more certain of my decision to not tell him, that's for sure.

Catherine pulls on my hands. "Rub that half pound of butter all over the turkey, there's a love, and then line up the rashers on top. We want it to be nice and juicy." She washes the brussels sprouts before putting the turkey in the oven "for a few hours."

Des has a great fire going in the living room. He's sitting in his green chair by the Christmas tree looking like he's the king of the world, and at the age of sixty-five, who's to stop him acting like it? On the sofa is a pile of presents, and there are two much smaller piles on the floor.

"Una, that's your pile over there." Des points to the sofa. "When I say go, we'll all open our presents at the same time." And there he sits, grinning like a man who's up to something. *"Go!"*

Even the first present stops my heart. It's a crocheted baby hat, a lemon color, and it's so small even a football wouldn't fit in it. I look at Des with full eyes and turn back to open the next one, and then the next one, until I have a complete wardrobe for my child. My *child*. *My* child. At the end of the pile is an envelope. They're both staring at me now in anticipation, their piles long since opened and sorted. No matter what happens, my reaction matters here.

The outside of the card is of baby Jesus in a manger, a halo around his head. Inside is some writing.

*Una,*

*The greatest present you could give us this Christmas is your presence. Not just yours, but your baby's too. What we're asking you for today is this: Will you do us the honor of staying with us after the baby is born? You and the baby, of course.*

*We never thought we'd be grandparents, and you've brought so much happiness into our old lives. It would make us so happy if you said yes.*

*Love,*

*Des and Catherine*

My legs won't hold me up anymore, and I fall onto the sofa's pink and green flowers along with my tears. "Really?"

"Yes, really. This is a chance we've been given to help

two lives." Catherine's wiping away her tears too.

I have no words. I lean in to her shoulder and keep weeping until I start hiccupping and Des says, "Hold off on that. We haven't even started on the whiskey yet!"

Catherine looks at her watch. "Oops, I have to turn the turkey over, and John will be here in an hour." She jumps into action while Des opens the door of the drinks cupboard and pours himself a small glass. I gather up the baby clothes and bring them into the bedroom, where I lay them out on the cover and stare at them for a while with a silly smile on my face, before I remember that I should probably wash my eyes in cold water to get rid of the red blotches around them. After all, one of the men who saved me, us, will be here soon to munch on those twelve pounds of lard.

And I'm pretty sure this baby will enjoy his fair share of the feast. And as soon as I think it, there are his feet pushing out my belly again. He'll be here in no time, or she; either way, he's all mine. As Sunshine Radio keeps telling me, no doubt the universe is unfolding as it should.

Three hours later and we're all sitting here smiling and laughing. John's telling us stories of times he was called out to people's homes to stop fights and pray over dying animals, while Catherine's getting up every other minute to get more food. My hand keeps slipping down to my belly to feel the kicks, and my mind keeps slipping to Donegal, to where the whole family is sitting over the same meal without me. Are they talking about me, feeling sad? Do they miss me as much as I miss them?

"Catherine, would you mind if I used your phone to call home?"

She gives me a huge smile and nods.

They'll be lying on the sofa, stuffed to the gills, with *Chitty- Chitty Bang Bang* nearly over. Then it'll be up to Ellie to get the Christmas cake ready. She'll fill up the kettle and get the plates out on a tray. Maybe she'll be swinging around to pull a knife out of the drawer when the phone rings. Maybe she'll be the one to pick up again.

She's laughing when she picks up the receiver. "Gallaghers."

"It's me, Una. I'm still fine. Happy Christmas to you all." I hang up before I say anything. I can see Ellie standing there, frozen to the brown flower pattern on the carpet with the phone in her hand, icing on her fingers, trying to remember if *64 works for calling someone back. Even if it does, I won't answer.

*And to all a good night.*

# 1984

# 10

## Una

### March

It's the end of March and I'm two weeks overdue, lying here on a hospital bed with a belly that feels like it's about to blow up. Two different nurses have come and gone, and the gynecologist has just stuck what looks like a ginormous pair of pliers up inside me, and then I heard a crunch before black water starting flooding the place. Apparently that's bad, and they want to help me have this baby quickly and make sure it's okay.

I lie here for what feels like hours with the water, or whatever mucky-muck word they call it, dribbling out, and my whole belly squeezes me about every minute and a half. Looks like that's bad too. Catherine's been great. Good thing she brought a book though; it's pretty boring, even though it's exciting at the same time.

A doctor and nurse come in with a tray and an IV bag. "We're going to start you on a drug called Pitocin. It's going to help your contractions and push this baby out faster because it doesn't seem to want to meet us all yet, and we need to make sure everything goes well."

Long hours pass until it's seven o'clock and I finally feel like I want to push, even though they gave me an epidural hours ago. It's like my legs are completely paralyzed but in a good way. I hate pain. I'll always, always be a wuss and beg for mercy. I push, breathe, push, breathe, squeeze Catherine's hand, breathe, and then the baby slithers out of my legs and into the nurse's waiting hands. She holds a tiny body up for me to see. I can see his bits dangling, and so can everyone else.

"It's a boy!" She wipes him with a towel and puts him in my arms for a minute. He's so still, so complete. "I'm sorry to take him away so quickly, but he's a bit pale and we need to make sure he's healthy." She bends her arms down for him. And he's gone again.

Another older nurse comes forward. "Sorry, love, but you split a bit down below, so we're going to have to sew you up so you don't bleed." She hunches over at the end of the bed with a needle and thread, along with a student nurse, inspecting my bits like they're on sale at the butcher's shop.

"Ow!"

"Oh, quit your griping. Women in Africa go squat in bushes to have their babies, and you've had an epidural. You can't even feel this. Shouldn't have opened your legs the first time if you didn't want any of this."

There it is again—the shame that's been following me around Dublin since I've started showing. Yeah, I know, I know, but it's all a bit pathetic. I mean, the deed is done, right? None of the dirty looks can rewind the tape to where I'm back at the party and I turn into the Virgin Mary and don't even touch a drink, let alone start a snogging session with Cullen. I close my eyes and shut up.

The old nurse snips the end of the thread, puts the needle in a kidney dish, and pushes the trolley away from my bed. They bring me some toast, which I throw up almost immediately.

"Can I have my baby back now?"

The nurse shakes her capped head. "Sorry, but we're going to have to keep him overnight in the unit to make sure he's okay. Some of his oxygen levels are a bit off, but we think he'll be fine in the morning." She leaves the room, as if there's no space for hussies like me to ask questions.

Catherine coughs loudly after her and glares at her back. She sees it too. "So did you decide on calling him Conner or Kieran?"

"I think he looks more like a Kieran, and the book said his name means 'dark-haired one.' Did you see all that hair in the few seconds they let us see him?"

"Kieran Gallagher it is." Her face is alight. I haven't seen her happy like this before, and it warms my heart. There's no shame in her face, no shame in her house. Kieran Gallagher is going to be loved well. Gallagher. I wish his last name could be Breslin, but it's far, far better that he have my name than the name of some adoptive parents who'd take him away forever. I just hope he's going to be okay tonight and that they're not playing down anything serious.

I'm woken early in the morning by a nurse pressing her fingertips to my wrist. She slips a thermometer under my arm as well and scribbles something on the chart. She presses her cold hand on my belly, for what I have no idea. Do some bits not come out? It's while she's checking out the blood loss that I ask her, "Where's my baby? Is he all right?"

"Give me a few minutes and I'll bring him right to you." Sure enough, she wheels him in and gently lifts him out of the see-through box and puts him in my arms. He's so small and perfect. Everything moves in slow motion as my hands find his fingers, stroke his hair, and touch his soft cheek. He smells of talcum powder and love. His hair feels like the baby feathers you find in the garden in springtime. Tiny eyelashes, teeny tiny lips, little ears.

I lift up the side of the hospital gown and bring Kieran's mouth up to latch on. He's so sleepy, he does nothing for a few minutes, so I tease his mouth open and try it different ways until his mouth starts moving. His mouth keeps slipping off, but I'm determined to keep trying, just like the leaflets showed. I fold back the edge of the gown to watch his face and make sure nothing is covering his nose, and out of nowhere guilt crawls all over me. *Cullen should be here. You should have told him. He should be here to see his son.*

The voices are right. Should, should, should. Well, should never won a race, and I'm on a new track now, should be damned. But.

There's a card beside the bed, ready to post. I'll ask Catherine to send it on her way home.

*Hi Mam.*

*You're a granny now. His name is Kieran, and everything went well.*

*I miss you all.*

*Love.*

*Una*

FIVE DAYS AGO I was able to see this gorgeous little fella for the first time. We're upstairs on the sofa with the cushions stacked around me, a beach ring under me, and the radio on low. I watch his mouth move in and out, even though he's not even sucking anymore, see his eyelids flutter to a close, and I stare at his soft face and have to hold back from touching his thin curls so he doesn't stir.

Who'd have thought I'd be looking forward to him waking up for hugs and kisses? I'm not saying I'm cured, like, but when I'm looking into the eyes of innocence like this, I'm not afraid to give back.

Catherine comes up beside us and rubs his cheek with the crook of her finger. "You doing all right? Need anything?" I shake my head, and we both sit there together looking at my little chunk of love. It's not easy being a mam, but it's very, what's the word, inclusive. I understand Mam now a whole lot more. I know why she wanted so many of us.

Ruthie, Owen, Charlie, Ellie. I think about them all the time, about sitting around the dinner table together with Dad telling his bad jokes and Mam enjoying the temporary rest, about Ellie on the phone while Charlie yells at her to get off it because he has friends too, about lying out in the sun out the back with our baby oil on to see who can get browner. But sitting here with Kieran was worth it. Yes. I lean down and kiss his velvety skin, letting my lips linger on his peacefulness. So worth it.

# 11

## Una

### April

"Tell me about Kieran's dad," Catherine says from the front of the shop. We're doing one of our big cleanups after closing. Kieran's in the pram with a stuffed belly and a few of his toys tucked around him. I say a few, but the truth is he has far too many. That's what happens when you have grandparents around all the time.

"Well." I stop and try to see Cullen's face, try to remember the way he talked and laughed, the way he worked that dimple in his cheek. It makes me sad every time I try this because my memories of him are getting paler by the day. I feel as if I'm speaking from inside a cloud. "I've known him for forever. When I started school, all the children on our road would walk in together. Mam was worried about me walking on my own, so she asked his mam if he'd walk with me for the first few days until I had some other friends to walk with.

So we walked to national school every day together until we were twelve.

"He's always been a great listener, but he's clever too, and we talked about lots of stuff. Whenever I'd be thinking about something and wanted to learn more, he'd go off and find things that would help me understand. One time he got a book from the library for me about eggs because I wanted to know why some yolks were more orange than others. Another time he dragged branches from all over to a big tree in the woods and showed me how to build a ladder up the trunk. We spent ages up there. Years."

I can see it all again—me reading bits of the latest book I'd taken from Mam's bookshelf to him because the words were so good; him giving me little gifts all the time, like snowdrops tied with a bit of long grass or pieces of toffee from the big jar in the newsagents. We were connected back then, so close in the way we'd think through things and process our own lives and the lives of our friends. He was always there for me, no matter what was going on at school or at home. Why did I love him? I've thought about it for so long now. I think it's because I felt complete with him, like I'd never need anyone else but him in my life and I'd be okay.

I dust the handbags again, even though they're dust free now, and watch the feathers dance around the leather.

Des cuts in. "You know, Una, I think you might have thought too little of your boy Cullen. We men, when we're in love, we're willing to do things. Do you think, maybe …?" His voice trails off when I give him my "back off" look.

My eyes start filling up. "I forgot something

upstairs," I mumble, and I run up before the feelings surging up inside me start screaming too loudly. I can hear Kieran start waking up, but I run into my bedroom and shut the door before opening the wardrobe and taking the only photo I have of Cullen out of a coat pocket. It's a class photo from when he was in fifth year, and I've studied it ever since, imagining what it would have been like had I stayed, had I told him he was a father, had I told him I loved him.

"Cullen, I'm so sorry," I whisper. "I'm so sorry." I grab the towel from the back of my door and blow my nose into it. The only boy I've ever loved, the only one I wanted to be with, could be sitting on a carpet somewhere with Kieran while I look on. Our family would be whole, and all I feel right now is pieces.

I've been missing Dad a lot lately—his quiet way of always being nearby in the evenings, the way he looks at me when he thinks I'm sad and he just waits for me to talk, if I want to. I don't think I ever appreciated him enough. He felt solid, dependable.

I've decided. Come June, as soon as Kieran is three months old, I'm going home. Mam won't be able to make me give him up then. She's all hard words but mush with a baby in her arms. She was born to have babies, so I'd be helping her obsession really. I'll get work in a shop now that I have some experience, and while I'll let Cullen think Dylan's the dad so he doesn't feel obligated to give his life up for us, at least I'll be able to see him again and tell him how I really feel.

And if miracles really happen, he'll have come around to the thought of us while I was gone, and I can finally be myself again.

# 12

## Ellie

It's Easter Sunday and we're all standing in our pew at Mass making Mam look good. She's finally let me start wearing trousers to Mass, but not today, oh no. But it's not so bad because today we can finally start eating biscuits again. Mam said that we should all do Lent together this year, and eejit that I was, I said I thought it'd be great. I couldn't believe she didn't make a single flapjack or buy even one packet of Jaffa Cakes for the forty days though. I mean, come on! Lent's like a diet— you say you won't eat something and then you scarf three times as many of the thing you say you'd rather die than eat when the kids have gone to bed. I've raided the shelves at the Spar. We'll all die of chocolate Easter egg poisoning this year, so help me God.

So anyway. Father what's his name is going on and on about some water well in Africa and Jesus being water and stuff, and my eyes are wandering. I'm freshly single after Philip said he didn't want to go out with me anymore, which was all right with me anyway because to be honest, I was getting really bored with his Adam Ant obsession. He could only look one way when he could have been changing that hair and makeup every time he went out. So now that I'm ready for love again, it's only right that I should keep my eyes peeled on the local talent. I've only one year of school left now, so if the right one came along, I might even end up with him for life and be able to skip college altogether. I haven't mentioned that in passing to Mam though. She has plans—wants me to head up to Dublin and do one of them posh typing courses. Says I might even meet Una and give her what for.

My eyes keep traveling around the church pews. Well, hellloooo, Cullen Breslin, in your Easter best! Oh my.

I slink up beside him when we're walking out. "Hi there, Cullen. Remember me?"

"Ellie!" He takes my arm and sits me down on the pew beside us. "So what's new? How's the family?"

"Yeah, doing my Leaving next year, and I have no idea what to do after that, if I even pass. I'm bricking! What about you? Haven't seen you at the house lately."

"Ah, it's been great. Just have to get the Leaving over with and then Michael, the blacksmith I was helping out all last summer, agreed to teach me what he knows. It'll be a good job for me. I love the work, but it's Letterkenny, you know? Not like Donegal Town." He stands up and looks around at the emptying building. "Still nothing from Una, I see. Ah well." He holds out a weathered hand and I put mine in it to stand with him.

"She called over the Christmas, actually. Another one where she said nothing but that she's alive and well."

Cullen's eyes go wide. "Thank God for that, at least."

God, he's lovely.

"It's been great to see you, Ellie. Let me know if you

or the family need anything."

I take in his almost manliness one more time and turn to go, but I stop as my brain lights up the cells I don't use very often—the ones where I strategize. I breathe in and turn back to face him. "You know, Cullen, some friends and me will be at the Abbey on Friday for a bit of dancing. Maybe we'll see you there?"

He scratches behind his ear and then rubs his jaw before he tilts his head to one side and looks at me in a completely different way—like a woman instead of Una's little sister. His green eyes have me feeling warm all over. "Ah, sure, why not? We'll have a laugh. I'll bring Tom. See ya then, Ellie." And he walks out of the church looking like the king of the world.

## May

CULLEN AND TOM have been making us girls laugh for the last four Fridays in a row. He only gets dancing after a few beers, but he has us in knots laughing when he does. It's starting to be the only thing I look forward to. I wish Una was here to join in the fun.

## May 25

CULLEN'S ASKED ME TO HIS DEBS!! I'm screaming the words into my pillow. His debs! Janey mackers. It's going to take forever to find the right dress! I'll ask Nathalie if she'll do my hair and makeup because there's no way I'll be able to hack it on my own, and I want to look perfect. The other fifth years are going to be dead jealous. He said he was asking me as a friend, not a girlfriend—just like Tom's asked Nathalie, but I'm not going to tell them that, not on your nelly. And maybe it'll turn into something else if I look drop-dead gorgeous....

## June

MAM WENT ALL OUT on the dress and paid a woman in town to sew it for me. All Spanish red taffeta and puffy sleeves with a scooped neckline and a big flouncy skirt. I feel fake, like I'm wrapped in candy floss. My makeup turned out lovely though. I copied it from a photo in *Image* magazine, and it's all dark at the edges of my eyes and blue eyeliner all around, and I found red lipstick the color of the dress—hussy color, Charlie called it. Rude.

"Ah, aren't you lovely." Mam's standing in the doorway of the living room so she can be the first to see me. "Seamus, have a look at Ellie there."

Dad turns around on the sofa and hesitates when he sees me before standing up and walking over to Mam's side. I can see a glint of something in his eye, but it couldn't be a tear. No. Dad only ever cried when he was drinking, and he doesn't do that anymore. Well, only on special occasions.

"Seamus, stand there beside her while I take a photo of the two of ye." She picks up her Instamatic and mutters and sighs before pushing us out the door into the twilight. "Kids," she yells back through the front door, "come out and see your sister before it all goes to hell."

Owen runs out first and stops. "Whoa, Ells, you've got a lot of makeup on your face."

Ruthie whispers as she feels my taffeta skirt, "You're like a princess."

I rub her soft curls, checking to make sure she

doesn't have something sticky on her hands. Mam starts barking out more orders. I suppose she doesn't take photos that much, so we all humor her, line up, and swap places for a few minutes until we hear Cullen driving in in his mam's car. Owen starts singing loudly,

> *Ellie and Cullen*
> *sitting in a tree*
> *K-I-S-S-I-N-G.*
> *First comes ...*

I slap his ear and turn to look at Cullen as he steps out of the car. God, he's lovely when he's dressed up. He's working that dimple by his lips and Mam is clucking around him like he's the new son-in-law, pinning his matching flower to his tux and talking about the chocolates he's brought me. I feel a bit awkward all of a sudden, to be honest. He's been just Cullen for so long and now he's *Cullen*. He walks up to me and puts his lips next to my ear.

"You're looking lovely," he breathes, ever so casually, and my legs turn into jelly and I try to hold in my chest so he can't see how quickly I'm breathing. Panting really. *It's disgusting, Ellie. Get a grip.*

Mam bosses us around for a bit more so she can show the photos off to her friends when they gossip over their tea next week. She'd be happier if they were here right now, but we can't have it all, now, can we. I hide the chocolates in my room so the wains can't find them, and we wave our goodbyes, laugh at all the bad jokes about what we're going to get up to, and head for the hotel to join about forty other lads and the girls they've talked into coming.

The hotel room looks lovely—all white tablecloths and fresh flowers around a big dance floor in the middle for later. There's a DJ setting up on the right and a bar at the back of the room for the lucky buggers who are over eighteen. We find a table quickly, and a few girls come up and say hello to Cullen. I know what they're thinking—how did I get so lucky? And I really don't know. Chances happen and you take them or you don't. But it's just for the night and I'm doing him a favor, so he says, so there you have it.

"You really do look gorgeous, Ellie," he says as we sit down. I don't know what to say, and you could normally never accuse me of being short of words.

I laugh. "That's what makeup and a dress'll get you."

"No, really, Ellie, you look fantastic." He leans back in his hotel chair and smiles at the girl next to him before holding out a hand. "I'm Cullen." And they start yakking while I shakily pour myself a glass of water.

He's really the best person. He has everyone around us chatting, and Nathalie's giving me a look like she wants a lot more to happen tonight for me and she's dead jealous at the same time, even though Tom's sitting right beside her. Tonight it's like she wants to be our matchmaker with all her pointed questions. I watch him laughing each one off. He gets it, and even in the way he looks at me as he answers, I feel like he gets me too.

I don't think I've ever felt like that with anyone else. Not that I've had many boyfriends. There was Philip for about six months, and the Australian who was in town for three months before that—the one who hasn't even bothered to write to me since he left. Yeah, true love. But I got over him quickly, so I suppose it wasn't love after all. And my first boyfriend, Michael, who said I talked too much. One of us was plenty.

They've cleared off the tables, cleared off the dance floor, and now we're sitting beside each other in silence watching everyone else dance. I can hear Nathalie laughing like a hyena in some far corner of the room. I bet she's drunk. I'll admit, I've had a few that I've begged other people to buy for me, and it gives me enough bravery to ask Cullen to dance. He hams it up on the dance floor and makes it all a big joke until the slow dance starts. I pull on his arm and lean into him and think about Whitney Houston saving all her love and me spending mine, and I let myself melt into him. I'm pretty sure he can feel my heart beating past his thin shirt, but he keeps swaying and moves his arms a little tighter into the curve of my back.

All around us girls are lip-locked with their fellas, and I think about how great it would be to do the same thing with Cullen. I lift my head up and find him looking down into my eyes with this strange look on his face, like he wants to but doesn't want to.

"What?" I say.

"You have lovely eyes."

I smile and put my head back on his sweaty chest. I suppose this is enough for now. He pulls away at the end of the song and heads for the bar. I should probably get more water, but I can't think about much right now with all these people around me snogging in the dark as the disco lights turn their lips shades of purple and green, so I follow him.

"Water?" he asks when he sees me sit down beside him.

"I'd murder a Stag."

He looks at my face for a few long seconds. "Let's

wait a bit." He says it as if it's decided, but then he gets off the bar stool and reaches out that huge hand and I put mine in his and we walk out into the hallway together like we've just robbed a bank and we're trying to act cool. And that's when he cups my face in his rough hands and he kisses me ever so softly right in the center of my lips. And then stops. And rubs the back of his neck.

"I'm sorry, Ellie, but I have to go now. I have an early start in the morning—said I'd help Michael out at the forge—and I should have told you I'd be leaving by midnight." He doesn't even wait for a response, and he walks back into the ballroom, picks up his jacket, and walks back past me to the front door of the hotel.

I follow him, my taffeta swishing like the wheat ready for harvest in my rush to keep up. "Did I do something wrong? Do you think I drank too much? I'm sorry for drinking so much!" But the words follow him like the smoke on a candle when you blow it out.

He doesn't look back and I sink to the floor and decide to sit there for a while rather than go back into the ballroom without him. It's one thing to be alone at a debs. It's quite another to be left alone as if you're the last person in the world a boy would want to be with.

I lean my head back against the wooden panel, close my eyes, and try to hold the crackling shards of my soft heart together.

# 13

## Cullen

I'm lying on my bed back at Mam's place. What the hell just happened? I'm playing with a sixteen-year-old's emotions, and I'm messing with my own. Why did I say yes? Why do I feel guilty as hell for wanting to kiss her, for kissing her, for wanting to kiss her far more than I did? There's nothing wrong with being with a girl two years younger than me. There's nothing wrong with fancying her. But for some *stupid* reason, I feel like there's some kind of code between me and Una that says I shouldn't go out with Ellie.

The look on her face when I ran off, and I had to go back in to get my jacket and drag out the whole leaving thing. Aarrgh! Enough already. Una's gone. She's been gone for too long. I owe her nothing. So why do I feel like shite? I haven't thought of her for months, and now here she is again, rattling my brain. What would she think? What would she tell me to do? It's been nearly a year now since she up and left. It's not been easy. There've been so many times when I went to call her or hang out with her those first few weeks and then I'd remember. I get back into normal life and I forget, but then I see something or hear a song and she's right back there again inside my head like she's never left. Una not caring anymore? I've twisted it around my head for too long, and I'll never understand it, but I think she'll always care. No matter what she left for, I've always trusted her. I still do. I'm sure she had good reason for hunting down the father and not telling us where she'd be. I only wish her the best. But she's moved on to live her life with her little one, so I suppose I should move on to live mine. Even Jesus rose from the dead.

I like Ellie. She has a big laugh, she's funny, she's sweet. So what's the problem? I turn up the radio and close my eyes, breathing in and out until sleep manages to fog up my thoughts and help me escape for a few hours.

The phone wakes me a few hours later. I look at my watch and it says it's seven o'clock. Who's ringing on a Sunday at this godforsaken hour? Mam's irritated voice bangs through my door. "Cullen, it's for you. It's a girl."

Ellie's words are sharp enough too. Not because she means them to be, but because she's too nice, and sometimes kindness cuts clean. "Hi, Cullen. I just wanted to say how sorry I am for drinking so much last night. I didn't mean to scare you. Sometimes when I get to drinking more than two, I get a bit too happy or something. Anyway, I'm sorry for waking you up. Your mam sounded a bit cross, but you said you had an early start and I wanted to make sure to catch you before you left."

*Ah yes, I did say that, and now it turns out I'm a liar as well. Well, aren't you the fine one, Cullen?*

"You're fine, Ellie. You weren't too bad with the

drink at all, but it all just got to me that here are all these fellas going off to college to do great stuff and I'm just learning to be a blacksmith, and I just couldn't hack it, so I left." Not a total lie, but not the truth either. I stare at the dirt on the phone cord, waiting for her to say something, anything, that will make me feel like less of a bollox, but all there is is silence for the longest time.

"Well, then, I suppose it is what it is. Thanks for asking me anyway. Have a safe trip up to Letterkenny, and I'll see you when I see you." I hear a click and she's gone. I lean back on my pillows and stare at the four walls for a bit, then pull out a Twix from the box under the bed. I have to forget her for my own peace of mind.

But for some reason, for the next few weeks, all I can think of is Ellie Gallagher's eyes when I leaned in to kiss her and how her lips felt under mine. She wanted me, needed me, and that's enough to set any man's trousers on fire.

All the more reason to stay away.

I think.

# 14

## Una

I've decided to do a test run to see if I can handle being home again with Kieran. I'm going to go alone and leave him here, though, test the waters, like. I need to talk to Mam and see how she'd feel about it, and I can't do that on the phone when I haven't even talked to her since last year. And I need to see Cullen, hear his voice, be close, see if I can stand not being closer. I couldn't do it before, so I don't know if I can hack it.

I pack the last few things into my bag and pull the zip closed—the same bag I ran down here with, only now it's filled with hope instead of fear.

Catherine walks in. "You're sure you're okay with us looking after Kieran? Old doddery people like us?"

My heart feels warm. "I can't think of anyone who loves him more. He'll be spoiled rotten and won't even want to look at me when I get back. I know your sort."

She laughs, loud and clear. "All right then. Get on with you, and all the best." She turns back. "Call me when you get there so I know you made it up. Three rings."

"I will." I throw the bag handle onto my shoulder and we head down the worn stairs together, weave past the chunky tables and through the doorway, and make it to the front door of the shop. Her hug is wide and all-encompassing, as usual. I'm used to them now.

"Don't you worry about a thing. As you said, my granny spoiling power is strong. See you Sunday."

I WAKE UP when we're almost in Donegal Town, my neck twisted sideways and drool sitting on my chin. Lovely. My heart has been beating overtime practically the whole five hours, and my insides are a mix of hunger, excitement, and dread. The bus pulls up to the stop outside the Abbey Hotel, and I jump down the stairs, feeling almost weightless without Kieran in my arms. My hood is pulled well over my head. I don't want anyone to see me and call home in advance. I want to surprise them all.

There's a break in the traffic and I run across the road, heading for the phone box on the other side of the Diamond so I can call Catherine. There's a wild noise of laughter and talking at the hotel behind me, and I look back for a second to see ... to see *my* Cullen in a tux holding the door open for my Ellie, *and his eyes are only on her.* She looks amazing. So does he. What the bloody hell ...?

It's right about then when my brain hits my heart and it falls apart.

*Think, Una. Think!*

The coins clink through the phone as soon as she picks up. "Catherine." I'm sobbing. "Change of plans. I'm getting the seven o'clock bus back. I'll tell you everything then, but can you pick me up from O'Connell

Street?"

"Of course, love. I'll see you then. Is there anything else I can do for you?"

"No thanks. I just need to come back." I grip the black phone unit as if it'll give me my legs back, but no such luck.

"Okay. I'll be there."

I'm really nervous now about standing outside the Abbey for the next thirty minutes, but I keep my head bent over and keep wiping my sleeve under my nose, making snail tracks like they're at the races. I scuttle onto the bus and pretty much cry the first hour until it turns into whimpers. I can't come back now. There's just no way my heart could keep beating up here. No way.

# 15

## Una

### September

It's 8:45 a.m. and I'm kneeling on the floor of the hallway in Kieran's new crèche on his first day. It's a brand-new one that's close to the shop, and the prices are great. I'm so scared. Will he like it, will they love him? Will he love them more than me? Other moms are all around me hugging the last breath out of their children before pushing or carrying them into the room that matches their age.

"Kieran Gallagher."

"Yes." I wave like an eejit and set him down on the floor in his room, his teacher smiling with motherly love at them all. Gillian Faulkner is her name. She says she's going to do water play, music play, story time, and all the things perfect mammies should be doing 24-7.

I sized her up as soon as I saw her last week. About five foot six with freckles everywhere and a raspy voice that means she was probably a jazz singer on her days off; hair like mine—vehemently disagreeing with her efforts to tie it back. She asked me that day how I'd been doing without a father around for Kieran.

"Excuse me?" I'd asked in as strong a voice as I could force out so she couldn't see my fear rising up behind my wall. "What are you trying to say, Miss Faulkner?"

She leaned in as if she didn't want anyone else to hear. "I'm a single mam too. That's my Ashlinn over there."

I put my arms on hers and for a moment shared that temporary helplessness, the feelings of not being good enough, the inability to give our children a more *normal* family setting.

She rubbed her eyes. "Miss Gallagher, you understand the other half of my life. Let's be friends." It was more of a declaration than an invitation. "And call me Gilly."

"Una," I said, "and I'd love to."

KIERAN AND I get home after I've picked him up and go through the new routine of an earlier bedtime. This'll be it for the next seventeen years. Eat, bath, story, bed. Once his tiny snores come through the door, I shut it and start in the bathroom with the green eyeliner, followed by some neon bracelets on my arm and a pink, pin-striped minidress. I finally feel my age again. I agreed to a night out with Gilly, and she's waiting for me. I'll be late, but at least Kieran is asleep for Catherine. I'd feel guilty if she had to put him to bed.

I finally run up to the entrance to Switzer's, panting, only to stand there like loose change while she rearranges her scarf, using the shop window as her personal mirror.

"Una, I have to ask," she says, "where in God's name did you get that handbag?" She strokes its flap with love.

I look down at it proudly. It's a simple design, just

one big piece folded over on itself and stitched down the sides, with a big buckle on the front, but Catherine let me use really soft, red leather, so it looks expensive. "I made it myself, so it's not the best stitching, but it's part of last year's collection we put together for the Christmas season. You should come by some time to see the others."

Her eyes are expanding. "You're messing with me. You made this? It's beautiful!" She touches it again before looping her arm through mine. "Right, enough with the leather. Let's go and find you a man!"

I giggle and feel like I'm fourteen again.

We head to O'Rourke's, which she says has the most eligible bachelors in Dublin. Sadly, eligible doesn't seem to mean gorgeous. A band is playing some Chieftains songs in the far corner, and though I'd rather have snagged two seats at a tiny table near the window, Gillian is on a mission. She walks up to a half-decent-looking guy standing with a friend and says something. He laughs and looks in my direction. I curl up on the bar stool like a fern at night. Minutes later, we're all hanging out together in the smoke. One of the guys has pushed a drink into my hand, and he's asking me about other things I can do with leather. I should have known.

Gillian catches the look of murder on my face ten minutes in, so she grabs her bag and my hand. "Sorry, fellas, we have to go." She rubs her tummy and makes a face. "Time of the month. You know how it is." The look on their faces is priceless. We march out into the rainy mist and she keeps walking. My legs are growing goose bumps rapido, and I hope we'll get into a bit of warmth soon.

"Gilly, where are we going?"

"Foyle's," she mutters, and keeps walking. "I know a guy."

Minutes later we're in another haze of cigarette smoke and barely able to hear each other. A waitress pushes by me with a tray of pints and some of it slops over and into my cleavage. She doesn't even notice. I run to the toilets to wipe off the stickiness and when I come out, Gillian is at the back of the pub where two pool tables stand, with the promise of £25 coupons for Superquinn on a torn-out sheet of paper on the wall for the winners. "Tonight Only," reads Gilly, giving me the "we really should be impressed" face. She hands me a stick and she lines up the balls perfectly before giving them a wild whack that sends them running all over the table. "Lads," she yells into the smoke, "who wants to give two country girls a game?"

I back into the corner as the eyes around us give us the lookover, while desperately wanting to scratch the sticky beer I missed off my boobs. Two men swagger forward. "We win and we get to buy you drinks."

"You're on," she says.

How does one person get so much confidence? One thing's for sure, she's the boss tonight.

THREE HOURS LATER and boobs shiny, I'm in my bed thinking about Robert, the fella I ended up talking to while Gillian snogged his friend in the corner. We sort of fell together because once the other two locked lips, we were invisible. Robert was such a gas man, and great company. He gave me his boss's business card so I could call him at work. Said he'd love to meet up again for lunch or something. He fixes bicycles so he can eat during the day, but also said that his mammy's very good at looking after him the rest of the time. To top it off, he wants to be a lawyer, and he's in his second year at Trinity, four more to go. I felt like I wasn't at his level at all, but we had a rare old back and forth about life, and my ribs hurt from laughing so much.

Granted, I laughed more with each Stag, but it's been a long time since I felt free like that with a guy. I stared at his face for much too long at one point, drank in the way his skin puckered up around his eyes when he smiled, imagined how his perfect mouth would feel under my fingertips, under my lips.

Gillian is this determined to find me someone. Did I find him already? Is this all just a chance thing? God, if you're listening, Robbie seems to be pretty all right. Delicious, actually. Maybe I'll call him in a few days and see what he's like in the daylight hours. He's lovely-looking, all blond hair and taking the mickey out of my Donegal accent. Such a big smile. He'd be great in a comedy film with his full repertoire of faces. He just seems focused, like he knows what he's about, which scares me a little.

## October

I LIKE ROBBIE, A LOT. Catherine likes him; says he has nice teeth and should be in a boy band. She says he could sell snow to the Eskimos if he wanted to with all the charm he has on him. But he has a lot more going for him than that. I like the feeling that life's not so serious and that I'm allowed to have fun and act my age. He's so normal with Kieran too. He doesn't put on that awful high voice some people do with kids when they're uncomfortable with them either. He makes him laugh so much.

109

His mam's lovely, all perfume and big hugs; and his sister, Annie, always runs to take Kieran off my hands so she can mother him. I've been going over a lot just to be near Robert. I feel greedy about it. Kieran likes being over there too because Robert's mam saved all the toys for the grandchildren. She's delighted with herself when she sees Kieran playing with them.

"See, Paul, just look at this. And you said I was an eejit for keeping it all." She licks her lips in satisfaction. Paul's a huggy dad too. I suppose they're all huggers.

His mam, Liz, loves her lip gloss, and I wouldn't be surprised if she had one in every flavor. "You can never have enough," she confided in me one day, before she tried to give me a tube the shade of ripe cherries. "It tastes like summer."

I've told him I'm not interested in going out with anyone right now but I'd love a friend, even though that's a total lie. I keep replaying that night we met, imagining it happening again every time I look at his lips. I watch him now, sitting on the sofa with his dad while the rugby's on, the soft curve of his cheek trailing down to the light stubble on his chin. He's wearing the scarf I knitted him; well, I knew I'd give it to someone if I ever finished it. It's massive, and he's drowning in it. He's very sweet.

He stares at me sometimes like he wants more. It's just that every time I look at Kieran I think of Cullen and it breaks me all over again, and I keep daydreaming about finding out Ellie got bored with him and has moved on to her next boyfriend. And then I feel guilty for even spending time with Robbie and think that if I lead him on and then Cullen shows up … well, it just wouldn't be fair because I'd pick Cullen.

YET AGAIN Robbie shows how much of a dab hand he is with the buggy and strapping Kieran into the car seat of his mam's car, and we drive back to the shop. "Did you hear the one about the farmer with the spade in his hand? His name was Doug. Did you hear about his cousin who hadn't got any spades at all? His mammy calls him Dougless."

"God, that's so bad!" He sounds just like Dad, which makes me feel homesick all over again. It's little triggers like this one—I find myself whizzing back in time and I'm a little girl and I'm loved just because I *am*. I think I feel this way with Robbie—accepted, intelligent, like I'm a good person even though I'm a single mam, like he likes being with me. He stands at the door while I open it.

"Right then, I'll be out of your hair. Thanks for today, Una. It was lovely." He stares at me for a minute and lifts his hand up to my chin, turning my face to the right and left. "I love your face, Una. If I were an artist, I'd pay you as my life model anytime."

I'd stay here swimming in his loveliness, but Kieran wakes up and cries, loudly. So much for, um, friendship.

Catherine's in the kitchen, ironing board out and a pile of shirts on the kitchen table. "Hot chocolate?"

"Mmmm, I'd love some."

She starts the milk on the cooker and puts two huge spoonfuls of Cadbury's in two mugs, ready for the magic. "What's going on in that head of yours?"

I fiddle with my necklace. "Just thinking about Robbie and how nice he is. He's just so different to Cullen, you know? He goes after life, always jumping to the next thing to do, and he's so bloody funny. Cullen was just there with me, enjoying the minutes."

111

I get up and start pouring the hot milk into the mugs. "Sometimes I feel guilty for hanging out with Robbie, like I'm doing something that's going to end up really bad for Kieran, but then I remember the way Cullen looked at Ellie that night and I have to talk myself out of it. It's like I want to let him go but I'm horribly scared that if I do, he'll be gone forever, which is so daft when he's mad about Ellie."

Catherine purses her lips. "It's been nearly five months since you went home. Do you think they're still going out together?"

"Jeepers, of course they are! She'd be really stupid to dump Cullen!"

Catherine wraps the shoulders of another shirt around a hanger. "He wouldn't get tired of her?"

I almost choke on my hot chocolate with the laughter and start coughing. No one ever gets tired of Ellie Gallagher unless they love silence.

# 16

## Ellie

Eight months of school to go and I'm supposed to know already where I'll be going next. Mam's still talking about Dublin, but I can't imagine anything more boring than sitting at a typewriter and answering phones all day. I have two plans. A–I'll get shitty scores and do a FÁS course in Letterkenny for computers, and then I can get a job in some office somewhere. B–I'll get nothing less than a C in everything and I'll get into Letterkenny Hospital and do nursing. C–I'll completely ignore everything every teacher and parent has ever told me about making enough to live off and do a hair and beauty course somewhere. I've had Letterkenny on the brain all summer, and if I'm going to be completely honest with myself, yes, it's because Cullen is there. Yes, I still fancy the arse off him. Yes, if I can accidentally on purpose bump into him someday while I'm walking around town, I will. Nathalie thinks it's a great idea and, of course, I do too. I mean, what man in his right mind wouldn't want to be with someone who can mop his brow when he's sick or fix the computer in his shop when it's broken?

"I *know*, Nathalie. He doesn't even come back for the weekends, and I feel like I'm an alcoholic with no booze in the house. If I could just see his face, I could last another month ... maybe.

"I haven't seen him anywhere around town since the debs; that's four whole months ago! And I hate school. I haven't a clue what the hell I'm supposed to know to pass the Leaving, and we have a big exam in a week. I haven't told them at home yet, but I might fail everything if I can't get my act together. Maybe I should have just worked in the hotel and left after fifth year. Mrs. Hyland offered me a job there and all."

"You never told me that!"

"I did too. You were probably too busy looking in the mirror to listen. So anyway, what am I going to *doooo?*"

"Well, I'll tell you what you're *not* going to do. You're not going to not even try. You're going to find out exactly where that boy works in Letterkenny, and you're going to dazzle him with those eyes of yours and he'll never run off on you again."

I laugh. "I meant about the Leaving, ya eejit. Boys, boys. Is that all you think about?"

"Well, that's a silly question, now, isn't it, and asked by someone who says she's my best friend. Let's just say I have plans, which is more than you have. I'm telling you now, find him, feed him, and give him a Frenchie and let him feel your boobs, and he'll be the one chasing you instead. And with the Leaving, I know you have it in you. You always did okay in the classes you understood. Just try and understand it."

I sigh. "You're right."

"Of course I'm right. I'm always right. Now be a good girl and do everything I told you to and I'll see you at Halloween. I have to go. I need to be standing outside McGee's at exactly four o'clock because that's when Tom gets off work and I want to 'bump' into him. See ya, bye."

I put the phone back on the cradle and do what I always do when I feel like life is too much for me. I go and watch TV. There's nothing on, though, and I start thinking about what Nathalie's said. She's right. I need to do something deliberate to see Cullen, and even if I hate looking like an eejit, I'll feel worse if I do nothing. But if I see him and he runs away again, then what? Sure I have to give it a lash. Tomorrow I'll sign up for maths and English grinds. It's the only way I have any hope of even passing.

"THERE YOU GO, Ellie. Do you see it now?" I'm a bit distracted by Mr. Wright's massive ring on his right hand, but I'm listening. "Fractions are like LEGOs." He spreads a few more LEGOs out on the desk. "Sometimes they all come together like soul mates to make a perfect whole, but most of the time, especially on maths tests, they don't. On the bottom you have to put how many parts would make up a whole one, and on the top you write how many parts you actually have out of that whole number. It's like a tragic love story that you have to keep winnowing down to get the star-crossed lovers as close as possible."

*Mmmm, lovers.* Yet again, Cullen's eyes make an appearance in my mind.

"You know, Ellie, I think you'll do well in the Leaving. Just concentrate on turning everything into pictures and put a story behind them and you'll be fine." He pats me on the back like I'm a good child and takes off his reading glasses to clean them on his jumper. "Now be off with ye before it gets dark and I'll see you again on Friday."

The bus ride home takes forever. There's a pregnant mother and her little girl sitting across the way, and the girl keeps looking at me to make sure I'm looking at her.

"That's a lovely dress you have on," I say. She responds by putting a leg out into the aisle to show me her pink patent shoes, and we keep up with her showing me every single thing she has on until they get off the bus at the stop before mine. It's a bit like what I think Cullen will feel if I show up outside his place, like I want all the attention, like I want him to notice everything about me.

And to be honest, *I really do.*

Una would have had a plan. She'd be going out with him already if she wanted to, but it's so hard for me to ask for anything. I want him to see me and ask me. Going to the debs didn't end well. What would Una do? Nathalie went to stand outside McGee's to meet the fella she likes. Una'd probably do the same thing, but I can't stand outside the blacksmith's place. He'd know I wasn't just *there*, you know?

I stop in the church before turning onto my street and light a candle like I always do for Una, and this time I light a second one for Cullen so he'll find his way to me and not get lost again. Maybe St. Anthony will help him and then I'll start going back to Mass with a bit more hope for him finding Una.

Then again, maybe not.

116

## Halloween

IT'S NINE O'CLOCK and Cullen looks like he was ready to put the sweets away when his fine self opens the door to us. He's got that bit of scruff on his chin and I can smell his aftershave—it's just lovely, like his face. How did I not notice this when he was at our house all the time? What a gorgeous specimen of a man!

"Hi there, Cullen." Nathalie and I made sure we were in quite the getup, all black shiny tights and leotards. "You've great legs there, Ellie. I'm dead jealous. Let's show them off tonight," she said. So I did.

He's smiling. Good, because all I feel is embarrassed ever since the debs going down the way it did. All my insides are blowing like autumn leaves in a storm. What if he shuts the door? Nathalie's looking straight into his face to see what his reaction is. His Adam's apple is moving in and out like a blowfish. Is it because her blond hair whipping around her face in this wind is *too* witchy for him?

"Well, hello, Nathalie." He throws his hands up in the air. "Oh God, you're not here with the results, are you?" She looks daggers at him. "Oh wait, you're back to pick up the socks you left on your way to my bedroom?"

Now I'm in shock, on top of the shaking I've been doing the whole way here. Nathalie looks like she's ready to strangle him. Is she really here to see him herself?

Cullen coughs. "Ah, I'm only messing with her, Ellie. What are you girls up to, going around the countryside in this getup?"

"Sure you know yourself, Cullen, we only do this sort of thing for the blacksmiths. It's in case our broomsticks break—we can have a blacksmith like yourself ready to stick a hot iron rod into the fire and get us riding again." Nathalie doesn't hold back, that's for sure. "But they're working just fine right now. Want to come fly with us for a bit?"

He's looking at more than our feet. I can feel his eyes roaming all over me, but he stops the second I look up at him and his ears turn pink. That makes it worth the effort. "Let me get my jacket." He leaves us standing in the doorway while he messes with the coat cupboard. Nathalie and I turn to each other with mouths open and a silent scream meeting in the space between us. "Right, then," he says from behind the cupboard door, "who's coming in my car?"

"Ellie's going with you. I'll be right there, but I have to go home first and ask Mam if I can have the car, I mean my broomstick, for a bit longer." Nathalie runs to her car, laughing that crazy laugh of hers all the way, and jumps in before I can stop her, so I just give Cullen a little smile and start walking towards his car.

He stands at the driver's door and looks over the roof. "So where are we meeting Nathalie then?" There goes his Adam's apple again.

"She said the Central, but I don't like it much." *Anymore—after you ran off like Cinderella's prince and left me there. But I'll hand you the other glass slipper.*

It's like he knows what I'm driving at. "Where would you like to go? Wherever you want." He climbs in and puts his hands on the wheel. "Donegal's going to be packed tonight," he says. Are his hands shaking? "How about Mountcharles? We might be able to find a seat in the back of one of the pubs there?"

"What about Nathalie?" I hear myself say. "Shouldn't

we let her know we're not going into town?"

The corner of his mouth curves up. "I think we both know she has no plans to show up."

I don't look at him, but I can feel a smile spreading into my cheeks.

He smiles back. God, that dimple! "I was thinking Mountcharles might be less packed, but now that I'm thinking about it, the moon is looking great tonight. Do you want to go to the beach instead?"

"Yeah." I lean back into the seat beside him as he takes the turns to St. John's Inlet and eventually parks on the grass at the top of the hilly path to the beach.

He shifts sideways in the driver's seat and balances his back against the door in what I think is an effort to look sexy. "So do you come here often?"

My dimples spring back into action. "You're daft, ya know that?"

He hangs his fingers over the bottom of the steering wheel to add to his cool factor. "I've definitely had worse things said about me. So tell me what you've been up to since I last saw you. Mam told me you were planning on doing some course somewhere after school."

*So he's been asking after me.* "Yeah, I've been looking into a computer course in Letterkenny." I look down at my nails and then rub one against my teeth.

"Really? Letterkenny?"

"Yeah," I say again, and then I look straight into his eyes for a second before looking out the window. "You want to go down to the beach or what?" Can he hear the tremble in my voice?

"All right."

The minute I open the door to stand on the sandy

grass, he's by my side. I'm already shaking a little. It was a daft idea coming in this getup.

He takes off his jacket. "Here." And without asking if I want it, he holds it open for my arms. As I put the second arm in, he wraps both arms around me from behind, and we stand together looking down at the moonlight on the waves for a long time. He's shaking too. I turn to face him and pray to God that this time he's not going to run. His lips are soft and welcoming. I can't stop kissing them. He holds me close and we let our mouths and hands do the talking for a while.

WE NEVER MADE IT to the water, and now he's driving me back home with one hand on the wheel and the other on my hand. I'm back to longer breaths, and I tuck my fingers inside his until he stops the car at the house.

"Right, then," he says as I clamber out of the seat.

I can't see much of his face now that I'm out of the car, so I go over to his side and wait for him to roll down the window.

"So, em, do you want to go out with me?" he says, not really looking me in the eye.

"Yeah, I'd love to. I'll call you tomorrow."

He waits for me to lean in.

"Me mam," I say sadly, and tilt my head to the front window, because for all I know, she's got her beady eyes zooming onto me from behind the living room curtains.

He nods, starts up the car, and heads out the gate with a wave of his arm through the window.

I run inside, wrap myself up in my duvet, and grab the phone for a long chat with Nathalie.

# 17

## Una

Everything's a blur these days, and the pain of seeing Cullen and Ellie together is only starting to soften, not to mention the blur of the last six weeks with Robbie. I keep daydreaming about him, even though I won't kiss him. I've enough to worry about without losing my mind over a boy again, although I think I am anyway.

At least having a baby helps keep me distracted. I don't know how Mam ever got a rest with the lot of us. Seven months old and he's jabbering away, and he laughs a lot, so my face is getting much more exercise than the rest of me from making funny faces. He doesn't like cuddling much, though, and he screams every time I try to put him in the baby carrier.

Mam said I was always fighting her, trying to do things my way. Well, Mam, it didn't turn out so badly, did it? I'm here doing things my way and I have a home, a second family, and the baby boy you wanted me to give up—like he didn't matter at all, like he wasn't even family, let alone your grandchild. I breathe for a minute.

It still gets me going to think of how I could have lost him. I had to lose so much more to keep him, but it was a sacrifice worth making.

It's been a normal morning for us all so far, despite it being Halloween. Granny (Catherine's new name) pushed Kieran to the crèche this morning, and she'll pick him up again at five, God willing. I got to draw out some ideas to go with some new belt buckles that came in. I spent an hour in the back room teaching some children from the school near here about how to work with leather while Catherine worked the front of the shop.

She comes up behind me and puts a hand on each arm. "Stay working in the back as often as you want, especially now Des's hands are a bit shakier. I'd rather have you working with the sharper tools, especially when he's not such a sharp tool himself." Her laugh fills the room.

"So make twenty key fobs and that's enough for the Christmas gifts?"

"Yes, catch the customers at the till with the small stuff. Two pounds here, two pounds there. That was a really great idea of yours. You're brilliant."

I take the tanned leather strip and measure off twelve inches, cutting it with the knife I just sharpened this morning, and smack my lips together in satisfaction. There's something so right about lining up these pieces against the ruler and marking off the exact cutting point under the template. Slice it, check it. Precision, focus— everything the nuns praised me for at school is now put to good use. Sure what use is all that head knowledge anyway? All that Irish history and theorems stuck in my head and going nowhere. Although I don't think Sister Bernadette would altogether approve of my job now. Her plans were bigger for me than Mam's.

I run my edge beveler down each side of the leather, then rub the edges with water and slick them with the burnisher until it's smooth—almost as smooth as Kieran's bum used to be. Yup, the right hole size is ready in the leather punch. Mark the spot on the leather to be sure to get it exactly centered. Now make five more exactly like this one.

Des comes into the back and stands behind me, proceeding to stay standing there staring over at the kettle for a long time. We've got used to his new habits, but I miss his old self. His jokes were wonderfully awful.

"Des, can you make me a cup of tea? There's a love."

He flickers back to life and moseys on over to the corner to get busy again. Catherine and I exchange a knowing glance.

"I'm out to get the wash off the line." She disappears out the back door.

It's a red dye mood I'm in, so I start putting on the dye until it all looks even. Then I put on the leather finish and they're all shiny and gorgeous, lined up like reindeer ready to fly.

At exactly five o'clock, I pull down the shop front and lock it to the ground. Then I head upstairs to start the dinner so Kieran will be in bed by eight. Will be, should be. I love him to bits. He has Des and Catherine wrapped around his little finger, and wherever we go, he makes people smile. Just like his dad. I can't let my mind go there. *Good thoughts, Una, good thoughts.*

It's just that every time I think of Cullen, the loss of him fills my throat with such a lump I can barely swallow. And it's not the loss of his presence and his company so much anymore, although that was a desperate feeling for such a long time; it's the loss of his heart. He was mine and I was his. We were hardly ever seen apart, and I'd naively taken that for granted and assumed it would never change. I fecked it all up, and even though Robbie is so, so lovely and funny, I don't know if I'll ever feel whole again without Cullen in my life.

Yet again I shut that thinking down and grasp at logic.

This shop is such an old building, but to me it's like the beginning and the end. Inside these walls are talent, art, love, and family. And the smell. God, I love this smell of leather. I'm learning a trade; I have a job that gives me a bed to sleep in and three meals a day, and my son has an older couple in his life that have willingly given us a home to make sure his first year is magical. This time thirteen months ago I didn't even know these people, and now I can talk to them about anything. I'm not sure I even did that with Mam, but a lot of that might be because of the wains. But Des. Poor Des. We laugh about him not being right in the head these days, but I'm wondering if it's more than that. I think Catherine is too. And that's one thing we haven't talked about yet.

I'm just about to dig my fork into the mashed potatoes at dinnertime, the melting butter creating more tributaries than the Nile Delta, when Des's face changes, with a look on him like he smacked into a lorry on his bike. "Catherine," he says, and then he stops for a few minutes to rub the place mat between his fingers before looking at her face. "I forget things." He holds up the knife, looks at it, and then puts it back down again. "I'm worried." He picks up the knife again. "I know what this is, but I can't remember what it's for." His voice wobbles. "I think I should go and see Dr. Walsh."

Catherine grabs his hand and gives it a quick squeeze. "I'll make an appointment in the morning. I'm sure it's nothing, but it'll be good to see the doctor anyway, won't it, Una?" She looks over at me with her eyebrows raised.

Now we're all scared.

I wasn't until he said something. It was easier to pretend it was just Des getting old. Sometimes you should just keep your mouth shut when things go wrong in life. That way everyone else can go on living their normal lives and you can protect them from yours.

IT'S BEEN A QUIET MORNING. I have the engraver in my hand when Des and Catherine walk in from their time with Dr. Walsh. Catherine's face crumples like a used tissue when she sees me, but she keeps her hand tucked around Des's arm and holds the handles of her handbag close to her chest with the other, as if it will hold her heart in place.

Des pats her hand. "We'll manage, love." He disappears up the stairs one sad foot at a time.

Catherine stands in the middle of the shop floor and the tears start falling, until her chest and shoulders almost look like they're being yanked around with her violent sobbing. I push a chair behind her knees and a wad of tissues into her hand. She waves me away. "I'll be okay in a minute. It's just, it's just …" She begins to moan. I do what any decent Irish woman would do in the moment and make her a cup of tea, throwing in a Coconut Cream for good measure. She takes a few deep breaths, grips the mug unmercifully, and looks up at me, mashing her lower lip in different ways as she gets the words out. "Dr. Walsh thinks Des has Alzheimer's."

I grab her hand and my breath comes in snatches, along with the tears in my eyes. *Nooooo!* We sit like that for what seems like ten minutes until we hear good old Des.

"Ah, come on, now, ladies. You're not rid of the old goat yet. I have plans for tormenting you two for many years to come, and if it bothers you, I'll just say I have no recollection of ever having said those words. It's the perfect setup." And there he stands, halfway down the stairs, in his puke-green Aran cardigan with the big brown buttons and a goofy smile on his face. We all laugh then, Catherine and I licking and wiping salty tears off our lips as he walks down the remaining stairs and we gather together for a hug. This man ...

## November

ROBBIE'S PARENTS are out and we're watching *Top of the Pops* from the sofa. Things are getting a bit intense in the heart-pumping department, what with my thigh being so close to his, so I move over a little. He turns to me.

"Right when I was getting comfortable," he says, and grins. I move my feet to the floor and start straightening out the colorful quilt over the sofa.

"Tea?" he asks while staring at my fingers as I puff up the cushions.

I nod.

He sinks in beside me again after a few minutes, the tea and two slices of his mam's sponge cake on the coffee table, whipped cream oozing around the strawberry jam. Now's the time.

"You've never asked me about Kieran's dad."

He looks straight into my eyes and smiles, the blue

and gray lines in his like the summer sky back home. "I knew you'd tell me if you wanted to."

Oh God, my heart. "I do."

It's not an easy story to tell, but it's the true version. The love I felt for Cullen, the party, how much I enjoyed it, the lies I told him, how ashamed I still feel. The Angelus comes on the radio as if on cue.

"And are you happy now?" He starts in on a piece of the cake, huge bites of it like it's a challenge to see how much he can enjoy in one mouthful.

Am I happy? What a question. "I'm happy right now, here with you. I'm sad every time I remember that moment when I saw them at the door of the Abbey. I'm happy I have Kieran. I'm happy I have a good job and a place to live with lovely people. I'm sad about Des. I'm sad I haven't talked to Cullen for so long. I miss him something fierce." I stop. But I want him to know. I want him to see this ugly part of me. "I think I still love him, if I'm being completely honest."

Robbie puts the plate down and starts walking around the room, hands in his pockets, his jumper ruched around his waist because he's sweetly a little too short for it. He stops at the velvet curtains. "So that's why you won't go out with me?"

I'm fighting everything inside me to stop myself from jumping up and saying a lot of pathetically stupid things. I want at least one person who cares about me to know everything, so I imagine glue between me and the seat and go on.

"After I saw them in May, I knew Ellie was better for him than I could ever be. I knew from the way he looked at her that he was smitten. And I knew that no matter what happened, I could never justify getting between them. So I stayed in Dublin and cried a lot and sang a lot of sad songs whenever one came on the radio. And whatever happened exactly, I don't know, but the more I let myself feel the pain of it all, the more I felt free, like, to hope for something new that didn't include Cullen."

"And here you are." His face is going through all sorts of twitches, but then it settles and he kneels in front of me, touching my fingertips with his. "Would it be horrible of me to say I'm glad he's with Ellie? Because I am." He gives me one of those huge, cheeky smiles of his.

I think I need a pacemaker, my heart's that out of whack, but I manage to throw a cushion at his head. "Yes, it would, Robbie Flynn, you mad eejit. Yes, it would."

CATHERINE'S BEEN ALL BUSINESS for the last few days, sneaking chats with Des at the kitchen table and on the sofa, and they both shush when I walk in. But apparently she has things all planned out now because she has us both sit at the table once Kieran is asleep to let me in on the secrets.

"Una, Des and I have been talking a lot over the last few days, and we have a proposition for you, but it's up to you as to whether or not you want to take it on. The thing is, with Des having Alzheimer's, we don't know how fast it'll progress." She grabs Des's hand and grimaces. "Which means we have no idea how long we'll be able to keep running the shop. It was a big job for two of us, and now, even with you here, it's hard work. So with Des possibly out of action in a few years, it's down to me to run things, and at sixty-six, I'm not up for it." She swallows. "So we've been thinking of selling."

I can feel my eyes opening wider. "But ..."

Catherine puts up a hand to stop me. "We have another idea, though, and that's where you come in. Des owns the building outright. His brother gave it to him back in 1946, and it's the only reason why we've been able to keep it going for so long—not having the expense of that. And if we knew that someone could be in the shop every day, no matter what happens with Des's health, and mine too, we could get in another employee to help you and keep it going and still have enough to live off." She stretches forward. "We'll get just enough with his pension, but we'll still have to sell if he, if he ..." She's crushing her fingertips on the table. "Because then I'll have to pay for the funeral and buy myself a little house somewhere, and for some silly reason, we never got around to buying a life insurance policy.

"So what we'd like to offer you, Una, is the opportunity to run the business until that happens, if you're interested. That would ensure that you and Kieran would have an income and a place to live." She taps the table with her fingertips. "We don't need an answer now. Let's just get back together to talk about it in a week's time, and if you say yes, we'll make it happen when the time comes. If not, we'll have to put the building up for sale once we can't manage things anymore." She puts both hands flat on the table. "We have to get a few things in order even if you say no—mostly find the papers saying the building is ours, stuff like that. His brother died a few years ago. It was very sad when all they had was each other for so long. Ah well, what can you do?"

Des nods in agreement.

"Either way," she iterates, "we'll be okay. Don't feel any pressure if this isn't what you'd wanted your life to turn out like. But we see you as a daughter, and this is our way of showing you how much we love having you and Kieran here. You've changed our lives in the best way possible."

Four hours later and I've been lying awake for ages staring at the moonlight pushing its way through the crack between the curtains to land, shimmering, on the wall. I never expected this. I never thought strangers would take me in and love me and Kieran and then care so much. I feel like I haven't done much in return, just been around the shop helping out with stuff for a while. It doesn't feel right. I'm no good at taking. I'm much better at giving. And what does that say about me?

What if I can't run the shop and I fail completely? I like the work. I like being in town and being able to walk everywhere. I really like teaching the children about leather and design, the odd time we have them in on a school trip. We even let the older ones make their own key fobs, and the happiness on their faces when they're holding that little thing is just lovely.

This would make me a shopkeeper for a long, long time, a job I'd do over and over, maybe even until Kieran leaves home. I don't have Catherine and Des's passion for running a shop. Aren't you supposed to love your profession so much that you want to do it for the rest of your life? And then there's Kieran. I don't know. I just don't know what to say. But without this shop, I, we, will have no security. In another way, I'm relieved. Without a husband for me to count on, this is all on me. From the day I walked out of my home, it's all been on me, and I've been afraid I'll be walking alone forever.

But what if, maybe, just maybe, this is where I'm meant to be? What if Robbie is my soul mate? What if the big man upstairs has been watching out for me all this time because he loves Kieran as much as I do and this is his big gift to us both? Would it be too much for me to just be grateful and happy and work hard and live a good life?

MY HEAD IS FULL of lists of things I might be able to do, but Catherine's only half listening and fiddling with something in her hands. My sweaty fingers slide over the six shapes Kieran's put out on the kitchen table. We have the heating up higher than ever so that Des is comfortable. He seems to be getting worse really quickly, and the doctor is worried.

Catherine pushes a brochure into my hands while Kieran studies his next move. "It's a place in Ashford with a nursing home and small houses. Des and I would live in the one-bedroom house and we'd have on-site help. And as soon as I couldn't manage anymore, they'd move him to the home, so I could still see him every day. We'd have just enough in savings to cover it for a few years."

I close my eyes. I don't want to look.

Catherine squeezes my hand. "You'll be brilliant running this place."

I manage to open my eyes and look at the pictures. There's even a path down to the beach in one. "Des will love that." The main house has a dining room and a living room with games tables in the back. At least Catherine will have some company and not be alone.

We both pick up a piece of Kieran's toy at the same time. He shakes his head bossily. Put in our place, we are.

IT'S A SURPRISINGLY WARM DAY for November, and we've all been packed in the car for the last hour, but we're finally on the long driveway in to the retirement place. The car jiggles over every stone while huge conifers lean over us, blessing our journey into Bags End, as Catherine has chosen to call it. "I'm practically an old bag already, so it's fitting," she said, closing her lips to hide her smile.

The car tips to the left on the hard curve and then it's just there, right before us in all its glory—the big house. I can already tell it's loved by the effort that's been put into its face. Huge rust and purple leaves run all over the walls, around the windows at their edges, and up to the roof. Windowsills are painted a happy red, and there are window boxes in some of them. A massive sycamore tree reaches out in all directions from the side, and a rope swing sways softly in the breeze. A white covering of daisies waves at us from the expanse of grass near the edge of the woods, gathered around patches of wild pansies bursting out late flowers before winter sets in for good.

The driveway shrinks somewhat on its way into the distance, and we keep driving along the edge of the woods until we reach the houses. I'm jealous. Seriously, who gets to live in a place this gorgeous? The houses are actually small rows of cottages that have been created out of the big house's old stables. They even kept the stable doors! Maud, our guide, waves at us from the door of one before walking up to the car window. She waggles her finger to the left. "Park anywhere and I'll be right here."

Des is having one of his "turns," and he's staring in every direction, trying desperately to grasp at something familiar. I squeeze his hand tightly, and we follow Maud and her fisherman's hat into the hallway of Des and Catherine's future home.

The living room and kitchen are combined in one large area, and it's bright thanks to the skylight and the sliding glass doors at the back that lead into a small garden. Maud walks over to them and slides them open, letting in a blast of November air and sunshine. "This whole spot is yours. Feel free to plant whatever you want, and you can bring your dogs and cats too, if you have some, although we have a limit of one dog per person, and they can't be barking all the time." She walks back to the living room and points her walking stick at the corner. "Every home has a solid fuel boiler like this one, and we'll deliver the wood as often as you need it. We all feel the chill in our bones at our age." She winks at Catherine. "I actually live in the cottage at the end, so if you ever need to share a pot of tea or walk the dogs together, I do love a good bit of banter."

Catherine glances my way and we both grin. Maud certainly looks like she enjoys a bite of gossip now and then.

"Now if you don't mind me getting into your car with you, we can head to the nursing home."

That's a different story altogether. It's a newer building with key-coded doors and the smell of bleach and urine. We follow Maud into the common room, where men and women stare at us from chairs and wheelchairs with empty eyes, some reaching towards us with hands that probably haven't felt family love for a very long time. I can feel the tears building up behind my eyes almost instantly and swallow them away. We knew, we always knew it would come to this, that we couldn't watch him anymore, but this ...

We're quiet the whole way home. Kieran—not so much. He's pissed we left the beach. I can't stay like this when he needs me, so I force myself out of my sad mood. "Oh no, oh no, you're not going to whine, you little monkey, because I'm going to get you!" And I raise my hands in the air and bring them down to his tummy for a grand tickle. I love this boy.

WE'RE ALL KNACKERED. Catherine wipes her hands on the tea towel and hangs it on the door of the cooker. "Leave those to drip dry, Una, and we'll have a game of rummy. I'd like to play something I feel I have some control over." She pulls the cards out of a drawer. "Des, want to join us?"

I can't imagine his mood is any better than ours, but he's a good soul. "As long as you don't mind losing horribly."

# 18

## Cullen

I smooth the paper out on the kitchen table again, trying not to be suspicious.

Dear Mr. Breslin,
   We have noticed your artisanship in a recent order you undertook with Michael Fox for the Grangers of Enniskerry, and we were wondering if you would be interested in a current need we have for a blacksmith familiar with this kind of work.
   The position we have in mind would be one in which you would design and produce gates and fencing with our team with the Killary House name on them. We would like to incentivize this offer by renting you a small bungalow to live in for the first

two months. We would also be
willing to offer you a fixed price
for your moving costs.
    If you are interested, please
call 819184 so we can answer any
questions you might have.
    Sincerely,
    *Jack Flanagan*
    Killary House Designs

Mam is practically skipping around the house singing, "My son is going to be rich! He's going to be famous! It's his mother's doing, of course." She dances back into the kitchen and looks over my shoulder. "Ah, sure look at you. You'll be on the *Late Late* before you know it."

"Mam! I haven't even decided if I'm going to take it or not."

She opens her eyes really wide and sticks her finger in my face. "Now, don't be an eejit, Cullen. This is your big chance." She pats her hair. "And besides, your fame and fortune will look good on your mother." A kiss on the cheek and a slap on the bum and she's out the door to tell her friends. You can't keep a secret in this town unless you leave with it.

I sit down and stare at the words until they start going fuzzy. Training, designing, and producing. A house. *Ellie!* I run my fingers through my hair a few times and try to sort through the thoughts running around like little ferrets. I'd miss Ellie too much. Stay in Donegal or move within a half hour of Dublin, where ...

I fold up the letter and put it in the back pocket of my trousers. No need to make the decision today. I grab

my coat off the back of the chair and head out to the car.
I've got work to do.

YOU'D THINK MAM didn't want me anymore. "Just
make a decision, for God's sake! Your mother's getting
on and needs to know she'll be kept in luxury in her last
years."

I roll my eyes. You'd think this was all her doing.

"Just remember, it is and always has been your job
to make your mother look good. Now don't let me down.
There's a good boy." She takes another bite of her baked
potato—that has enough butter on it to clog every artery
she has—and then puts her fork down. "But really,
Cullen, it'll do you good to get away. I know you're mad
about Ellie, but it's all a bit too fast for my liking, even
though she's a lovely girl." She stares at me for a minute
and then picks up her fork again.

"These spuds are lovely, Mam," I say.

She shakes her head and reaches for the salt. But I
know what she meant. Love has a stronger hold on the
mind than anything. I'm not one for complaining
though.

"If you're that scared of leaving your mammy, I'll
come and visit you." She cackles at her own wit. I roll
my eyes again. This woman is giving them more exercise
than they've had in a while.

I sit by the fire later with Ellie, the letter in her hand.
Thankfully Mr. Flanagan was willing to give me a few
weeks to think about it. Her eyes are shiny with hope for
me. "Don't you dare turn this down, Cullen Breslin!
Don't you flipping dare!"

I should have known. When has Ellie ever done
anything but give? I lift a hand, but she pushes it back

137

down.

"I think I'll survive without you as long as you come up every weekend." She cups my cheek in her hand. "I can't go without seeing this mug of yours for longer than a few days. I'm addicted." She moves her face in to kiss me.

It's going to be hard to leave her behind, and all this, even with coming back every weekend. Yeah, it's leaving all the memories, but I'd kind of wanted to hang on to them. I gaze at the flames for a while. Watching them curl, spit, die, and spring to life again never gets old.

"I'll call Mr. Flanagan in the morning after I talk to Michael and give him the news."

Ellie has a brilliant idea of giving her brother Charlie a go at apprenticing with Michael at the forge on the weekends so he's not left stranded. If Michael's up for it, I can even teach Charlie a few things before I leave. I won't know a soul down there, but I'm used to people leaving me. This time I'll be the one doing the leaving. I shake my head.

"What?" Ellie pulls her face back from mine.

I pause, thoughts rushing over each other. "I'm not sure I'll last five days at a time without you, Ellie. That's an awful long stretch."

She stands behind me and strokes my hair back from my forehead like I'm a cat. "Don't be daft. Now git. You have a lot to do."


IT'S A REALLY shitty day, but Charlie and Michael and Una's dad and I managed to pack all of my crap into Michael's car without completely drowning, and the wipers are still working. Ellie gave me a send-off like I was heading for a hero's landing on the moon.

Michael and I stop in Cavan and run like mad eejits into the chipper before heading on to Enniskerry. Of course we left it too late to skip the evening traffic, and Michael is forcing me to listen to his karaoke version of Kylie Minogue, complete with head flicks an' all, as we inch forward.

It's dark by the time we get to my new home. We're off to a good start; I can see that already in the rental setup. The "house" looks like four stone walls from the seventeenth century with a tin roof, and it's stuck in the middle of a field with some sheep for neighbors. One of them even came over to say hello, so I won't be starved for friends. The rain has cleared up a bit, and Michael helps me haul the bags in through the front door. I'm pleasantly surprised, though, when we walk in. Someone's done a great job with it all, with a dead comfy sofa in the sitting room, and the bed's already made up with a feather duvet, no less. "Well, I'll be damned," I mutter, and I hold off on calling Mr. Flanagan every bad word my mother never taught me.

Michael heads for the fridge and cheers. "He's even left you a six-pack!" I join him and have a look. There are some ham and cheese slices, a pint of milk, orange juice, and a carton of eggs too. On the counter beside the fridge is a loaf of bread with a map opened up and an X mark on it with the words *See you here at 10*. Michael starts opening up the cheese and I put the kettle on.

We sit on the sofa watching the telly until I catch Michael snoring. I throw a blanket on him and make my way to the bedroom. This could be all right, this could. I'll have to get a phone installed, though, or Ellie'll go bonkers.

MICHAEL STICKS HIS HEAD out the car window as he rumbles his way back out of the yard and yells goodbye. He's dropped me off at my new job, and a pretty girl is walking out the door of a building to see what the noise is all about. She's got freckles all over her nose, and her long hair is almost black. She must have done that crimping thing on it because it has little ridges all over it. She laughs at me staring and smooths it down.

"You must be Cullen." She holds out a hand. "*Very* nice to meet you. I'm Claudia."

A young guy walks out behind her. "Watch that one," he says with a laugh, jerking his head in her direction. She curls her upper lip at him and turns back to me. "Follow me. Jack said to give you a tour. He'd do it himself, only he got delayed."

She talks the whole time we walk around, but I'm a bit distracted by the spot where her leggings meet the end of her short jumper. Judging by the other fella's words, she must dress this way on purpose every day.

The place is huge, the main buildings being two barns, and there's a converted farmhouse for the forge. They all stretch back from the road, so the first thing you see is the forge, and as you keep going along the hedge, you come to the bigger yard for the barns. In one of them they do all the woodwork, and in the other they store all the finished pieces, which look amazing. The more Claudia talks and the more I see, the more loaded I get with doubt. There are so many men working here, all skilled, and I'm not sure if I can pull my weight in with the best of them. What if Jack was wrong about me? What if I let him down?

To the side on the left is the office Claudia first walked out of, and it's all very posh with double-glazed windows and fancy armchairs for the buyers. There's even a massive bowl of fun-size Twixes on a coffee table in the middle of them. That's where we end up after our walk around the place, and almost as soon as I sit down and reach out for the chocolate, Jack Flanagan walks in. At least, I can't imagine it's anyone else because he looks like a boss in his ironed trousers and buttoned shirt.

"Welcome to Killary House, Cullen. Let's go and have some lunch."

I'VE PUT IN a long day, showing the lads assigned to me how I've been mixing wood and metal together. Most of them are more experienced farriers, so they instantly offer some great ideas to do the job better and faster. I think this is how it'll go for the next few weeks until I get up to speed. I'm now lying in the hottest bath I can muster. It soothes the muscles better than any cream. Ellie gives great massages, even head rubs, but I'll have to get used to the bachelor life down here and make up for it with her at the weekend.

I close my eyes and picture my next fence. It's going to have thick black posts with cedar-stained planks of wood molded into single sheets, and then I'm going to have them cut circles into the wood and put steel in there instead. Jack says it's for a retired president, so we have to go all out. He says the connections alone will be worth a fortune as long as he doesn't die before we've delivered.

I think I'm going to ask Alan and Jimmy, two of the team I met today, if they want to share the rent on this place. It's too quiet, and they can have the extra bedrooms. Being alone isn't good for me, and I wouldn't put it past Claudia to show up at the door with a flat tire or something. I shiver. She sort of scares me.

## December

TWO MONTHS with this gorgeous Ellie and I'm
obsessed with her. She's written my name in neon green
in her schoolbook—to match all the other ones in
different colors—which means it's serious. It's been a
long week and a few more phone calls, and we stand
entwined in the Diamond for a few minutes to catch up
on hugging and kissing—my favorite.

"God, I think you look more gorgeous every day," I
say, before kissing each eyelid she's covered in pink and
purple eyeshadow. "So where do you want to go?"

She slaps me with her handbag. "I didn't spend two
hours after class doing my hair and makeup for *that.*"

I hold up a hand, laughing. "I know, I know. I'm
supposed to have it all planned out." I open the
passenger door for her and sweep my hand towards the
seat. "M'lady." She loves a bit of steak, so I'm taking her
to that fancy restaurant on the hill. I can't wait to sit
across from her and spend the next few hours together.
I can't see myself ever being with anyone else. Every
time I'm with her, I get giddy. I never knew I could feel
this way, that someone could be so clearly placed in my
life like this and I'd feel so alive. It's great being back
home for Christmas and getting to see her every day.

TO CELEBRATE our first Christmas, Ellie's given me
*The Hitchhiker's Guide to the Galaxy: The Original Radio
Scripts.* I love how she remembers everything I say I like,
even though it puts me to shame. I can't even remember
if I brushed my teeth yesterday.

She's talking about our first kiss at the debs, and I

can't believe she even wants to remember it when I was such a bollox. That's Ellie for you—all forgiveness. I don't get it. We're sitting in a coffee shop at the Abbey, and she's putting six teaspoons of sugar in her tea and stirring while staring into my eyes with that smile of hers.

"What?" I say.

"Just you. You're lovely."

Yeah, right. "Why?"

"Oh, your jokes, your smile, the way you look after me. Stuff like that."

I get busy buttering my soda bread. She's far too good for me. Sometimes I watch her almost dance through life, like she doesn't get how hard it can all be. Even with her grinds, no matter how hard it got, she was so sure it would all work out in the end. And it did. She passed that last exam. If it were me, I'd feel like crap because I'd only scraped through, but she was so delighted about it.

"What made you end up at the forge, Cullen? I always thought you'd end up in the Gardaí solving murders or big crimes, mastermind that you are."

"You know, Ellie, I think about that sometimes, and all I can say is that when you have a choice between being a bit soft and having muscles like these, it's a no-brainer."

Ellie laughs so loud it feels like everyone in the shop is looking at her and smiling. She's magic.

Sometimes I feel like I'm just watching *us* happen, like I'm an actor in a movie and all this love and stuff is part of someone else's life. And the next part of the move is where the guy gets married to the girl who loves him and we have two kids and God knows what else until we die. And if it was a blockbuster, we'd die hand in hand at a nursing home or something because that's how you go when you have a real love story. But then other times it feels real and bloody brilliant and I'm a bit scared it won't feel like this forever.

"What are you thinking about?" She's twisting her bracelet around her wrist and grinning at me.

"Ah, you know, about us, about the debs." I take another slurp of soup off the spoon. Mam'd slap my ear for that.

She yawns for the third time since we got here. "Sorry. I don't know why I'm so tired. Must be from dreaming about seeing you today at last. Thinking about you gets me a bit sweaty." She straightens up and grabs my hand. "I was thinking about that night on the beach, well, on the hill looking at the beach. That was a right snogging session. We should do that again sometime."

Yes, yes, we should. Actually, I'd like to do a whole lot more than that, but she says she's a good Catholic girl and that even though some of her friends are going all the way, she wants it to be special. Yeah. I still haven't told her. I don't think I'll ever tell her. I feel like shite about it most of the time anyway, so why would I want to make it even worse? Thank God she never really asks me too many questions. She likes to talk more than listen, which is fine with me. And if I told her, it'd change everything. Not that she wouldn't forgive me because she forgets things we argue about so fast, but because it's her sister, and she talks about her like she's one of the best things that happened to her up until that day she left us all. So there's that.

The whole getting-married thing. It's all Mam talks about, even though it's only been two months, but maybe they see what I feel. Her mam is up for putting in some hints too, like every time I'm over at the house, like it's a given. Ah, sure, it'd be great to be married to someone like Ellie. Life would be easy most of the time. But would she even want me if she knew? And would she even want someone who doesn't even have his own forge? No, I don't think so. But when I *am* sorted, that's what I want to do. I want to marry this girl. I can't imagine anything sweeter than waking up to this face every day.

"Come on, so." I grab my bag off the back of the chair and start heading out the door.

She snatches her handbag and jumps off the chair. "Where are we going?"

"Oh, I think you know. It includes sand." I give her a wink and keep walking.

# 1985

# 19

## Ellie

## March

I've been home for half term and I'm dreading going back to school when all I can think about is Cullen.

Ruthie and I are dancing around the living room to "The Irish Rover" when the phone rings right on the "two million barrels of stones" line. I stop and run to the hallway, panting a bit as I go. No PE all summer hasn't done me any favors.

"Hello, is this Ellie Gallagher?"

"Yes." I look back into the living room to see Ruthie still swinging her arms in the air and letting her mad laughter scare the dog.

"This is Dr. Kennedy, and I was wondering if you could come in today and see me. I'd like to follow up with you on those blood tests I did yesterday."

I'm still smiling at Ruthie, funny girl. "Oh, you can just tell me on the phone."

"No, Ellie, I think you need to come in for this. I'll

be open until five o'clock."

*Then the ship struck a rock, oh Lord what a shock*
*The bulkhead was turned right over*

My mind goes blank, skipping right over the lyrics for a few minutes before I shake myself out of it. Ruthie keeps dancing, keeps swinging, keeps laughing. *Cullen. I need to talk to Cullen.*

I know the number at the forge off by heart, and my shaky fingers turn the dial around and around, watching it swing back for the next one. The phone rings and rings for a long time, until I can't wait anymore. I have to go.

Mam's out the back taking the clothes off the line. "Mam, Dr. Kennedy called me himself and says he wants me to go in this afternoon for those test results. Can I take the car?"

She stops, holding the scrunched-up sheets in her arms before dropping them into the wash basket. "Oh, Ellie, is everything all right? Did he sound serious?"

I don't want her scared. She gets all jittery for days. "I think it's fine. He probably just has to tell me in person so I'll know how to take care of myself better. You know how he is."

"Do you want me to come with you? I'd have to bring the wains, but, you know."

"It'll be fine, Mam. He's just going over the test results. So I can take the car then?"

"Yes. Be careful."

Fine. I'll be fine. It'll be fine. My nerves are wired for sound.

I wish someone had heard the phone. That Claudia girl usually answers and gives him a message to call me back, but maybe she was at lunch or something.

The waiting room is half-empty. There's an older

lady in the far corner snoring, and one of the Brown brothers is looking at a magazine. I nod to him as I walk up to the window. Nathalie had a thing for him a few years ago, but the last two years haven't done him any favors.

"Ah, Ellie, how are you? I'll let him know you're here."

I give her the best fake smile I can muster. Joanna was in Una's class and got the receptionist job straight out of school, lucky sod.

"So how are you?" she prattles. "How's Una doing up in Dublin? And I hear you and Cullen are all serious now. Anything happening in that department?" She gives me an all-knowing grin.

"Ah, yeah, he's a great guy. We're moving along." And that's all I'm giving her because if I say anything else, it'll be all over town by teatime. Not that there's really anything juicy to tell her. We're all right, me and Cullen. We're more than all right. Unless ...

Her phone rings. "Okay, I'll send her right in." She waves her hand in the direction of the door. I'm not used to this kind of speed. It makes my insides freak out even more.

Dr. Kennedy's office feels like a box all of a sudden. I'm hemmed in by his four walls, a thing to lie on behind me, and a huge weighing scales that practically climbs the wall in the far corner. Half his desk is invisible under his piles of papers.

"Ellie!" He stands up to shake my hand and waits for me to sit down before he does. "Thanks for coming. So how are you?"

"I came as soon as I could." What else does he expect me to say?

He looks down at a piece of paper in front of him and won't look at me. "Well, Ellie, I'll spit it out. I got the results of both tests and I'll need to send you up to Dublin for some more tests. I'm a bit worried about the white cell count, and I'd like a professional opinion from a friend of mine at the Adelaide Hospital up there. I think you have a bit of a problem with your bone marrow, but it might be nothing. We'll find out once you get the tests done." He drums his fingers on his bottom lip. "Do you think you could get there by lunchtime tomorrow?"

I don't really remember driving home, but I must have because I'm now packed and swirling my hand in the bubbly bathwater to make sure it's not too hot for little Ruthie. All I can think about is wishing Cullen was here with me. Mam's spazzing out over what might be wrong, and she's down at the church right now to try and make it go away. I called Cullen's place, but they must all be at the pub.

"I love Cullen, Ruthie." She looks up at me and looks back at the bubbles before taking her toys and dropping them into the foam one by one and giggling. "He's perfect, Ruthie."

"Cullen," Ruthie says after me, only it sounds more like *Cowan*. I find myself smiling and start to pull off her turtleneck, grateful for this small bit of normal living before we head to Dublin in the morning.

"OWEN GALLAGHER! Get back here and put your bowl in the dishwasher," Mam yells. He traipses back, shoulders so slouched he could be Quasimodo, and throws the bowl in before giving her a look. It's never worth challenging Mam; she'll just yell louder, and at this

152

hour of the morning, doing whatever she says is a wise idea. She rearranges the bowl after he leaves.

"I don't like this. I don't like it at all." Her lower lip begins to wobble, and she quickly brushes her thumb over it.

"Ah, Mam, I'll be back before you know it." I'm not even convincing myself though. Sometimes even all my hope talk doesn't match what's in my nerves.

I'M IN THE CAR with Dad heading out on the road to the big smoke. Charlie's helping Mam with the wains. I've never been away from them for this long. It already feels like part of me is missing. I don't know how I feel. My insides are like peeling paint. Dad's not speaking much on the long drive down, but I chatter on, more out of nerves than anything. Eventually we pull up to the Adelaide, a huge old building that must have about six floors, and find our way to the outpatients.

I shut up while they're taking more blood, and then they want to do something called a flipping bone marrow aspiration, which hurts like the bejeesus, and the biopsy is even worse. Somehow I manage to hobble back to the car and we go for a sandwich.

Two hours later we walk down to the consultant's office and sit in front of his desk, Dad strangely holding my hand like I'm five again about to cross the road. The consultant has told us what he specializes in, and now we wait while the radiator gurgles like our insides. After shuffling through paper, he finally spits it out.

"I'm afraid I have some bad news." He takes off his glasses and rubs the lenses on his coat. I can feel Dad's grip tighten.

"Well, there's no other way to say it, Ellie, but it

looks like you have leukemia."

*Whoosh, whoosh.* My heartbeat is loud and strong. "But you can fix it, right? And then it'll be gone?"

"That would be fantastic, but leukemia is a disease in your bone marrow that's very hard to get rid of. It's a form of cancer in your bones, and it can spread very quickly. I need to get you into the hospital right away."

"Wait, cancer?" Dad sits forward on the edge of his seat. "You said it was leukemia."

My whole body is quivering.

"Yes, that's the medical term for bone marrow cancer."

"Oh." Somewhere in my brain it's registering as something that people can get better from.

"I hate having to tell you this, Ellie, but it's not good news at all."

"But I'll be okay, right?" I'm leaning forward now, my voice splotching as I talk.

He puts his glasses on the table. "I'm sorry, Ellie, but I can't promise you that. But let's wait and see." He hands me some blue papers with the words *What to Do if You Have Acute Lymphoblastic Leukemia* written at the top. "I'll need you to be admitted to St. Luke's Hospital immediately. It's a few miles from here in Rathgar. I'd like to nip this in the bud if I can. The sooner we stop this beast, the better." He puts his glasses back on and looks at us over the top of them. "I'm really sorry, Ellie. This is a hard one. I'll be in touch with you, Mr. Gallagher, as we figure out the next steps. In the meantime, Ellie, you focus on getting admitted and we'll see what's what after that."

I DON'T KNOW how Dad and I get to St. Luke's, but

the car turns into a short driveway and ends at a one-story building. This is not what I expected at all. It looks more like a big home with some extra bits tacked on. We go down a long hallway, around a corner, and into a ward with about twelve beds in it. A bed by the window has the sheets turned down, and someone's already put fresh flowers on the bed table.

Dad sits with me for a bit and we tell the nurse all the information she needs to know. She asks me about my pain level, and then she pulls the curtains around to see how much swelling I have in my armpits and all those other places lymph nodes live. I look at everything but her as she checks. Her name tag says Patricia, and her uniform is as white as they come.

"How old are you, Ellie?"

"I just turned eighteen."

She gives me one of those "sucks to be you" looks. Then she lets us into the nurses' office so we can use the phone. Dad's behind me, staring out the window, papers trembling in his hand.

"Leukemia? What?" Mam asks.

"Acute lympho something, Mam. The doctor says it's in my bones."

I can hear Ruthie jabbering in the background. "So what's next then? Can they get rid of it?"

"Ah, you know, Mam, it's just bone marrow that's not working like it should. How bad can it be really?" I swallow. "But I'm being admitted right now. He said I have to get treatment as soon as possible so that I can go into something called remission."

Dad drops his head.

"And if that doesn't work, sure, I've always wanted to go to France, and you can take me to Lourdes once

I've seen enough French hunks and eaten all their chocolate."

She manages to laugh. "Ah, Ellie, never change, will ye?"

DAD'S HAD TO GET on the road home because he has work in the morning. Professor Milton is checking out my legs with his fat fingers, looking at the bruises that I started getting from nothing. Then he starts feeling in my groin, humming and hawing, while the three young men in white coats, interns, I think, watch me blush all the way to my hair roots. He's already mauled my neck, stuck a finger over my gums, and asked about headaches and weight loss. He looks at his folder one more time. "I'd like to start a treatment plan in the morning." He's talking more to the three interns than me.

"Is it that bad?" I hear myself say. I sound like an echo from another room.

He rearranges the pens in his top pocket. "Well, now, Ellie, it could get very bad if we do nothing. We need to take care of this as soon as possible. It's not something we can play around with." He swishes his hand sideways, which I take to mean I can sit up.

"The nurse will tell you everything you need to know about your prep work. And if your mother is a praying woman, have her start now." Well, that's one thing already taken care of.

I called Cullen at work as soon as Dad left, and Claudia said she'd let him know, so fair dues to her, he's here now. I missed him so much after he moved up here, but now look at how lovely it is to see his face. He feels solid, calm, and everything inside me settles.

The nurse comes up to the bed as well with a wad of

papers. "Did Professor Milton talk to you about what the treatment is?"

I shake my head.

"Okay. I'll be back when I can. I have to go over a few things with you."

I sit on the edge of the bed and lift Cullen's hand up and around my head before leaning my head against his strong shoulder. His arm fits into the curve at the back of my neck perfectly, and I close my eyes. I don't want to think. Not here. Not ever.

The nurse comes back in. She seems much older than most of the nurses, and I can see a line etched between her eyebrows from overuse. "Ellie, what I'm about to tell you is going to perhaps come as a shock, but I want to make sure that you're prepared for what might happen."

Cullen sits up and straightens his back against his chair. Her eyes move to his face before she turns back to mine.

"Is it okay if your boyfriend stays here for this?"

I swallow and nod.

"So, Ellie, there's a Plan A and a Plan B we're looking at here. Plan A is the good kind—you get some chemotherapy that puts you into remission and this doesn't come back ever. The lab does a bunch of new tests, says you're good to go, and you go home in a few weeks and celebrate, although you'll keep getting chemo as an outpatient in Letterkenny. Chemo is nasty; you might lose your hair and feel very, very sick, but you can eventually get back to your life.

"But Plan B is not pleasant at all." She sighs and puts her hand on mine. "Ellie, if you don't go into remission, the doctors will have to give you all sorts of drugs, chemo, and radiation to try to get the cancer to go. And that still might not fix it. Some doctors are trying bone marrow transplants, and we're hearing back good reports, so keep your hopes up. You'd have to go to the treatment center in St. James and stay for a few weeks in a single room. It can take a long time to get your energy back." She sighs again and sits up straighter. "I hope, for your sake, that Plan A is all it'll be, but it's my job to prepare you for what could happen so that you're mentally ready for it, if it happens." She looks at Cullen. "And you'll need to stick around, even if you hate the sight of blood. Your girl needs you now." She inhales and exhales deeply and shakes the papers in her hands. "Now do either of you have any questions for me?"

# 20

## Cullen

We're at the pay phone in the hallway, and Ellie is lying through her teeth on the phone. "Yeah, Mam, he says he wants to start me on some IV chemo tomorrow. Would you believe it, doing it that fast? I didn't—a few little bruises like that! But I'll be fine, Mam. I'll be back home before you know it. The nurse said I can go into remission and then it might never come back!" I get it—she's always looked after her mam like that, but it's not right.

She hangs up and points her finger in my face. "Don't you dare, Cullen Breslin!" We walk back to her bed and she starts pulling out a few things—her Walkman, a few magazines I didn't know she read, some makeup, the teddy Una left her, and some tapes. That's Ellie in a bag right there.

But after the nurses have sent me home, I call her mam. God, I hate doing this on the phone, and I can't even think straight here I'm so upset.

"The nurse is after telling her that it's cancer in her bones and it could take her months to get better, if at

159

all. They're starting chemotherapy tomorrow." I'm running my fingers so hard through my hair that my scalp feels numb.

"Oh God. Oh God, oh God. Thank God you were with her. She made it seem like it was something they could fix easily, and Seamus couldn't tell me exactly what the doctor had said other than hearing the C word. Thank you for calling. I really appreciate it. We lost one girl. I'm not about to lose another."

I'M BACK AT THE HOSPITAL waiting to be allowed in. The nurses are giving me pitiful looks when they walk by. I ask the nurse at the desk if I can use the phone, but she points to the one on the wall and I have no change. Stupid cow! I want to call Mam. I can't stand this. I can't stand just sitting here feeling like everything's going to hell in a handbasket. What did Ellie ever do? And now I'm pissed at God too. Probably not a great move.

It hurts to think. I can't sit down anymore. The waiting room feels like it's shrinking around me, and I've flicked through every magazine here without remembering a single thing.

Mam answers the phone on the fifth ring. "Now tell me again what that nurse said might happen." So I tell her everything I can remember before I fall back into the silence of the waiting room.

I jump up when the nurse tells me I can go in. Ellie's sitting up flicking through a comic. There's a pump beside her with a syringe on top, sending whatever drugs to her body, I suppose.

"Looks like I'll be here for a few days," she says as she puts down the comic. "The doctor's been around twice. He says I might be able to go home for a few days,

160

but I'll have to keep coming back for each treatment."
She sweeps her arm by the window. "But sure look at
this view! Why would anyone want to leave this?" She
laughs with pure happiness. As if on cue, a robin hops
onto a tree branch by the window and cocks its head
from side to side. "Wouldya look at that, Mr. Breslin; all
the hope of spring right there."

THE WEEK HAS PASSED quickly, with Ellie holding
up like a champ. The professor wants a word before her
mam brings her home, so we're both in there with her.
He walks in, his hands turning his pair of glasses. And
he goes on to tell us all that Ellie, my Ellie, who only the
other day was laughing with life, might now have it
sucked away. Mrs. Gallagher is gripping my arm so
tightly as he talks. I stare at a faded picture on the wall.
She takes a tissue out of her bag and blows her nose. I
glare at the doctor's glasses and want to crunch them up
into tiny pieces. This can't be true. No way.

He mutters things about radiation, and he's using
words like "wait and see," "when these drugs work," and
"taking care of things."

"There's a difference between acute, which means
sudden onset, and chronic, which is long term. The
survival rate can be as high as 80 percent, but it changes
from person to person, so we don't know if radiation
would make any difference. A bone marrow transplant
might work, but it's always hard to find matching
donors."

Gail's grip on me tightens, her tears all over the
place. He stops talking. She waves her hand for him to
keep going.

"… six to twelve months if we can't get you into

remission. I'm so sorry." And he pats Ellie on the back and leaves the way he came.

ELLIE'S OFF HOME with strict instructions to stay away from anyone with even a sniffle. I'm back at the cottage and my thoughts keep going to Una, not because I'm still in love with her—I've forgotten about most of that now that I have Ellie—but because we talked so much. We figured things out together. She really was my best friend. She'd have a plan, and she'd be asking the doctors and nurses all the questions I can't think of right now. And the thing is, Ellie needs her too. She needs her big sister, and we can't fecking find her.

What would she do if she were in my shoes? What can we do to find her that we haven't tried already? She needs to know that her sister could be dead by Christmas, for God's sake! For all the reasons she had for running away, I don't think she'd stay away if she knew that.

And that's when I think of it. That's when I come up with something that might work to bring Una home.

THE RAIN IS POURING off the roof in sheets, and my runners splash their way into the smell of books and quietness. Enniskerry Library has so many shelves running around this little room, it's like a maze.

"Ah, Cullen, back for another big pile of mysteries? Or what can I help you with this time?"

It's always good to see Miss O'Donnell again, rooted to her usual spot at the desk in her red V-neck cardigan with books scattered in piles around her.

I scratch the back of my head for a second to gather my wits—what I have left of them. "Well, Miss

162

O'Donnell, it's not a book I'm looking for this time. It's information, and I need you to help me find it for Dublin."

She brushes an imaginary speck off her cardigan sleeve, like she's getting ready for action. "I'll do my best. Now tell me everything you know already and we'll go from there."

After two hours poring through books, I spend the rest of the afternoon at the house, my hand getting sweaty holding the phone so long. Trying to get in touch with the powers that be is murder. "So you might be able to do that, so? And when would I know if you can or can't?" I write down a few dates and mutter a few "holy mother of Gods" and one "Jesus, Mary, and Joseph." My respect for journalists jumped up a few points today.

WE'RE BOTH BACK UP in Donegal for the weekend, a welcome break from another week at the hospital.

She's still acting all airy and light, so we haven't pounded it home with her yet exactly how serious things are with her—that if she doesn't go into remission or find a bone marrow donor, she could be dead by Christmas. She was right there in the room when the doctor talked to us all, but her mam wants us all to keep pretending she's going to be fine.

Ellie's lying up against me on the sofa talking about going to Benidorm. "Once I'm better, I want to do loads of things, Cullen. Yeah, I'll still do my stupid Leaving, get more grinds to help me, but I want so much more, you know? All I'm doing every day here when I'm not getting chemo is eating and watching the telly. I'll be a chronic slob soon if I don't get out of here and do something!"

I choke a bit before I answer and pretend to laugh at the show the kids are watching. "Like what?"

"I've always loved makeup. Maybe I could take a few classes and learn about all the more advanced stuff. I could even do a Boy George number on your eyes." Her giggle is sunny, easy. "I could take art classes and start sketching you working at the forge. All those muscles and sweat and hot metal." She reaches up to my mouth and runs her finger on my bottom lip. "I don't think I'll be playing football anymore, that's for sure. I need to go to the loo. Want to help me?"

I roll off the sofa and move the walker close. She's been using one lately because she's so weak. This sofa has had years of children climbing all over it, so it's not the simplest to get up from, but we have a method, so we do. I lock my hands behind her and bend my knees. "One." I lift her a little. "Two." I lift her more. "Three." And she's up on her feet. I almost threw her over one time doing that. I stand to the side so she can lean on the walker and start pushing her way to the toilet. "And maybe I can get that puppy I've always wanted," she adds as an afterthought.

It's not the easiest house in the world for someone on a walker, but I put in a ramp on the three steps in the hall a week ago, and she works her way up slowly with nary a whimper. At least the IVs are out. She's like a regular bag lady with those.

"Don't forget I have another appointment tomorrow in Letterkenny! Can you come?"

"I can't. I have to go back to work tonight, remember?" I feel like shite saying it, but at least she has the family around. Her eyes fill up and we look at each other for a moment. "I'm sorry, Ellie," I murmur, and I kiss her on her shoulder.

"Oh well." She smiles. "It won't be forever, now, will it." It's a statement, not a question, thank God.

THE PHONE CALLS turned into nothing, so it looks like I'm going to have to write a few letters. I hate my handwriting. I was hoping it wouldn't come to this. Sod it all. I'm staying in a cottage of boys—all of us looking to save money and just have somewhere to sleep—so there's not much by way of extras.

"Hey, boys, anyone got any stationery I could use?" As I thought. I'm met with a few blank stares before they turn back to the telly.

Connor gets up. "I have some a girl gave me, but we broke up a few weeks later. I think they're in my chest of drawers. Hang on and I'll have a look." A few minutes later he's pressed some flowery muck into my hands, and there's a strange smell like gone-off perfume or something coming off them. "Yeah, I know." He laughs. "I think there are a few stamps in there too, if you need one."

It's the best I can get, so I sit down at the kitchen table and start trying to find the words that will get me noticed. I write a few words on a notebook first so I can get it right, and two hours later I think I finally have something worth sending. Miss O'Donnell gave me three addresses she said would be better than others she could find for me because more people work there, so I write out the letter in my neatest handwriting—which is not saying much—three times, fold each one exactly in half, and put it in an envelope smothered in roses. I'll drop them in the letterbox tomorrow. Here's hoping.

## May

I'M AT THE DOOR AGAIN, waiting for the postman like I do almost every day. Nothing's come. I never in a million years thought I'd have a girlfriend maybe dying and a best friend disappear all in the space of a year and a half. Each one fading in her own way. I can't give up. Not now, not ever.

THE FORGE IS COLD, as is usual at eight in the morning. I grab the apron and tie it in a knot behind my back, get the fire started, and start working with the others on the big order from Carnew—eight hinges, two huge knockers (how we laughed at that one), and some sort of poncey shamrock to hang off the front of it. They're Americans.

I like the challenge of forging the shamrock, and with what's going on in my life, maybe I can at least see one difficult thing through to its end today. I take a metal prong from the pile and watch the top of it slowly heat to a red-hot color before taking it over to the anvil. The heat is already leaving it, so I hit it over and over with short, pelletlike bangs of the hammer until it reaches a four-sided point. I push it forward, over the edge of the anvil, to start thinning out the rest of it, each black flake spitting in resentment as I keep slamming. Heat, hammer, heat, hammer, and so it goes on. The shamrock leaf slowly takes shape. I give a lot of attention to the texture. I move the last bit of hammering to happen on a piece of wood so as not to change the texture I've added, and the wood shoots small flames and sparks almost every time I hit the hot leaf into it.

I lift an arm to wipe the sweat off my face. I'm not

166

quite sure why I'm still here, working at the forge, when it feels like Ellie is slowly dying. *Bam.*

I was saving up because I thought Ellie and I would need a house. In a few months, she might not need anything, not even me. *Bam.*

I don't want to pretend everything's all right anymore. I want her to know we might only have very little time left. *Bam.*

I can't do this anymore. *Bam.*

God, if you're listening, I really hate you right now. *Bam.*

An idea drops into my heavy thoughts, one that I think will help Ellie keep fighting this cursed disease. For the first time in a while, I start to smile.

A WEEK LATER and it's ready. Everyone in her place has gone to bed and we're by the fire, the light flitting softly over her lips. I kneel in front of her and open a small box.

"I made this for you. I hope it fits."

Her mouth is hanging open like a drawbridge.

"I wanted to give you a claddagh ring so you can wear it and let everyone know you're mine. I'm a jealous man, Ellie, when it comes to you."

"Right." She laughs. "Every man in Donegal wants a pasty-faced girl with no hair in his life."

I put my hand under her chin and stare into her eyes. "Maybe not, but not one has your smile. So back to the ring.

"There's a lovely story about it all," I say, feeling my smile reach into my cheeks. I love giving her things. "There was this man who was captured on a ship and sold as a slave to a Spanish goldsmith, and while he was there, he made this kind of ring to remember his one true love back home. The heart was for his love for her, the hands were because they were true friends, and the crown was because he had promised to always be loyal to his promise to come back to her.

"So anyway, Ellie, I made this ring for you for the same reasons. I love everything about you, you're the kindest person I know, and I can't see myself ever being with anyone else."

She gives me a soft kiss on the lips and then has a look at the ring—silver, simple, and made with a hell of a lot of love. "It's gorgeous, Cullen."

"I had to get a friend to help me with it because I had none of the right tools, but it didn't turn out so bad. I just need to know if it fits or if I need to size it better. Try it on."

She puts it on her right hand with the heart turned in. It's almost exactly the right size.

"I'll fix that tomorrow."

Ellie holds her hand back reluctantly before letting me take it off her finger.

"I love you, Ellie Gallagher. Want to be my one true love?"

"I do, ye daft man. By God, yes I do."

# 21

## Ellie

I can't believe I'm still stuck at home. I was so sure I'd at least be in remission by now, dying of boredom and glazing over the words in a school textbook. I look over at Dad on his chair, laughing quietly to himself in his sleep. Mam is knitting yet another Aran jumper, all loops and cables running over each other. She gets twenty pounds for each one she does. It takes her weeks. Slave labor, if you ask me.

I'm so tired, so tired of this. I got my third blast of chemo and I feel like my whole body is a sewage pit. I still need the walker. The doctor said just last week that it was all "as good as can be expected."

"Mam," I say, "did the doctor say anything else about remission, anything at all?"

She keeps moving her needles, light bouncing off them in different places from the fire's flames. "No," she answers. "Why?"

"Well, I'm not getting better."

She chews her cheek and checks the pattern draped over the arm of her chair. "Sorry, I'm on a difficult bit."

CULLEN'S HERE! I straighten the blanket and wait. I love that big smile he has just for me. He sits down beside me and takes a hand, but then his head drops and he won't look me in the eye. "Ellie," he says slowly, "I'm really worried that you haven't gone into remission yet. That nurse said leukemia sometimes goes into remission after the first or second treatment, but yours hasn't."

I stare at him. "And? Didn't the doctor say they'd keep trying different things?"

He swallows. "When the doctor was talking to us in March, he said some people don't make it. They never get better...." His head drops again, but he's holding my hand so tightly that I can't feel the blood in it anymore.

"Bloody hell, Cullen. I'm not going to die!"

"No! I'm not saying that, but he said if you don't respond to the treatment, you might only have six to twelve months left, and as of today, you're still not in remission."

Mam lets out a sob and jumps up from the chair. Says she's going to bed. Says she'll be able to think more clearly in the morning.

Cullen sits there, misery embalmed.

I can feel the rise and fall of my chest get faster and faster. It's as if I've done a belly flop into the Arctic Ocean—naked.

Fear swells up in my chest and I fire its bullets. "I bloody well know I'm not in remission! Six to twelve months my arse! *You* ..." My hands are shaking. The tremor writhes up my arms and into my mouth. *"You ...,"* I say again, and then I can't help myself. I suck air to try to hold it back, but the torrent of fear crests and I can't wipe the tears away fast enough. I need him. I can't talk for the next few minutes, but then all the snakes slither

170

away. I breathe deeply.

"The nurse did tell me what might happen. You were right there beside me. But I want to let her words float on by." I shift my bottom back into the chair. "Can we not just focus on good things?"

IT'S MIDNIGHT, the fire is down to a few bright splotches, and Cullen's kneeling at my feet with his head on my lap. His tears have wet right through my stretchy skirt, and my own tears have dropped onto the back of his head. "Every time you spoke, your words were so full of the belief that you were going to get better that there wasn't any question about it. I had to make sure you were realistic about it so you could choose your own plans." He lifts his head to look me in the eyes. "That's it, that's all."

"If I don't say the words out loud, then I don't have to think about what 'might' happen. So I don't."

He pulls up a chair beside me and lifts my hand in his, kissing each finger one by one, wanting to make it all okay between us, wanting to pretend I'm not sick and we're back in the shop goohing over each other and thinking about what going all the way with him would feel like. The exhaustion of where I'm at instead smothers me.

"I'm going to bed," I hear myself say. "It's so late. Thanks for everything, Cullen, and for trying to keep me in reality. I'm lucky to have you. Really I am." I need some time alone though.

TEETH BRUSHED, nightdress on; I turn out the light by my bed and submerge myself in darkness. I'm eighteen. I'm too young to die. I move my fingers in the air one by one. My life. God, are you for real? You knew this would happen. Why was I even born if it was going to end like this?

My mam fake-smiles day after day. My sister abandoned us and left me to clean up the pain she left behind. And now I might never get to marry the one person I was willing to trust with my life. Piece by piece, my heart is resettling. I need to be there for them all. What I might want doesn't matter. Win or lose, I can add a little spark to their lives as I go through this.

It's too much to think about tonight though. I'm knackered. I close my eyes and dream of nothingness.

IT'S NINE O'CLOCK when I wake up, and my brain and my whole body feel like they're filled with clear water. I had a brilliant dream last night, and in it Cullen and I were playing in a river with our grandkids. So much laughing. So much love. The only words the doctor used were "maybe," "possibly," "might." That's not enough to give up on. I'm not going to die. I don't care how many chemo treatments I need. I'll do whatever it takes.

It's earlier than when I usually drag myself out of bed, but Cullen stayed the night on the sofa. I swing my legs and push the rest of my body into a sitting position. The frame is right there, and I begin the tiring snail walk to the bathroom, followed by the even longer shuffle to the kitchen. The mouth sores are the worst part of this because I can't kiss Cullen. The doctor says the feeling sick and tired all the time will fade away eventually, but then the next round will start it all over again. I'm just happy that it hasn't hit the old brain, not that I had much in there to begin with.

I walk in on Cullen and Dad. Cullen's washing up

while Dad is reading the paper. They both rush to get the chair for me, and Cullen pops some bread in the toaster. I haven't been eating bread lately because of the issues down below, but I say nothing. Having him here is magical, especially when I have another big trip to Letterkenny today to see a consultant.

"Are you up for this?" he says.

"I think so," I say, even though I'm completely wrecked just from walking in here.

"Nothing too hard on your tummy, I hope." He looks at me questioningly.

I give him a forced smile. "Sounds great! Can you help me with all my drugs though? This addict needs her pills."

It takes us almost an hour to get ready and get out the door, but it's worth it. I forget what it feels like to be free and sort of normal sometimes. The sky looks like six layers of turquoise with a layer of ice between each one, so if you could fly, your wings would be powered by the frost flakes each time you broke into the next dimension until you reached heaven. Makes me want to see what putting icing sugar on my eyelashes would look like.

I can feel every bump as Cullen drives, even though he's slowed down his driving these days. We park in the handicap space and he helps me into the wheelchair, the sagging leather seat and back offering limp support, but it's better than walking.

THE CONSULTANT has his back to me. "So, Ellie, how have you been?" He fiddles with the bits of paper in front of him, and the nurse hands him my blood and pee results. "How's your energy level?"

173

I push myself up straighter. "Here's the thing, Doctor: I want to know if I'll survive this."

"Ah, that." He peers at me over his reading glasses. "All my patients have more chance of a remission if they're under the impression that they're getting better. Hope is an amazing little gem we doctors don't maximize enough." He rubs one eye with his little finger.

I don't think I've ever felt this small, like an ant trying to tunnel my way up to the grass while he watches. I finger the rosary beads in my pocket before my next question. "So how do things look now?"

"You know, Ellie, I don't like saying anything specific because everyone's different. I only put months on it *if* we can't get you into remission. That's a big if. Every single person who has sat where you're sitting has reacted faster or more slowly to chemo. Your age, weight, health, fitness level—everything matters when your body tries to fight this thing."

I glare at him and set my teeth in place like I'm making a mold for the dentist. "Please tell me what it looks like for me."

He rubs his other eye for a while, as if a midge has flown into it. "As far as I can tell, we can do another bone marrow test today to see if you are in remission, which I think you might be, thankfully, based on this blood test."

I close my eyes and focus on breathing while my heart taps on my chest with wild abandon.

He continues. "But because A-L-L is so aggressive sometimes, I'm afraid that if you don't get a bone marrow transplant in the next three months, you might only have a few months left. Then again, you might have years. We never know, so we need to move quickly." He moves some papers around on his desk. "If the bone marrow aspiration looks better than it has, I'd like you to go up to Dublin again to have some radiation. It'll help deter the partially formed cells that are doing all this damage and put your body in a better place to receive a transplant. In the meantime, I'm going to have to get you to take some chemo pills to try to double the effect of the chemo without destroying your red cell count, and I need to get you on the bone marrow registry as a recipient."

I can feel my face pucker as the salt water builds up in my nose. Hope has its way.

ONCE I'M BACK IN ST. LUKE'S, it's like I never left.

"Hi, Ellie," the nurse says. "Welcome back. Here are some of the chemo pills. We'll give you more before bedtime. Dr. Hooper will have a look at you in the morning, and he'll outline a more detailed plan to you then. Hopefully we'll have you with a donor within weeks. I hear your parents got tested last week." She lifts my duffel bag off the floor. "I'll put this in the cupboard out in the hall with your name on it. I'm off to supper now, but I'll be back soon to talk to you about your radiation treatment and what to expect." She pulls back the curtains and walks away.

Mam is still here. She brought her knitting, but she's packing it into her bag already. I swallow the pills and lie back against the pillows. Mam leans over and gives me a kiss on the forehead, her hand cool on my bald head.

"I'm heading to Aunty Margaret's now, but I'll be back in the morning before I head home. Sleep well." She gives my hand a squeeze and I watch her flat shoes walk slowly out of the ward.

I don't feel abandoned though. Something big's about to happen here. I can feel it in these cancer-riddled bones.

DR. HOOPER is a short man with hair that looks like the Burren on a windy day. I'm itching to cut it. The pockets on his whiteish coat are stuffed with pens, a notebook, and what appears to be a piece of chewing gum, which is now in his mouth. Mam would be disgusted. He's not one of those doctors who stands at the end of the bed and speaks like he's a lord of something; he's on the chair by the bed, and he's waving his big hands around as he tells me what's ahead.

"Ellie, only about one of four family members might be a good enough match. Even though you have four siblings, only one of them is over eighteen, right? That leaves us with your parents and the oldest girl. I'm delighted to tell you that your mum and dad have done the blood test, and an aunt, I think. Now we have to look at each person's results to see if their human leukocyte antigen system matches closely to yours." He pulls one of the notebooks out of his pocket and starts scratching four squares on a page with a pen.

"See these three shaded squares? We want as many of the HLAs to match yours so they don't start fighting the new bone marrow when we introduce it. If none of them are good in all four people, then we have to wait for a stranger to match you with."

*Or Una. Una could be a match!*

He pushes all his bits and bobs back into the pockets that seem to have space. "We'll do some blood workup here, and hopefully we'll have some good news for you in the next few days." He runs his fingers through his hair like they're a rake, but it doesn't help. "If all goes well, we can send you across to St. James and set the ball rolling." He reaches into another pocket and pulls out a tattered brochure. "Here's why. Let me know if you have any questions, or ask any of the nurses." A penny drops on the floor when he stands up, and he picks it up and throws it to me. "See a penny ...!"

There are loads of photos of doctors and nurses on the front like a welcome committee.

THE STEM CELL TRANSPLANTATION (SCT)
SERVICE
ST. JAMES HOSPITAL
FOUNDED IN 1984

On the next page, it says they have a post-transplant team that works with a recipient for two years. *Two years!* They have a room for getting the bone marrow, a room for storing it, and then a bunch of one-bed rooms where I'd stay, if the big team I'm looking at decides I'm a good candidate. Feck's sakes. Two years?! But feck's sakes—there's hope!

# 22

## Una

We rent a lot of old black-and-white films from the video shop around the corner. Des is a lot more settled when we watch them together. It's *Murder on the Orient Express* tonight. The doctor keeps talking about the move, trying to speed it up, especially after Des putting the electric kettle on the ring when Catherine was on the loo and nearly burning the place to the ground. We crack jokes when we can about it all. It's easier than crying because Catherine and I both know. We just can't bring ourselves to say it out loud, even though we've been sorting and packing for weeks.

Catherine staggers to the kitchen table with yet another box covered in dust that hasn't seen light since 1969 or thereabouts. "This is the last one," she gasps. "Thank God I don't have to bring these down to Ashford. The only space we have there is under the bed and a tiny cupboard in the hall."

We shake each bit of paper to make sure the mouse droppings and chewed-up corners fall on the lid and then lay the paper in piles by year. Catherine's lips are quivering as she holds one up in her hand and places it in mine. A letter signed by Tony Pringle that confirms he's given Des the building. I pull a plastic bag out of the drawer and seal it in before putting it in an accordion filing box in my room. Then I grab two wineglasses out of the cupboard, fill them generously with some white wine SuperValu had on sale, and we clink and knock it back in celebratory glugs. Catherine stops to examine the empty box before putting it by the door.

"So many memories." She turns her head away and goes to stick her hands in the sink, lathering up enough suds to get the dust off, but she turns to point at the last piles. She waves her hand in the air, a single bubble escaping and floating into Netherland. "They can all go in the fire too."

We could have sent smoke signals to America with all the paper we've fed the fire in the last month. This will be our last message: THANK THE GOOD LORD IT'S OVER. I stick paper by paper into the flames, each one a memory of the way business was done so long ago. So many handwritten scraps. *So what now?*

It's like she can hear my thoughts. She wipes her damp hands on her tweed skirt and pulls a stool forward. "Here, give me half those." She sways as we watch. "Des was so handsome then," she murmurs. "We met at a greengrocer's orange stand. I was with my mother, and we were both so excited because it was the first time oranges were being sold after the war. He held one up to my face and said, 'Sunnier, prettier, and you smell quite delicious!' Mum whipped around to see who was talking to me, but he had her wrapped around his finger within minutes, so she invited him to stop by the house. The rest is history because my dad couldn't turn away a young man who owned a building in the city at the age of twenty-seven, and I was close to being a spinster in those days at twenty-six."

She's smiling now. "He had this charm that made me want to be with him all the time, this easy way of being himself that made every day one I looked forward to." She takes my hand. "Una, no matter what, choose a man who keeps you smiling. It matters more than you think."

"That's right, love, prettiest girl at the market," says Des out of the blue. "My orange girl."

We both go back to watching the flames sway and curl around the logs as together we turn decades of her and Des's life to ash.

I'M WATCHING TV with Kieran. I feel like a horrible mam sometimes. But my feet hurt and it's so easy just being here with him on the sofa, and I can keep an eye on Des this way too. We've set up an alarm so that if he ever opens the door, we'll be able to run after him. But Catherine's here, we've had Sunday dinner, and I need to make the most of my Sundays with Kieran, what with my working all the time.

"Catherine, I was thinking about maybe us all going to the park and maybe even getting an I-C-E-C-R-E-A-M after. What do you think?" Kieran's all ears.

He bounces up from the floor and starts pulling on my jumper. "Abababababa!" He stops for a moment and searches my face. "Abbababa." I smile. This love hits me at the best times.

In a way, heading out for a few hours makes me feel more connected with the family back home. I've wondered so many times about everyone. What did Cullen end up doing with himself? Is he mad about Ellie?

I hope so. She doesn't lie and kidnap children and hide secrets. I hope she treats him well. I hope so many things.

"Okay, Kieran, I need to go and get my shoes on." I check my face in the bathroom mirror and add a bit of lip gloss and some eyeliner and find myself singing "Against All Odds" without even realizing what I'm doing. Robbie's face keeps dropping into my mind, making me smile.

Maybe I'm over Cullen.

And maybe not.

I call Robbie to see if he wants to meet us there. Kieran adores him.

IT'S MONDAY MORNING and we're all downstairs in the shop. The heater is going in the back, all swishes and plashes, and Des is back there with the nurse and the *Gerry Ryan Show* on the big radio we got so Des could be near us. He loves it.

Gerry starts a new topic off. "So today we're going to talk about runaways. We've had letters over the years from different people all over the country about missing loved ones, and I thought it'd be a great thing to read some of these letters to you so that if by chance you know the person, or if you're the person I'm reading about, you can get in touch with your family. Please, please do, just to let them know you're all right. I can't imagine how terrible it must be to have a child run away and you have no idea if they are okay, even years later."

I edge closer to the radio, body stiffening.

His voice continues. "This one is for Bríd Kinsella."

*Bríd,*

*I don't think you know how much pain you've put us all through since you left, without even saying goodbye. Every Christmas for the last ten years we've put a present under the tree with your name on it. We're so sad all the time because you're not here, even ten years on.*

*We're sorry. We love you. We miss you. Please come home.*

*Your mam and dad.*

He reads through two more and my body starts to relax. But then ...

*Una Gallagher,*

*Your sister is very sick and we need you to come home. Can you please call us, or even just call RTE to let them know you got this message? Your family needs you right now.*
*Cullen.*

I put my face in my hands and lean into them. I can feel my breath coming in short, sharp shots.

"So as I said before, if you're out there and you are one of these people, please let your family know you're okay. There's possibly nothing worse than not knowing where your own child has gone or if she's dead or alive." Gerry clears his throat. "It's the least you can do."

The ads come on. Catherine's looking at me. Why is Cullen the one writing? Am I even safe here now? The phone rings. It's probably Sinéad from the crèche asking if I was listening. She's always on top of everything. Probably told everyone on her street already. I ignore it.

"I'll make you a cup of tea," Catherine says, and she heads into the back.

Des is back to listening to the show. I stay in that

position until the tea sits cold on the counter, weighing every single reason I gave myself to stay away from my family, but no matter how true any of them feel to me, no matter how scared shitless it makes me feel, I know what I have to do.

"Tanya? It's Una. Una Gallagher. Yeah, I know, it's a long story, but before I get into it, I have a favor to ask you. Do you have any idea what's going on with my sister?"

"Una! Thank God you called. Yeah, your Ellie's very sick. I ran into your mam at the SuperValu just the other day and asked if she'd ever heard from you after that call she got from you at Christmas, you know, and she told me that Ellie's got leukemia and she has to go up to Dublin all the time. She's heading up there again really soon to get some radiation to try and help her out a bit before her bone marrow transplant, if they can find a match."

"Leukemia?" *Oh God, oh God, oh God.* I try and reach out for the table, but I miss and wobble in the rebalancing. My eyes are completely full and I can barely get the words out. "Do you know which hospital?"

"She said something like St. Luke's?"

I recognize the name. Gillian had a great-uncle there last year for radiation after they took out his voice box. "Is there any way you can find out when she'll be there for sure? I need to see her. I can go as soon as she gets there."

"I'll do my best, Una. Sorry. It's a really awful thing to happen to anyone."

I sit on the carpet and take off my slippers, trying to earth my feet to the floor. Mam must be in an awful way over it. The whole family. "How did Mam look?"

"Oh, you know, as well as can be expected. But she's having a hard time with it all. Made me wish you were here again. Anyway, I'll let you go. It's great to hear from you, but this call is costing you a fortune, and I'll let you know as soon as I hear about those dates."

"Thanks, Tanya, and can you do me a huge favor and don't let on that you ever talked to me? I just wanted to be prepared before I called Mam."

"Right you are."

I head for the kitchen and put on the kettle. Not Ellie. Not our Ellie!

I can feel the fear swell up inside me until my head starts pounding. I put my hands over my ears and try to gather my thoughts. This makes no sense.

I could pretend I didn't hear anything, stay hidden, keep Cullen's mirror image here in Dublin. I could avoid Cullen for the rest of my life. I could keep never having to really deal with the truth that my greatest love is with my sister.

But running hasn't helped me; it's just kept me in the avoidance mode I started living in when I realized I loved Cullen. If you don't talk about it, it's not happening. But that's not true. Cullen is probably still going out with Ellie. Ellie might die.
Everything I'm afraid of facing is in Donegal. I was ready once, but this time the thought of going is so much harder because it means seeing Cullen pour his love around and into someone else. But Ellie needs me. I need Ellie. Decision made.

But first I need to talk to Robbie. He's somehow able to take mountains of information and condense it to a few points that make so much sense, and it's annoying that something that simple never crossed my mind.

He's at the door within thirty minutes, his arms ready to scoop me up and hold me tight. I sink into his arms and stay there for a long time, but eventually I pull myself out and tell him everything. Sure enough, he does exactly what I expected. He'll be a great lawyer.

"So one, Ellie is really sick. Two, she's going out with Cullen, who you haven't seen since you left and who has no idea about Kieran. Three, you have to see her so you'll have to see Cullen and your family. Four, you're afraid Cullen and Ellie might find out about Kieran.

"The good thing with fear is that most of what you fear won't happen. So Ellie probably won't die, you won't be struck by lightning when you see Cullen, and it might be easier than you think to see them together when you've got this hunk of burning love to come back to."

I laugh. He's very hunky.

"As for Kieran, that's always been on your mind, and this is forcing you to face it."

Well, yes, that's the part I didn't want to deal with.

"But all you need to do right now is see Ellie and do whatever you can to help her get better."

He gets up to get a glass out of the dishwasher and fill it with water. "Life is about one single step, one single decision at a time. Take care of this first step with Ellie and shove the other stuff back into the brain cupboard until this step is over with. You can't let what-ifs get in the way of what is, or you'll never take care of anything; and you'll feel guilty at every turn and accuse yourself of being lazy, when all you really are is scared shitless, and that's no way to live."

He has to leave then, but not before he peeks in at Kieran to see him "in his ethereal state when he can do no wrong," as he puts it.

It would be so easy to grow old with this man.

THE WEIGHTY CURTAINS the color of dandelions are pulled tightly together, with ne'er a crack of night creeping in. Gillian and Ashlinn are slumped sideways on the sofa. She stayed for moral support while I get this phone call over and done with, but I suppose she wasn't able to stay awake with a sleeping child on her. I've done it often enough myself.

I can't stop my hands from shaking, but this is it. This is when I grow up for good.

"Hello?"

"Mam?" I say. I can't say anything else. My nose has just flooded with tears and the air isn't getting through to my lungs. I open my mouth and gasp a bit.

"Who is this?" There's a pause. "Una? Is that you, Una? *Oh God. It's Una!*" I can hear her shouting, see her yelling into the sitting room. "Where in God's name are you? Are you all right? Oh, thank God, thank God. You're okay. *Seamus, come here. It's our Una. She's on the phone!*" I can hear Mam sobbing now, deep gulps of years of pain matching my own.

"You're sure?" I can hear Dad now, ever the skeptic.

"Yes, I'm sure! Don't you think I know my own daughter's voice?"

"Una?" His voice is quivering, the scratchy sound of an older man who's weathered much.

"Hi, Dad," I manage to say, before wiping my hand all over my nose. *Damn, I should have brought tissues.* "I'm sorry, Dad. I'm so sorry." I'm heaving now, my whole body scattered in all directions yet trying valiantly to pull itself back to its core.

"It's good to hear your voice," he says, the words

interrupted during their delivery by ugly sniffles.

"It's so good to hear yours too." Now I'm a complete basket case, rubbing the tears out of my eyes like a madwoman and snorting back everything that's threatening to come out of my nose. Kleenex would have a field day if this was an ad. "Dad, I'm coming home for a few days. I have a lot to tell you all, and it's too much to talk about over the phone. I can't wait to see you."

"Same here, love, same here."

"Can I talk to Mam again?"

"Hi, Una."

"Hi, Mam. I was wondering if it would be all right if I come up this weekend. I'll be coming up alone, what with the news about Ellie. I heard about it on the *Gerry Ryan Show.*"

She doesn't even pause for a second. "We'd love that, Una. We really would, but Ellie's in the hospital in Dublin for another few days, but you'll be wanting to see her first. Here, write down this address."

Forget tears. This is a flood. I blubber through the wetness. I put the cap back on the pen. "Thanks, Mam. I'll go and see her and call again soon."

I lean against the wall and swallow more tears, then finally get up and go sit on the sofa by Gillian's leg. She doesn't budge, so I get some blankets and put them over the two sleeping beauties and leave a pillow on the floor in case she wakes up with a sore neck.

My bed is so welcoming tonight. Thank God that's over with. But that was only step one.

I DON'T KNOW what I'll say, but I have to see her, secrets be damned.

It's a gorgeous day, but when I walk into the hospital

and ask for Ellie, my whole body is shaking with fear.

"Are you a relative?" the nurse asks.

"Sister." It feels refreshing on my tongue, like raindrops.

I follow her to the middle of the ward, where I see Ellie sitting by the bed, legs up on a footstool and some magazines on her lap. I have to choke back a gulp when I see my old teddy on her bed.

"Una!" she gasps, and she jumps off the chair and flings herself at me.

I should have expected her to look different, but I wasn't prepared for how much older she'd look and how different without her shiny hair. She was sixteen when I said goodbye and ran out the door. It's insane how nearly two years can change a woman's face. Hers is thin, but her smile is the same. I wrap my arms around her body and hold her tight for a long time while the tears fall.

"So," I say.

"So."

"I take it you heard Gerry Ryan then?" Ellie asks. "Has anyone told you anything else?"

I shake my head and sit down on a stool beside her. "Mam told me you were here. I haven't talked to anyone else but the family, but yeah, I heard Gerry all right."

"So apparently, I might not be okay," she says abruptly, "but I think I'll live." Her fingers squeeze her blanket.

No words come out. Probably for the better. My mind is buzzing too loudly, too many thoughts crashing into each other at once. "What do the doctors think?" I'd like to feel a thin hope of a cure coming. Not this flat despair. Ellie always plumped things up. I'm more likely to dehydrate them and pack them away.

"It's a thing in my bone marrow that's supposed to make new blood cells but instead it decided to make shagging cancer cells that thought they were on a trip around the world, and they decided to have an all-nighter in every town. Doctors say I need a bone marrow transplant." Her voice sounds like ripping cardboard until she perks up again. "I might be fine by the spring next year! Cullen tried so hard to find you. He wanted you to be able to see me just in case, you know …"

I can't see, the tears have surged so high. "Oh, Ellie." All the usual things I could say are useless. I'm swimming without a life jacket and there's no driftwood to reach out to.

"And Cullen? You two are hanging out?" I'm hoping, praying.

"Oh!" Her eyes start to sparkle. "He'd be here today, only he had to go to some farrier thing in London. We've been going out for about six months now. I'm mad about him. He's even given me a claddagh ring already. Can you believe it?"

And that's the moment when I feel I will truly drown.

# 23

## Ellie

Una starts talking and I study her face. She's changed. Her Donegal accent is all but gone, and she sounds like someone from the rich side of Donnybrook now. Even her clothes look like they come from somewhere far better than Penny's.

She's talking about her job and about how the old man has Alzheimer's and it's getting worse. About a woman called Catherine who treats her like a daughter. About the building she lives in and how she hopes to run a shop. It doesn't sound like anything she talked about doing after school, and it sounds strange—like she's trying to convince herself that it's all she wants. I don't understand any of this, but I don't ask. Except about Robbie. Now, he sounds lovely. She glows when she talks about him. Not going out with him my arse!

Una stays for as long as they let her. Even after I'm in bed and the lights are low, she sits there by me. I'm lying here thinking about the last few hours. Thinking about Una and how she's different. Wondering why she's so hard and sad mixed together. I thought it would be just the same as before if I ever saw her again, well, except for me being sick and all, but it's all a new world to us both now.

"Una?" I whisper through the gray. "Why did you leave us?"

I hear her body turning toward me and then nothing, followed by a long sigh. "It's a long story, Ellie, but none of it matters now."

I prop myself up on one elbow and feel myself about to head into a hissy fit of major proportions. And then I realize she's right. None of it matters now. She's here. Never mind that she's only here until they kick her out. She's here and the two of us are talking to each other long after I should have gone asleep. I rest my body back down and tuck the covers around my neck.

"Una?"

"Yeah?"

"Thanks for coming." I stop. "This isn't easy." I can feel my breath start to shudder, and before I can inhale again, she's climbed onto the covers beside me and is stroking my head, just like she used to do when I had hair. And I let the tears drip onto my pillow without shame.

The nurse comes by and clears her throat. Una rolls off the bed and stands by me.

"I'll be back tomorrow," she says, before bending down to whisper. "And remember, you're going to get better."

I blow her a kiss, and I'm already looking forward to tomorrow. As soon as she leaves, I reach into the nightstand for the Bible I found in there. The priest at home says it's too hard to understand, but I'm reading all the bits in a book called John where Jesus is talking, and they're just beautiful, the words that came out of his mouth. I feel like I'm getting to know him for the first time in my life.

UNA'S PUT ME in a wheelchair so we can sit outside for a bit. I have enough layers on me to cover Russia. We're sitting by a pond looking at ducks quacking softly in the water. I'm not really sure what we can talk about with her keeping mum about why she left.

"So will you be able to come back home?" I really want this to happen. I want us to all be together again to make up for those shitty years we had without her.

She looks down at her hands and twists the ring I gave her years ago. "I can't, Ellie. It's not that I don't want to, but I have a new life here in Dublin, and Catherine and Des really need me now."

"It's okay. You don't have to. I just miss you so flipping much." I reach out for her hand and she lets me hold it for a minute. "So tell me more about Robbie."

She starts laughing. It's good to hear her laugh. "Ah, Robbie. He's lovely—funny, so good to me, helps me with … with everything I'm going through at the shop."

"So when can I come and see you at your posh leather shop?"

It's hard not to hear the drops of silence before she answers. "I'll have to meet you somewhere in town. You'd never make it up the stairs on that yoke." Her hand lands on the wheelchair.

I leave her be. The last thing I want to do right now is make waves.

# 24

## Una

I've made up my mind. I'm going to tell her everything. All I've been thinking of this whole time is how to protect myself, how to protect Cullen. Ellie needs to know why I left, why I never let them know where I was, why all of this happened.

Although maybe it won't quite be everything. Because of Cullen. He has a good life carved out for himself. He's in love with Ellie. I'm a ghost from his past, and if I insert myself and Kieran in this now, it'll make a mess of Ellie's recovery, maybe even set her back. So I'm going to do the next best thing. I'm going to almost tell her the whole truth, because what better lie is there than one that grasps at truth's edges so finely?

I sit on the tight hospital bedcover and take in a long breath before I begin. "Ellie." I chew my lip and look into her eyes. "You asked me why I ran away, why I stayed away. I want to answer that question now."

"Oh, Una, it's okay. You don't need to."

I wave my hand. "Actually I do, Ellie. I need you to know, to understand it all. Do you remember that day I climbed in through the bathroom window after you gave me a towel?"

She nods.

"Well ..." I pause, "I needed that towel because I'd just puked in Mam's car, and I puked because I was pregnant."

Ellie mouth falls open.

"Remember the next day, when Mam left me a letter? I'd told her about the baby, and in the letter she said I had to give him up for adoption. She didn't give me any choice. And that's why I had to go. That's why I've stayed away." I stare at my jeans, waiting for her to judge me.

"I'm an auntie?" Her smile radiates, like child-drawn heat squiggles from a radiator. Then she shakes her head at me like it makes no sense. "But you could have come back after you had it." She leans forward, fists knocking each other in excitement. "Boy or girl? Name? Have you got a photo?"

"Boy. Kieran. No photo."

"This is so exciting!" She rearranges her blanket. "When can I see him?"

There's that claw machine in my throat again. "The nurses said I couldn't bring him while your immune system is so low."

She nods trustingly. "I'll see him soon. I know it! But why didn't you come back, Una?"

"But I couldn't come back, Ellie, and here's why. The boy I had sex with? I was at a party and I was really drunk, and there was this really cute guy there who started kissing me. And I'd always wondered, you know? And I was so drunk and I just didn't care. And all those warning bells you usually get when you're sober? They weren't ringing that night." I trace the pattern of the rug with my finger. "And the guy is someone practically everyone in Donegal knows, but I hadn't even told him I was pregnant." I pause. "And I never will."

Ellie's shaking her head. "I still don't get it, but I'm kind of glad you're not telling because then I'd be staring at him in town and I'd go puce red and then he'd know that I know something he doesn't. Why wouldn't you go and marry him? Is he horrible?" She laughs again. "But sure you'd drive any boy demented."

"You're right there!" We laugh for a while until I get all serious again. "I thought about it, thought I was ready to come back, but changed my mind at the last minute because up there I'd always be known as the slut, the one who had a one-night stand, who couldn't keep her knickers on for one night. Because Kieran would be stared at every time I took him out. Because I have a good life here in Dublin. Because I've brought no shame on the family by staying here." I think about Kieran and feel my heart twist. "Because here I'm still an okay person."

She nods but then stops and looks into my eyes. "So who's the dad?"

"It's too embarrassing. I don't think I'll ever tell anyone, to be honest." *Is it obvious? Is she slagging me? Am I looking away? Does she know?*

"Ah, sure it's all right. I'll take it to my grave." And she smiles that Ellie smile.

But I still don't tell her.

I wheel her into the sunroom. Thank God I haven't run into Cullen.

I want to tell her everything in this snatch of time, but she deserves this dignity, this feeling that she's the only girl for him, that she's special. I don't want to be the big blot on her life's canvas. What do you tell your desperately sick sister? I tell her I love her. I remind her of all the good things I've ever seen her do. We laugh about the funny memories. I tell her I never forgot her smile in all the months I was away. I hug her for a long time until my heart feels like it's cramping up after a long run.

She has no dates for the bone marrow transplant, but she'll be in St. James Hospital for who knows how long once they find a match. I'm not sure if I can even go into the room or if she's just kept away from the other patients, but maybe there's a window I can wave at her through.

And then I walk away and I can't even see where to put my feet, the tears come so fast. What happens now? How can we save Ellie?

# 25

## Una

Killary House Designs,
Enniskerry,
Co. Wicklow
May 1st

Dear Una,

It's been a long time since we talked. Feels like years. I hate that I missed you at the hospital, although I'm sure you and Ellie had a bit to say to each other. I'm glad you told her about the baby. It was very hard keeping it from her, but you asked me to, so I did.

Anyway, I'm hoping we can work together now on getting her better, what with you being the organizer of all things. You always were good at that.

I've missed you all this time, and I can't wait for us both to catch up and to meet the wain. I bet

197

he minds his p's and q's rightly. How old is he now, one and a bit? Is he a handful? But sure no better woman for the job of being his mammy.

Are we good though? Are we talking? You can call me at the forge most days. 712569.

Love,

Cullen

"Una. Una? Are you okay?" Catherine stands in front of the till. I hand her the letter.

"Oh," she says after folding it up again. "He thinks you can pick up where you left off."

I sink onto the high stool behind me and whisper a yes. "I have to be okay with this, Catherine. I have to let it go. I have to pretend I've never loved him. It's all about Ellie now. I have to protect her from our past so she can have no mental obstacles to her future."

Catherine places her fingers over the edge of the counter and looks into my eyes. "I believe in you, dear. You know what's best for your heart."

It's not that I don't love Robbie. Oh, wait. Love? I loved Cullen—his smile, his love of books, his curiosity, the way he looked into my eyes like I was the only one who mattered, the way I'd find him in our spot in the woods most days after school because he liked being with me. I loved how "liked" I felt with him. But even now when I think about Robbie, my insides melt a little. It's like he sees past the words that come out of my mouth and he sticks the tweezers into my soul and pulls only the good stuff out to inspect it in the light. He makes me feel like I can do anything. Is that love? Is it really only about how others make me feel or is it more than that? Is it about how alive I feel or how safe I feel or both? Or is my happiness with a man like icing on the happiness I should already have in myself? I felt contented and safe with Cullen. I feel alive and safe with Robbie.

That's what I can use as my mantra whenever I'm with Cullen. "I feel alive with Robbie."

"I just need to run upstairs for something," I yell at Catherine, and I take the steps two at a time before reaching my lemon room and pulling some writing paper out of a drawer. Once I'm back downstairs, I grab a pen and write as fast as I can before I change my mind and make a shagging mess of the whole thing.

*Dear Cullen,*

*I agree. It's been a long time.*

*I didn't let you know I was back because I was a bit emotional already, what with catching up with Mam and Dad and taking in all Ellie's news. I should never have asked you to keep the baby a secret, but it is what it is. Thank you.*

*I'm happy to do whatever needs to be done. I talked to Mam just a minute ago and she says her and Dad have had the blood test. I did mine at the hospital. I'm sure you were the first one to do it.*

*I'll be seeing her next week again, I hope, so maybe the nurses will know what else we can do. I wish I had something to do right now. I keep feeling like any day not doing something is like not trying hard enough to save her.*

*Kieran is the best thing that ever happened to me. I think you'll like him. He loves his books and he's into everything. As for Dylan, it's a long story I might tell you some day, but life here is good. We just need to get Ellie better now.*

*Yes, we're good. I should have called or written. Let's start over.*

*Una*

I have to pretend I'm okay talking to Cullen again. We have to save Ellie's life.

I need to go home. I need to see Mam and Dad and everyone. I need to feel connected again. I made them a promise that I'd go up as soon as I'd seen Ellie. And I know Cullen's staying down here for Ellie, so I won't run into him if I do this now. Family is the most important part of my life, and I've treated it like the least. If I can repair the damage, I need to do it now.

IT'S ALL BEEN SORTED. I'm on the bus heading out on the Navan Road to the unknown.

The bus bends around the last corner of our journey before leveling out at the hotel. "Donegal Town," shouts the driver, just in case we're not sure. I let everyone else off first—the three Mormon missionaries who got into a heated discussion with another woman near the front, the couple behind us who were more interested in hanky-panky, and the old lady across from me who obviously has bad arthritis. I help lift her bag and follow her out, my nervous feet dragging all the way. I want to forgive Mam, and this is not all her fault, but she's the biggest reason why I ended up where I did.

The bus pulls away and there she is—Mam, waving at me from the car in the middle of the Diamond, her tweed skirt poking out from under her anorak. I can't make out any expression on her face from here, what with the rain and everything, but I run across the road with the break in traffic and hope for the best.

I'm not two feet away from her when she opens up her arms and pulls me in. She steps back and looks at me. "I'm so sorry, Una. I'm so, so sorry." Her apology looks genuine. Maybe she regrets everything she said after all.

She runs her fingers over my face with shaky hands and then hugs the breath out of me again, tears messing up her blusher.

We climb into the car and she starts with the questions every Irish mother in existence asks: "How was the bus ride up?" "Are you tired?" "I saved you some lunch because I thought you'd be hungry." It fills in the awkwardness because I just don't know what to say from here.

The tires scud the gravel as we turn in. The house looks just the same. The rain flies in towards the windows like machine gunfire. And there's Dad standing by the front door with an umbrella. He half runs and walks towards us, opening the car door first to make sure it's really me. He places his hand behind my head and tugs me awkwardly into his arms.

We run together to the front door before he leaves me to go back to Mam. I squeak open the door, but there's no one in the hallway.

"They're all at school," says Dad, as he comes back in, "and Ruthie's at a friend's." I should have expected his face to age. It's been over a year and a half since I ran out the door without saying goodbye, and all the skin on his face is a little looser, his lines deeper.

"Do you want to eat yet?" says Mam—food being the fixer of all ills.

"Thanks, Mam." I follow her into the kitchen, where she's made a big effort to welcome me—flowers on the table and even napkins—stuff I only ever saw come out at Christmas.

Mam and Dad sit down with me. I keep the conversation light in this testy air. I have to make this right. They tell me all they know about Ellie and her treatment. We share tears and hugs, and their relief over me seeing her, and doing the test to see if I'm a match, is profound.

We talk about Dublin, Kieran, my job—everything we could have shared in weekly phone calls and weekend visits—until lunch is over.

The tin of biscuits is in the middle of the table. The tea is nearly at the bottom of the mugs. This. This is home.

I've added a box of tissues to the mugs and biscuits. Not going to skip that this time. I learned my lesson. I wait until Mam settles back down.

"Mam, Dad, you know I ran away because I was pregnant. I didn't know what to do, and I didn't want to tell the father because I wanted him to have a good life— one without a kid weighing him down. I didn't want you two to be the talk of the town either. So I left. I got the bus to Dublin and found a place to stay with Catherine and Des." I put my hands around the bottom of the mug.

"I can't tell you who the father is ..." I pause, heartbeats smacking the inside of my chest wall. "... because he doesn't know himself."

"Oh my God!" Mam claps her hand over her mouth, and her eyes are wide in shock. "I thought you were living with his family. Catherine and Des aren't his parents?"

Dad puts a hand on the table to steady himself. Mam's face is working overtime.

Without mentioning any names, I give them the whitewashed version of that night at the party and watch understanding fill their faces. Mercy falls. I can almost see it sprinkle around us like a fine mist. My heart feels like someone is unwrapping its scrunched-up form and smoothing it out.

Dad reaches across the table and curls his fingers around mine. "I'm sorry you felt like you couldn't trust us, that you had to go through that alone."

Mam looks away while her hand reaches out to find a tissue. How long must she have fought with her guilt?

"I'm sorry too, Dad. I would have told you, but I was scared you'd be back on the bottle in no time if you knew I'd brought that on the family. You always thought I was so brilliant, and then I wasn't."

"Mam?" She turns her head towards me. "I'm sorry for running, for not calling as soon as I got to Dublin, for not being here for you with everything Ellie's going through. It was a really selfish thing for me to do."

She sniffs and shakes her head. "We're all sorry, Una, and how were you to know? Such a waste, such a loss all around. Well, sure, what can we do only make the best of it from here?"

"Thanks," I whisper, and stuff about four tissues

under my eyes. Mam and Dad get up and surround me. To feel this support here, now, goes far beyond my expectations.

THE EARLY LIGHT has just started to tiptoe through the curtains, and I can hear Mam rambling around the kitchen already. I'm exhausted from everyone crowding around me all night asking questions and telling me all their news, and Ruthie wanted me to read to her for ages. I've missed this noise.

I get dressed and join Mam. I head to the cooker to stir the porridge, and I add a bit more milk to it while she sets the table and fills the French press from the kettle. The radio is on low, classical music filling the empty space between us.

"I'm sure you're a great mam. You were always so good with the wains." Her voice trails. "I've thought about you nearly every day since you left," Mam says. "That phone call you made two weeks in, and on your first Christmas away—you have no idea how relieved I was to know that you were all right." She takes the wooden spoon from me to stir the porridge again. "Your dad too. And your card letting us know the delivery went well and your baby is happy and healthy was a big relief too." She turns off the gas and puts the lid on the saucepan.

"So you two are not"—she wiggles her finger from left to right—"together?"

"God no, Mam."

She stands there stiffly in the middle of the floor, fiddling with her watch. "Why did you run away, Una? Why didn't you even try to talk to me about it all?"

"Aw, Mam, you know there was never any talking to

you. We weren't allowed to ever question you."

She purses her lips as if it's not true and walks over to the coffee press. "I wish ... Do you have any idea of what it was like after you left? I couldn't tell your dad about my letter because I was terrified how he'd react. I had no one to talk to because I knew it would get out about you being pregnant if I did. You did this, Una. You broke up our family that day you ran away."

I can feel my head shaking vigorously, warm blood racing to my fingertips and making them tingle. "No, Mam, running away was one of the best things I did. Keeping Kieran is the best choice I ever made. And you could've told Dad what you did and let him forgive you, but you never did. You shut him out too." Then I see her heart instead of her words and soften. "But staying away was the worst. I never gave you a chance after that letter. I wrote you off and cut you out of our lives. And I was the one who ended up broken because of it."

"Oh, Una, we're both a mess really." She takes in a big breath. "Well, if you want to move into this defective home with Kieran, you're both welcome here." And then she runs out the door.

# 26

## Una

I finally land back at the shop on Sunday night to a welcome committee of Kieran and Robbie. Kieran's face is smeared with chocolate, and Robbie holds a single chocolate button on his hand out to me. "We saved one for you," he says with a smile.

What I want to do is push his hand to one side and wrap my arms around his neck, and wrap the rest of my body around his too. Just be friends, I said. Stupidest idea ever. Or not. Instead I avoid his eyes because I suddenly feel all tingly and focus on Kieran instead, reaching out to hug him.

"So?" Robbie says later. I feel the deepest sigh escape my lungs. I don't have words. The next minute I feel his arm behind my head. He pulls me to his chest and I start sobbing. I stay there until I stop hiccupping, which is quite some time later because I don't want to leave this closeness, and I had more tears inside than I thought.

"How did you know that's what I needed?" I whisper into his jumper.

"All ice eventually has to melt somewhere. You looked like you were ready to defrost."

I wallop his arm and snuggle in some more, if that's possible, but he shifts himself to a standing position. "I'm afraid I have to head home. College tomorrow."

I nod and we walk downstairs together. It's hard to let him go tonight. I stay next to the window, watching him walk away while my breath steams up the glass. I draw a heart in it and groan. I'm either a complete idiot or very, very wise in staying single, and tonight I don't understand what would be so terrible about signing up for more. Much, much more, please God.

CATHERINE APPEARS IN THE DOORWAY, face drawn. "There's something I have to tell you, Una. We knew it was coming because the doctor was practically begging us to move weeks ago, but the home help told me yesterday she can't look after Des properly anymore because of his antics, so we need to move quickly. Either way," she says, "he can't stay here anymore."

I walk back so I can feel the bed against my legs and let my body sit, the duvet cushioning around my legs. I wish it would swallow me whole. "How soon?"

"Tomorrow."

She looks so small and fragile as she says that one word. I stand up and wrap my arms around her. "You're doing the right thing. You're the best wife."

She clings to me before taking a deep breath and standing back. "I'm glad I still have him from time to time."

DES'S BAGS are in the hallway. They're heading down in the morning. Kieran is in bed, finally asleep, and I tiptoe back to the living room. Catherine and Des are wrapped in each other's arms on the sofa while Catherine bawls her eyes out.

Des pats her back. "There, there. Shhh. It's all okay."

I sit in the armchair beside them and wait for Catherine's hiccups to stop. "I'm really going to miss you, Des. I can't even begin …" The words get stuck in my throat along with a deep ache I can't swallow.

Catherine grabs more tissues from the box to dry her wet face. "I'm not going to sit here and cry me a river. Every tunnel has an end and a new phase of the journey, and I'm going to keep going." She reaches out a hand to Des, who looks confused but puts his hand in hers anyway, and she heaves him to his feet. Hand in hand, they walk to their bedroom, leaving their warmth behind. I shift over on the sofa to sit in it and soak in the short-term remains of their presence before heading to bed myself.

IT'S BEEN A WEEK without Catherine and Des here. It's like living someone else's life. Frank, the new guy, is sitting at the table cutting more leather. Scrawny fella, with a head of curls so tight I could mop the floor with him. Catherine got him on a recommendation from a friend of hers, and he's been working out well. He does things right the first time, and I don't have to tell him what to do from one minute to the next. He has the best smile, and he knows all the words to every song on the radio.

We're singing along with Madonna while I'm planning the next schoolchildren's visit to the shop when I see the time.

"I'm going to get Kieran, Frank. Back in half an

hour. I'll get some milk on the way home."

He gives a thumbs-up.

Kieran's sitting in the playroom with the other kids, and when he sees me, he gets up and does his awkward baby run over. Ashlinn waves at me before going back to her board book—bit of a bookworm, that one. Gillian makes a phone sign with her hand at me, so as soon as we get home and I've given Kieran a snack and stuck him in front of his toys, I call.

"You'll never guess what!" she says. "Remember that fella I was telling you about, Sam, the one with the big chin?" I don't remember because Gillian seems to be with a different guy each week. "The one I met when we were doing that musical." I can hear her clicking her fingernails on the table.

"Oh yeah," I lie. "Him."

"Yeah, him. You have no idea who I'm talking about, do you?" she hoots. "Well, anyway, we've been having a lot of laughs together, and he's coming over *tonight!*"

I almost throw down the handset. "Really? I thought you said you'd never do that."

"I *know*, but I think this is it, Una. I think he's the one. He thinks I'm hilarious. He's funny, he's really sweet, and he wants me to move in with him. I know, I know, it's all very quick, but I told him I'd think about it. He has to pass the Ashlinn test first. And I think he'll do fine with that because he has loads of nieces and nephews already. And he introduced me to his mam and dad last week." She stops to breathe.

I have a huge smile on my face. "I'm really happy for you. That's fab news. You deserve this. So when do I meet him?"

"I'll make it happen. I promise. Have to dash. Mum's

all jittery and wants the place to be clean for him so we can pretend we're this tidy all the time."

I hang up and lift a leg over one of the boxes Catherine has been half packing. Who knows if she'll manage to ever fully move out all her stuff, what with her promise to keep coming back up for a day here and there of work and spending time with Kieran?

I peek into Kieran's room and lose myself in his tiny snores before walking into the empty kitchen, my one plate long since washed and dried and Kieran's high chair wiped clean.

Things could have been so different if I'd stayed in Donegal, if I'd told the truth, if I'd carried the shame. Cullen and I would be in a flat with a little garden off Main Street. Round about now he'd be in the bathroom brushing his teeth while I sat in bed reading. We'd be poor but happy. But I thought I knew better, and here we are.

Run, hide, pretend, disconnect again? Or stay, be seen, be real, connect? Ellie needs me. Mam and Dad need me. Catherine needs me. What do I need?

Who is Una Gallagher? And when I figure it out, will I even like her?

# 27

## Ellie

D
r. Hooper leans forward on the bed table at the end of my bed. His nerdy smile is infectious.

"Great news, Ellie. Your sister is a match. I honestly don't think you could get a closer one if we wanted, so we're moving you over to St. James today. She's agreed to head that way this afternoon for some bloodwork to make sure she's the picture of health, and we'll get this done as soon as possible."

I almost keel over I'm so excited.

Nurse Patricia helps clear out my bedside locker and gives me a face mask for the trip. She says my immune system is in enough of a state without picking up something weird on the way over. Two hours later, I'm in the hospital van with her, and inside I'm about to burst with pleasure. I see kids running to the bus stop, women pushing their prams, white clouds racing to the edge of the world, and I'm running and pushing and racing with them all. Today is such a good day to be alive!

Patricia pushes me to the main reception area, and

we're sent from there down a long hallway to a ward with a bunch of separate rooms. I'm in number five, which is so great because it's my lucky number. There's a lovely big armchair in the corner, all blue with wooden arms, so I park myself there by the window and look out at the busy carpark.

Patricia pushes my bag into the locker with a grunt. "I'm heading off now. I'll just give your new staff nurse the lowdown and I'll be praying up a storm for you." She hesitates before reaching into her pocket and pulling out a piece of notepaper she's written something on. "Here's a little something for one of my favorite patients, but don't read it 'til I'm gone, okay? It's by a poet called Rumi, and all our conversations over the last few weeks made me think you'd love it."

I dutifully wait until the door closes over and open up the paper, reading the lines slowly.

> *Lo, I am with you always means when you look for God,*
> *God is in the look of your eyes,*
> *in the thought of looking,*
> *nearer to you than your self,*
> *or things that have happened to you.*
> *There's no need to go outside.*

I close my eyes and put the words over my heart. Nearer than myself.

THERE'S A KNOCK on the door and Una pokes her head in.

"Thank God you're here. I'm dying of boredom already!" I shout.

She laughs and turns her big handbag upside down

over the bed. "I stopped by Eason's on the way and bought up all their romances on sale. Danielle Steele, Belva Plain, Judith Krantz, and Colleen McCullough are waiting for you to feast your eyes on their words and transport your heart into moments of exquisite, um, love." She sits on the bed. "In other news, I did the blood tests, and they'll let me know when to come in for the bone marrow donation. They said it depends on exactly when your body is ready for it, so they can't tell me right now." She picks up one of the books and opens it on a random page. "His eyes caressed her body before he slowly lifted his hand to her heaving bosom." She slaps it shut. "Ellie Gallagher, you'll have to tell me how this one ends. I can already see Sylvester Stallone as the hero."

I laugh but then get quiet. "I know this messes up your work and having to find babysitting and everything. I want you to know how thankful I am that you were my match. After this, your bone marrow will be swimming around my bones and you'll never be able to leave me again!"

She sits on a stool by the tight, green bedcover all hospitals seem to have and takes my hand in hers, running a finger over my claddagh ring. Tears pool in her eyes. "I can never make it up to you for abandoning you the way I did, but at least this way I can start mending that bridge I almost burned." She lets go of my hand and turns around to tidy up the books and put them in my locker. "There's one other thing I want to do," she says, "but it's a surprise. Hopefully tomorrow it'll happen."

"Give me a clue!"

"Nope, not one tiny word about it because it might

not happen at all." We hug goodbye and I pull the first book out after she leaves. It's not Stallone in my mind as I start reading. It's Cullen in all his glory.

IT WAS HARD to sleep, but today one of the nurses has wrapped me up and wheeled me out to a tiny courtyard with a patch of grass in the corner and a little oak tree starting to give shade. Una's there at one of the iron tables. A tiny breeze seems to scoop down into this pocket of freshness and flitter by my face. A baby is crawling on the grass, and I point him out to Una and smile. She smiles nervously back.

"That's your nephew, Ellie." She lifts him off the grass and carries him to her lap. He looks up at me and starts blowing spit bubbles.

"Kieran, say hello to your aunty Ellie." He stares at my face for a moment, bubbles on hold, his eyes an ocean blue. He oozes peace.

"Hi, Kieran. You're such a big boy!"

Una's watching me like she's afraid she'll do something wrong. I wonder if she thinks I'm judging her, but how can I say anything bad about such a cute baby? "He's gorgeous, Una. Tell me more about him."

He starts twisting his body to get down until she gets out the chocolate buttons. "A bribe," she says, relaxed now.

A nurse comes out to tell me I'm needed inside. Argh! It's too soon, but I take Kieran's tiny chocolate-smeared hand in mine and give it a squeeze. "Bye, Kieran!" I give Una a long hug. "Thank you," I say in her ear. "This was brilliant." Who knows how long it'll be before I get to see my only nephew again? It makes me want to have Cullen's kids all the more.

I want to stay longer and ask her what it was like to have sex and all, but I'm afraid she's going to say it was horrible. I don't want to hear it was that bad because I think I could go all the way with Cullen. When I went out with Tomas, I let him kiss me and all that, but he wanted to put his hands all over me and I told him not to do that, that God was watching and I wanted to be good. I had to say so many Our Fathers and Hail Marys after the last time he was at me that I told him after that I didn't want to be his girlfriend anymore. I told him he was a randy bugger, and he was too. Cullen would be so different.

"ISN'T IT WEIRD how you and Una always miss each other?" I'm twirling Cullen's hair while he sits by the bed, his exhausted head on his hands. I hope he never cuts it so short I can't do this, especially right now when I can't twirl my own.

"It makes sense," he says. "She has her baby in a crèche and I have to work until six."

"Yeah." I get out of the bed and look down into the carpark, people running to their cars in the rain, puddles everywhere soaking up the hard drops like they'll never drink again. "I could dance in that," I say, but I get no reply. All I hear are the little ripply sounds he makes through his nose when he's asleep. I reach over and rub my fingers down his back, his muscles hard and shaped under the tight T-shirt. They remind me of a scene in one of the books I've been reading, and it makes me long for normal life again—some Chinese, a pint and some great music, some snogging in the car.

The noise stops for a second or two and I lift my hand so as to not wake him, but then it starts again. It's almost time for him to leave, and he'll get on two buses just to get back to his gaff and then he'll be back in tomorrow night. This is the love they don't show in the films.

I'M SITTING IN THE BED eating my hospital toast and boiled egg when Dr. Hooper shows up in the room with the staff nurse beside him. He's bouncing a little on his toes.

"Great news, Ellie, you're right at the level we need for the transplant! We've called your sister and she's on her way, so we'll make sure your central line is in perfect shape and do the transplant tomorrow afternoon at about three. Then we'll wait and see how it takes." He nods to the nurse and she writes it down. "Any questions?"

I shake my head but put my hands together like I'm praying.

"Yes, yes," he says, "and do that too."

Thirty-seven hours later, I'm hooked up to a bag of Una's donation. It's quite strange imagining it traveling into my chest, around my body, heading for my bones. I imagine her cells racing around going *pew, pew, pew* like in *Star Wars*, destroying every single bad thing in my body that has me here away from home. And thanks to Una, I'll get back there soon.

# 28

## Cullen

It was a long walk from St. James, but here I am, having a goo at Una through the shop's smudged glass. I look at her face and see the same girl I knew so well with a woman's face now, only her smile is a little harder, her shoulders a little stiffer.

She looks up, takes a step back, half smiles and stops, and comes to the door. The bell tinkles as she opens it. I lean towards her to give her a quick hug, but she moves away, so we stand awkwardly close and stare at each other without really seeing.

"So how have you been?" I offer.

"Ah, not so bad. And yourself? You look great."

"Thanks."

She shuts the door with another tinkle. "Yeah, yeah, well, it's a long story." She won't even look at me. I follow her into a back room full of leather and tools. I say nothing.

The room smells of machines and leather and tea, and Una walks through it all with her shoulders higher and a walk I've never seen in her. A confident walk. She sits at a table and I scoot the chair in across from her, finally getting a better look at her. Her hair is a bit longer, curving around her face with a haircut that's thinned out all the wild bits and given her a tailored look. Warmth spreads across my chest while I take her in, and her face gets pink. I look away quickly and focus on the table.

"Cullen ...," she starts, "... I know you probably have loads of questions, so I don't want to sit here pretending everything is grand when we both know it isn't. Okay?" She drops a lump of sugar into her tea and stirs. "So I'll get straight to the point. I had a baby, Cullen. I ran. I chickened out of real life and made a new one." She sweeps a hand around the room. "Welcome to it."

I know people say this, but it's true: it's like all those years between you disappear and you pick up straight from the last time you saw each other.

But then someone comes into the shop and she turns into someone else. Her voice, her way of turning a question into a sale, the way she talks to the other fella working there. It's not bad, but my chest fills up with an ache for the years we lost together.

She comes back to the table and starts fiddling with a piece of leather, turning it over and over between her fingers. I put my hand on hers and she jumps, suddenly standing up and saying into the front, "Frank, can you take care of the shop for a few?"

He grunts and raises a hand in acknowledgment.

"It's high time you and Kieran met," she says in my direction, practically running up the stairs as I follow. "Catherine comes on Saturdays for Granny time.

"I'd love you to meet her too."

Kieran's in a high chair in the kitchen sticking his hand into a bowl of potatoes and carrots and inspecting each finding before he rams it in his mouth. He stops from time to time to stare at me, like I'm a museum exhibit, but his food is apparently much more interesting. He has a sweet face that's very much like Ellie's in her baby photos.

Catherine's all business, getting me tea and biscuits and asking me about Ellie and work. It's a bit of a relief, actually, giving her the updates instead of Una, who's all jumpy and weird. I can't quite nail what it is, but then I realize that she always used to look me in the eye and now she can't seem to.

Kieran's food starts landing on the floor, blobs of orange and cream rejected forever. Catherine rinses out the Ajax cloth and starts wiping off his face and hands, then his table. He slaps the table with his wiped hands and starts laughing, his smile wide and catching as he reaches up for Catherine.

"We're off for a bath. Cullen, feel free to stay as long as you want. You two have a lot of catching up to do."

The bathroom door closes us off from the happy yelps and water running into the bath. Someday I'll get to have that myself, please God.

"So," she says, "you and Ellie, eh?"

Just hearing Ellie's name makes me smile. "Yeah. Who'd have thought, all those times over in your place and you two yelling at each other?" But then I can feel my face pucker, my lips start to shake, and I put my hand up over my eyes to hold it all together. She hops over to me and rubs my arm. It's a few minutes before I can gather my thoughts again. "You're not freaking out because I found you, are you, Una? Because she needed you."

"God no," she says. "I would have hated myself forever if I'd found out too late that ..." The warmth of her hand lifts and she sits back across from me. She takes a deep breath.

"When I ran away, I didn't do it to hurt anyone. I just, I had to make a choice or I would never have been able to keep Kieran at all." She rubs at her eyes. "And you probably figured it out by now, but Dylan isn't Kieran's dad. I made that bit up, but I still had to leave. I would have told you who it really was, but you would have gone to his house and made things even more embarrassing."

I press my lips tightly together. She mustn't know about my trip down after she left.

"And the more I thought about it, the more embarrassed I was about, about how we weren't even going out together." She scratches her arm. "Me and the guy. And then I thought it wouldn't be fair to lump a kid on him with me seventeen and clueless." She swirls her hair into a knot behind her head and holds it tightly. "I thought I could take care of things on my own."

"And?"

"Those first two weeks were really bad. I was so cold, afraid. But I had to keep going. I had a baby to look after. And then Catherine and Des saved me." She walks around the kitchen wiping the countertops, putting plates away.

"You're a good mam, you know." I mean it. She's soft around him.

"How can you say that? You've never seen me with Kieran until today."

"I know you, Una. You've always cared about the

important things, and I know you care about Kieran
more than anything else, ever. I see him in your face,
hear him in your words. He's your whole life." I slurp
back the last bit of tea and stand up, mug in hand. "You
finished?"

She shakes her head. *Just say it already, Cullen. Just ask
her.* I follow her into the living room and stand in the
doorway, watching her pick up Kieran's toys. I might as
well do this the Una way and spit it out.

"I need a favor."

Her head shoots up like I've switched on something.
If there's anything Una loves, it's helping. I rub my chin.
"I know we're only just now talking and all, and it might
be awkward, but with Ellie in St. James and me coming
up every night on the bus, I was wondering if I could
stay on your sofa on Fridays and Saturdays. It would just
be until she's better, and it would save me an awful lot
of hassle."

The corner of her mouth turns down a bit, just
enough for me to know it wasn't a good idea to ask.

"I could help you with Kieran if he wakes up in the
middle of the night, or get up with him in the morning,
help around the shop." Her face has gone a bit pale. I
put up my hand. "It's okay; I just thought I'd ask. I can
see it's not a great idea."

She sits down on the sofa and moves her fingers in
and out of each other before talking at the telly in a
distant voice. "Um, that's okay. I'll talk to Catherine and
check. She might not want any boys here at night. She's
a bit old-fashioned."

I take a few steps back and lift my jacket off the hook
in the hallway before I stand back in the doorway. "No
pressure. I need to head back now anyway—last bus an'

all that."

She walks me down to the door, the shop music bouncing off the walls. This is weird, the way she's holding herself back, like she's here but not here. I suppose if she's up for letting me stay, we can iron things out, but this is not the way I remember my best friend after all.

There's a note for me by the phone when I finally get home.

> **Someone called Una called and said Catherine said it's fine and she'll see you Friday.**

ELLIE'S LOOKING BEAUTIFUL, as always, the next day, with her head scarf covered in sunflowers cheering up the room. She has her legs up on a stool with a pillow on it, back pressed into the big blue plether armchair, and a green-covered novel on her lap. I pull over a chair and gaze at her face, studying her lips, the spread of freckles that run almost from one ear to the other, her eyes that sink slightly into their tired cradles.

She flashes a happy smile. "Doctor says he's delighted with how things are going. Says I just need to keep doing well for thirty days and I can move into a room with another patient."

Yet again I release a breath I never realize I'm holding in until it escapes.

"I have some news too." I have no idea why I'm nervous about telling her. "Catherine, the woman Una lives with, says I can sleep on their sofa on Fridays and Saturdays instead of having to go back to Enniskerry every night."

Her eyes rest on my face. "I thought Una told me Catherine and Des had moved to Ashford."

"Yeah, but Catherine comes up to pack more and spend time with Kieran every Saturday. She said I can kip in a sleeping bag on her bed when she's not there."

"So you saw her then? What did you think?"

I pick up the book and run my fingers over the raised gold title. "She's not the same girl I knew—not in a bad way, just different in a way I can't really explain." Closed off would be the words I'd put on her now. I keep thinking back to yesterday at the shop and how displaced it made me feel, like I'd been part of her life completely and then cut out—like she'd taken a scissors to a photo of us and stuck her side back on her corkboard.

And then Ellie jumps into a totally different conversation. "Cullen, do you ever think about dying?"

"What?" I can feel my head freeze and I don't know where to look. "I never had to, but I suppose I do now, you know, with ..."

"Yeah." She closes her eyes for a moment. "I think Jesus is real. I even think he likes me."

Jesus? "But what about all that crap the priest goes on about, like it's our joy to suffer for him?" I can feel the anger rising already.

She smiles that Ellie smile. "I think he laughs at that because it's not our cross to bear. That bleeding heart of his has already done all the bleeding. I don't think any of this is his doing at all."

"Then why? Why did you get sick? Why do so many young people die? Why you, when you're so perfect?"

She laughs and takes my hand, kissing my fingernails one by one. "Sometimes in life you have to stop and say, 'It just is.' This is one of those times." She stops to catch her breath. "It just is, Cullen. And if God is real, then he's in this with me, and it'll all work out. I can feel it." She grabs my other hand as well.

"And, Cullen? It looks like I'll get through this now, so I can say what I was going to tell you. If I'd gone, I'd have wanted you to go on living, okay?" She bends forward to look into my face. "Like with other girls and all. I'd be floating around with my harp and cheering you on. And if you messed it up, I'd make sure to send a sign, like a stray cat or something, so you'd know."

I can't help but laugh. My Ellie is a ticket all right. If God's all she seems to think he is, that ticket'd grease her way in for sure.

"You know, Cullen, every day I feel more peaceful inside, more in love with life, more appreciative of my family and you." She rubs my cheek with her thumb. "Sweet Cullen. Even thinking of you warms me up." She struggles to shift her body towards me more. "Everything's working out for the better. Una's come back to us. You have a chance to stay at her gaff for a bit and get to know wee Kieran. He's a dote. You were set up by the big man upstairs to be in Enniskerry at just the right time. And look at all the books I get to read!"

God, how can she be so cheery and talk about death at the same time? But I nod and squeeze her fingers. She has so much thinking time in this box of a room, it's no wonder she's filling her head with bits of everything. But Jesus? I suppose they kind of go together—death, life, hope.

# 29

## Una

I look up at the clock for the umpteenth time, as if it's going to rush forwards and ping before Cullen walks in the door. As it turns out, I'm sweeping in the back, fingerprints pressing into the wood, when I hear the door open. Everything inside me zings in fear that now that he's this close, I'll tell him everything. But Robbie's upstairs, thank God. Cullen doesn't know it's because I'm afraid of myself, afraid of what my heart and then my mouth will do. Afraid of destroying Ellie's life. Afraid of never being able to pull myself back into what I've built here because I'm not strong enough to lose everything again.

Like right now.

"I got some Chinese," he says behind me, and I swear my feet leave the floor for a second. "Your favorite."

I turn around and there he is with his sweet grin, boxes of food in a plastic bag.

"The lady said to just cook Kieran's veggies for a bit longer so they're soft enough."

My lips won't work, but I point at the stairs. "I just

need to finish up here, but the boys will be delighted. Thank you!" I stop and manage to look at his face. "By the boys, I mean Robbie and Kieran. He's a good friend of mine." I need to clarify.

I watch him climb the stairs and knock on the door, stand there patiently until Robbie opens it, and try to see Robbie's expression as he invites him in. Robbie knows everything. He's already jealous. Can I trust him? I take my time locking up, emptying the bins, wiping things down before the slow walk upstairs. Only to meet Cullen at the door.

"Gotta run with those visiting hours. I'll be back later."

All my muscles relax when I hear the door shut, and my legs follow Robbie's laughter and Kieran's giggles. There's rice everywhere, but I don't care. The worst is over, I hope.

Robbie walks straight to me and wraps his arms around me, resting his lips against my hair. Then he releases me like he's on a spring. "Right," he says to Kieran. "Are you ready for a bath? Bubbles?" Kieran smacks his hands together and tries to push himself out of the high chair. Robbie grabs him from behind and holds him out as he walks to the bathroom. "I'll start," he says. "You eat your Chinese before it's cold."

The fortune cookie looks like it needs to be opened first.

IN THIS LIFE IT IS NOT WHAT WE TAKE UP, BUT WHAT WE GIVE UP, THAT MAKES US RICH.

I scrunch it into a tiny ball and aim it at the bin before working on trying to avoid thoughts about Cullen while I savor his gift of dinner.

Robbie and I are on the sofa when Cullen gets back, my head on Robbie's shoulder as we watch *This Is Your Life*. I feel the cushion sink beside me as he joins us, and I shut my eyes and pretend to be asleep while the two of them make random comments. It's not that I want to snog his face off. It's all these ties made of laughter and conversations and books and childhood trust and sex. How do you extricate yourself to feel like a singular person again when you never cut the ropes, when you just hid and wished them all away? That's the thing about ties. They have knots.

Then I feel the cushion move back to its normal position and hear him say he's heading to bed. Thank God. Catherine will be here by lunchtime, and I won't have to go through this again until next Friday.

What I hadn't counted on is this, an hour later. Now. I can almost feel Robbie's body heat surging up from the floor where he's sleeping, imagining its tremor in the air the way petrol fumes shimmy out of the petrol can in summer. Without thinking, I lie on my tummy and reach out to catch it. Without thinking, I let his fingers lock through mine. I peek over the edge to stare at the outline of his jaw in the darkness. He moves.

"Una Gallagher, will you go out with me?"

The words dance over me, through me, the way they do every time he asks. My thoughts fly to Cullen in the next room in love with my sister. Me in this room with a man who has wanted to go out with me since we met. He has no fear. But it would mean more ties. How can I hoist a new sail when I'm still on the old boat?

He pushes himself up on one elbow, flattening his palm against mine like we're on opposite sides of a window. I'm amazed he can't hear my heart like it's under Edgar Allen Poe's floor, but he mustn't because he's still waiting.

I wait for a few minutes before answering this time, but it's the same reply. I lie back, staring at the curtains furrowing in the night breeze.

He sighs heavily and lies back down.

"It's not that I don't want to. I always want to. It's just ..."

"It's still Cullen, isn't it?"

"Yeah," I say. I want to explain, but I can't explain fear and how it threads through my heart and up through my brain and then into my reactions. That's the thing with fear. It never makes choices, just reacts when it's sparked. My worst enemy.

I hear him get up and walk down the hallway. I put on my dressing gown and slippers and follow him in.

He's sitting in the armchair across from me, pulling at the loose threads in the arm, the fire to his left spitting and popping from the new log he just added. I stare at the flames because if I look at his face, I might cry. I'm so tired of being half a real person.

"I don't want to lose you too."

"Too? Like I'm second prize?"

I finally look sideways, and I can see the layer of water waiting to drop from his eyes to his cheeks. He coughs. I quickly look back at the flames, so fervent in their quest to burn brightly. My flame is at "low fuel in the lighter" level, a lighter you burn your thumb on trying to get the flame to show up. *Turn the wheel, Una. Tell him what you're feeling.* But my thumb keeps scraping the ridged wheel of my mouth, and it won't spark the words I need. How can I be real when even fake me can't succeed?

Robbie puts both hands on the arms of the chair and pushes himself forward. "I think, Una," he says, trying to hide the choke behind the words, "that it would be good if we took a break from 'us.'" He picks another log from the basket and adds it carefully to the weak spot in the fire, waiting until it roars its thanks before standing up again to face me. He cups my face with his hands and moves his lips to mine, giving me the softest kiss imaginable.

I start to respond, but he pulls away, shaking his head. "I just want to remember it like this."

He climbs into the sleeping bag he's brought from the bedroom and puts it on the sofa and shoves the cushion under his head. I watch his eyes close, shutting me out of his life.

It is not what we take up, but what we give up that makes us rich. So where's the richness in this?

I'M WAITING FOR the nurse to let me in to see Ellie, just like they do every day I make it here, which is only when Gilly or Sinéad can watch Kieran and it's not raining. That's when I can get on my bike and take it up Dame Street, with all its traffic, to the cathedral, where I stop for a minute to get my breath back, and then freewheel down most of Thomas Street—past the stinky Guinness Brewery and on down to the main entrance. I have to try and find a hiding place for the bike because even though I have a brilliant lock for it now, the area doesn't exactly feel safe in the evenings. Even the shops close at five and pull their iron bars over the windows.

Ellie's watching telly when I come in, and I watch the end of *Emmerdale Farm* with her. "So what's new?" I say when the credits start, emptying a bag of colored wool onto her bed as I ask. "My news is I got this from the sale basket for your new hobby."

Ellie picks up one of the balls and holds it against her face. "My color?" It's puke green, and we both laugh like two seven-year-olds until I start crying. She puts it back on the bed. "What's wrong?"

"It's Robbie. He dumped me." I grab a few tissues from her box and blow my nose, dropping it into the special red bag we're supposed to put in anything that might make Ellie sick.

She stares at me waiting for more, but I shake my head. It's too painful because it's all my fault, and besides, I don't want to depress her when she's trying to get better.

"I have something that'll make you feel better. Look what Mam brought me!" She waves a crimper in the air. "Sit down, Una Moona, and let me turn you into Cyndi Lauper. You'll have to wait until I get out of here before I can make your hair pink, but at least we can have some fun now, and I can't exactly do it on my own head." She chats about Cullen, the latest novel, all her shows, the doctors and nurses who work there as she works. I have no idea how she never runs out of steam. "Ta-da!"

I gape at myself in the handheld mirror she gives me. My hair is standing out sideways. "I can fly home with aerodynamics like this."

She waves me goodbye, and I can almost feel my head bouncing before liftoff as I walk to my bike. There's no one like Ellie to cheer up a girl.

Which is why the phone call is so horrible when I get home.

I LIE ON MY BED staring at the patterns on the ceiling in the dark. Kieran is down, and I finally have time to process what Catherine told me. Edward Wallace, the shop's accountant since they opened, has been fudging the books almost since he started. A little here, a little there, until he started taking out small loans with the building as collateral. Swing forward to today and Catherine and Des now owe about three-quarters of what the building is worth to different banks. There's barely enough for the house and Des's nursing care once it's all paid off, and they have to sell as soon as possible because the interest on the loans keeps rising.

I close my eyes because it feels weird not to when I'm talking to himself. *I'm not much of a one for praying, but, God, if you can hear me right now, I need you to do something big.*

"THE BASTARD!" Gillian has never been one to mince her words, which I love. I need backup, and she's it. We're sitting in Bewley's Café for the heat and the great sausages. Some days here you wouldn't know it's meant to be summer. This big room with wooden panels on the walls and the patterned carpet is a bit like a huge family dining room. Mam would love it for all the eavesdropping opportunities.

"So what are you going to do if the building is sold?"

"Pretend it isn't happening."

"Yeah, that'll work great, so it will. I mean really, Una, what will you do?"

"Well," I mutter without much hope, "I could teach a class on how to run away from all your problems. And I can work a cash register and pretend to be nice to people who drive me up the wall, and I know how to make a lot of stuff with leather.

"Well, if you get into some of that S and M, you could beat the crap out of people with your creations and you wouldn't have to pretend to like them at all. I hear it's all the rage in some of the dungeons in Dalkey."

I give her a look.

"Just kidding." She laughs with that husky gargle of hers. "It's Blackrock, not Dalkey." She puts both hands down flat on the table. "But really, Una, you're brainy. You work hard. You're a great mam, which means you can get stuff done. Anyone would be lucky to have you working for them. What about working at the Brown Thomas department store? You know a lot about leather now, and you'd be really good at answering questions all those Foxrock women would have, now that you're one of them an' all."

I slap her with one of my gloves. "I'm in mourning. Stop trying to make me laugh. One day my life is all sunshine and my future is locked in place, and then Robbie disappears and this bastard ruins it all. And I can be okay, I know that, but for Catherine and Des? I'm so angry! This is such a load of bollox; excuse my French."

Gillian takes a sausage off Ashlinn's plate, who looks like she needs it more than her mother. "Eat your beans, love," she tells her, and turns back to me. "Una, dear, it is what it is. You thought you had a lot. Now you find out you have nothing but yourself and your Kieran. Is that such a bad thing? Life is built on failures. Hell, look at me, twenty-three, separated because he liked some floozy on the side, and the only boyfriends I could get disappeared after a few weeks. I lived with my parents until a month ago, and Ashlinn here has more of a mother in her granny than me."

I start to interrupt, but she puts up a hand. "Una, I'm telling you now. Suck it up. Don't you always have a plan?"

She's right. I know she's right. But everything's all piled up in my brain until I can't even think straight. The last thing on earth I want to do is start over again. I look sideways at Kieran's precious little face. I'd do anything for him.

*Anything? Would you tell him who his dad is? Would you tell his dad he has a son?* The strength of the voice inside my head surprises me. I play with it out loud.

"Gillian, I know you've told me what a loser your ex is, but if you pushed yourself and what he did to you right out of the story, what's he like as a dad?"

She looks me straight in the eye. "Honestly? Not bad. The floozy he moved in with has two kids of her own and she looks after Ashlinn all right. Kevin's good to her too. I don't spazz out every time I think of her being over there with the two of them. And to be honest, it's nice to get a break now and then. I just wish ..." She lifts her heavy mug and swirls the liquid inside. "He was a nice guy, you know? He just had his demons, same as us all, and now this new mot has to deal with them. I wish them the best, but I think he'll be with someone new within the next two years, and I can only hope Ashlinn will still be in his life when he settles in with her. Every kid needs a dad."

I swallow. It's true. I was able to tell myself that Des was a good replacement father for Kieran early on, but not now, not now that he's become like a dysfunctional child again himself. And Robbie was good with him, but he's not Cullen, and he won't be around anymore anyway. I can feel the sadness start to overtake me and swallow it all back down. Why do I always think I know what's best when I suck at everything?

"So you think I should tell Cullen then, now that I'm about to be homeless? But I can't! I can't break Ellie's heart."

"Ah, sure, Una, who am I to tell you what to do with your life? I'm as fecked up as they come. You don't want to take advice from me." She leans in, though, and whispers, "I'll tell you what, though, if it was me and Cullen wasn't going out with my very sick sister, and I still had the hots for him, I'd be in there in a snap. Sure what would I have to lose? A—I'd seduce him all over again and move in with him and I'd finally be out of my mother's house, or B—he'd tell me where to go and I'd be right where I am today, shacked up with my man."

I inhale deeply and instinctively reach out to stroke Kieran's hair. "But he *is* seeing my sister. And it's not like I haven't thought about this like, all the time."

"But sure I'm Team Robbie. Now, there's a beautiful man." She has her head tilted to one side, looking at my face. "Ah, no, Una. Don't say you let him go!"

"I did. I don't want to talk about it."

"Janey, Una, if you were my sister, I'd beat some sense into you."

We sit like two nutters there in the middle of the Bewley's tables with our babies for another bit, the smell of rashers and beans long since crept into our jackets, until I check my watch, sigh, and haul myself off the chair for the trek home. But how long will I be able to call it that?

UPSTAIRS IS SO EMPTY without Des and Catherine here, but Kieran runs in and out of every room and hugs my leg each time he passes. I grab him, and he and I sit by the window so he can wave at everyone as they walk up the street. He runs back to the telly once he gets bored, but I stay there mulling over how lonely I feel. Other people have kept my life moving forward for so long, it's like I've forgotten how to really live.

I turn around and look at Kieran, the only love of my life right now. His baby curls have gone since that first haircut, but his eyes still shine with delight, and he giggles a lot, especially when he's being naughty. All of a sudden the cartoon he's watching on the TV spits out the words "You'd cry too if your daddy was taken from you when you were a baby." He's still sitting there watching as if it doesn't mean a thing, but the words wail through my soul like a banshee. *Your daddy was taken from you. You'd cry too.* My lower lip begins to shake. Not only did I take Kieran from his dad, *I took his dad from Kieran.* The truth, the bottom line, is that I'm a taker, not a giver. I really do suck as a human being.

I think back to 1983—the year when I was so infatuated with Cullen. I was so happy to see him every day. He made love feel easy. Why did I throw that away?

I keep remembering, letting all those feelings come rushing back—the ones I've managed to keep at bay all this time. I wipe and rub at the tears that threaten to never end, and hours later I'm lying on my bed with a very wet pillow and eyes as red as overripe tomatoes. I did all this. I made the decisions for Cullen. I didn't even respect him enough to give him a choice. Kieran could have had his dad holding him, loving him, raising him all these years. And I'm the stupid, pathetic, selfish bitch who wrecked it all.

# 30

## Una

The shop doorbell rings, and I add a receipt to the growing pile on the spike against the wall. The customer looks like one of the horsey crowd, probably wanting some of those custom-fitted gloves we had an ad in the *Irish Times* for—silk scarf on her head, oilskin jacket covered in dog hair, ankle jodhpur boots. I take her coat and ask her to hold out her hands so I can measure them, and while I'm curling the tape measure around her wrists and fingers, Catherine walks in—red, drained skin around her eyes. She fiddles with her handbag before looking up at the wall behind me.

I give her a nod and walk to the back of the shop to get the last customer's measurements. Glove lady has small hands and wants the softest leather I have in stock, so I suggest an extra layer over the spots most likely to get worn. We go over some leather swatches until she seems happy and then I close the sale, although I hate calling it that.

Once she's left, Catherine comes up beside me to grab the box of tissues and goes back to a chair. "Des sends his love. I left him on the sofa watching reruns of *Bracken*. The home help is with him and her knitting." She doesn't lift her head, but the muffled words creep through her cardigan. "I've hired a real estate agent."

All sorts of thoughts are careening through my brain again, a repeat of last night, none of them good. No job, no shop, no future, no way to care for Kieran. I'd become indifferent to the way it had all panned out, but now that it's being threatened, fear is scratching my insides. And then it hits me that I'm only thinking about myself again. Catherine's livelihood. Des's mental state.

I keep my mouth shut and wait for Catherine to speak some more, but her silence rings loudly, and I eventually turn back around and begin to cut some leather for the order until the kettle clicks off. I squish the tea bags in the water and throw a few flapjacks Kieran and I made last night on a plate. She's probably hungry.

Catherine slides one around the plate. I kneel in front of her. "Catherine, if it's me and Kieran you're worried about, don't be. You've taught me loads. We'll be fine. And if worse comes to worst, I can go home. Mam's already offered." Mam actually has no idea what's just happened, but she did say I could come back if I wanted.

Catherine dabs at her eyes, her face a little less tense. "Okay then. I'll go pack some more things. Let me know when the estate agent gets here." Her feet lift slowly up the stairs. So much for being happy and living a good life. Now we're all miserable.

CATHERINE SITS DOWN at the table and shuffles the cards before dealing out seven each.

I bring over the tea and take a sip while I think through my card-playing strategy. I already have three nines, and I spread them out on the table with a smirk. In response, she spreads out all seven cards—from the ace to the seven of clubs. "I wish getting our money back was this easy," she says as I sweep them all up.

"You just didn't shuffle them properly!" A thought crosses my mind—one of those flashes I've learned to pay attention to. "Hey, Catherine, what if we fought back? We get the news that the money's gone and we fall over and play dead?"

She tips her glasses on her nose and looks at me over them. "Una, what more can we do? The lawyer would know, surely."

I shake my head. "There must be more to this. If Edward Wallace took all that money, surely there's stuff he bought with it we could fight him for. What did the letter say?"

"Well," mutters Catherine as she splays four threes over the plastic. "I'll mention it next time I see David and see the letter for myself. He said we owe a lot of money, but maybe there's a way to hire a detective or something." She jabs a finger at the pickup pile to get me to take a move. "Again, I'm so sorry for all this."

I hate seeing her guilt on display, when all she's done is give. "I'll be fine." I gather up the cards after losing yet again. "We'll be fine." But I'm not fine, and I don't know if I ever will be. I can't even afford a bedsit once I lose this job. I can't move in with Catherine—no one under the age of sixty can live there—so basically no one in Dublin can help me. Des doesn't count because he's often oblivious. I almost envy him. Almost. Gillian said she'd ask her mam if she could give us her sofa for a week or so if we were stuck, but we'd have to find a place to go after that.

Robbie would have some great ideas, but I can't call him. Just thinking about him in my bedroom asking me for the last time makes my heart seize up. I miss him wild bad. But I can't keep drifting back to memories as if they'll save me. I'm here, now, and all I can see in my future is me stuck in Donegal with no job and a boy who looks more and more like Cullen every day.

# 31

## Una

### June

I'm staring at the sky, hoping the black clouds won't drop everything they're holding in one massive dump over our good clothes.

"A detective!" states Gillian excitedly. "I know a fella at the Bank of Ireland. He owes me. And I went to school with a fella who's already high up in the AIB. Want me to ask them to check if they can look into old Wallace's accounts?"

Ah, Gillian—she knows half of Dublin. "But wouldn't they get in trouble for that?"

"Yeah. But can't they force banks to give over information if there's a charge against someone?" Her eyes get brighter. "Ask Robbie!"

"I can't." She knows why, but it doesn't stop her trying. She keeps attempting to get us back together, even though we were never together together.

We're surveying all the different department stores around town today, gawking at the women in charge to see who'd be easy to work under. We've cut it down to three because the other places aren't big enough to give me a chance at moving up the ladder, according to Gillian. She picks up a calfskin glove and winks at me. That's the sign to look around the room and see if we get a witch's glare or an offer of help.

"What if," Gillian continues, with one eye on alert, "the universe is looking out for you and all the money *is* tied up in stuff that can be sold?"

A woman walks up. She's wearing shoes that lift her about four inches off the floor, and her skirt is so tight, I can't imagine it's easy for her to pull it up if she's dying to go to the loo in a tight stall. "Can I help you?"

Her posh accent sounds fake. Ugh. Everything about working here is a big fat no. Is this where my life is going? Am I destined to be a bogus, bunion-ridden blonde?

"Yes," says Gilly, holding the gloves practically in the woman's face. "Do you have these in any other color?"

The girl obviously hasn't a clue, based on the blank look on her face. "I'll have a look," she says, and vanishes behind a wall. This would be my job.

We scarper before she can make it back, waving our hands and gasping through the invisible smog of perfume from the makeup booths before we get out to the street.

"Time for a drink," announces Gillian, and she quicksteps her way to the nearest pub before I can argue. At least they have pub grub, though, so I dig in while she downs the good stuff.

"So. How long do you think it'll take to sell again?" Gillian takes out a nail file and starts on her thumb.

I purse my lips. "The shop can keep running until we find a buyer. It'll look better if there's already a business in place when people come by for a tour."

"And you're supposed to drop everything and pack, once the deposit is down?" She's on her little finger already with that nail file. "Have you found a place yet? Although you would have told me." She leans over, takes my left hand, and starts to file. I just let her. That's how we're such good friends.

"There's a bedsit on South Circular Road I went to see yesterday. It's the size of a stamp, but it has a shower an' all, and it's a hundred and fifty a month. Kieran an' me would have to share the sofa bed."

"That's no good. He wouldn't be near school or anything, and you'd go batty in a place that small."

"I know. But I can't think of anything else." I stir the last bit of soup and dip the buttered bread into it.

"And if you don't get a job?" Always the hopeful one, our Gillian.

"Then we're country bumpkins after that one week with your mam."

She blows on the file and puts it back in her bag. "I think you should talk to Cullen. Ask him if you could stay at his gaff until you get a job. You were friends once, and it sounds like he was a bit soft on you fadó, fadó."

I run my thumb over the freshly filed nails. "I don't want to bother Cullen, to be honest." My voice catches. Saying his name out loud is so different to letting it whisper in my soul. But if I'm really honest with myself, I'm more afraid of what I might say when he's around than feeling what I used to feel.

"Yeah, but you said he was always ready to help. If you told him how desperate you were, even?"

"I suppose," I sigh. Talking just rinses hope of being able to stay in Dublin even further from my heart, and I don't know how to find it again.

I DIAL CULLEN'S NUMBER as soon as Kieran's asleep before I lose my nerve.

"This is Cullen."

"Hi, Cullen. It's Una."

"Oh." He's silent for a minute. "What's going on?"

"Well, I have a big favor to ask you. It looks like I'm going to have no place to live and no job in a few weeks' time. Long story. And I never asked you how you were doing, where you were living even."

"So you want to know if you can stay here for a while? I don't know, Una. I owe you for the weekends up at your gaff, but I have two other blokes in the house with me, and the two lads would have to kip in together. And it wouldn't be just you either." He sighs. "To be honest, I'd have to ask the lads, and I'm not sure they'd be into that." He's silent again.

"Okay so. I'll work something out."

"Are you sure?"

"Yeah, I'll be fine. Sure how hard can it be to find a decent job?"

"Well, let me know how you get on, and I'll ask the lads in the meantime. Good luck."

Now I'm the silent one, but I hang up quickly so he won't feel bad with me hanging on. I hate asking him. I wish I had a way out of this that didn't have to include him. But I made my choices and he was my last hope.

# 32

## Cullen

I've been rubbing my head for so long that it's going to need a good old wash in the morning. The lads weren't too happy about giving up a room and the thought of having a girl and kid here. And Kieran—will Una expect me to act like a father to him? Won't that be weird?

With all Jimmy's drinking and cursing, it's not the ideal place for a little one. I'm picturing it already—the three of us lads having to clean up, watch our mouths, and not walk around the house in whatever we want. They've said they're okay with them coming if she's really stuck though.

Una needs help. I know for sure that she wouldn't ask if she wasn't desperate. She's always liked to do things her own way, and this is probably killing her. I haven't even asked her what's going on.

"I'm going to have to let her stay here, lads. I was thinking about just having her come down for the weekends, like, and getting her used to the three of us and our ways. And the boy." I fiddle with the toast I just slathered with marmalade. "Well, lads, you'll need to clear your shite out of that room." They groan loudly while I'm walking out of the room to the phone.

"So, Una, the lads and I had a bit of a talk, and we know you're sort of in a bind, so we'd like to help you out until you're sorted. We thought maybe the two of you could come down on Saturdays after I see Ellie and then come back in with me for Sunday afternoon hours. You could get used to the place that way, maybe bring a few of your boxes as well?"

"Yes, that'd be great. I know—"

"Una, it's fine. The lads have said yes, and we're clearing out the bedroom for you right now. It's okay." I clear my throat. "Just know it might be a bit much for the baby."

It's only now I notice how thick the dust is on the shelf over the phone. One more thing to do before she gets here.

"Yeah. Thanks, Cullen. You're a lifesaver."

"So you'll come back down with me on the bus then?"

"I'll let you know. I might be able to get a ride down because of the boxes."

"Okay then. See you Saturday."

CATHERINE GETS OUT of the car first, and Una gets Kieran out of his car seat and into the buggy. I follow her with her bags.

I can see it all through her eyes as she stands in the living room—a mustard-colored sofa that's probably from the early '70s, a telly on the floor, and an old table and chairs at the back of the room. It was good enough for us, but I'm suddenly embarrassed I didn't try harder and at least buy some cushions or something.

"Right," she says.

Catherine stands in the doorway. "Thank you so much for helping Una like this."

"Oh, no worries. Can I get you a cup of tea or anything?"

She shakes her head. "Thanks, but I have to get back to Des."

I shut the door, following it with a shove with my shoulder—doesn't ever shut quite right the first time—before I go back to Una.

Kieran starts to cry. She closes her eyes and straightens her back. I leave her to do her thing and take her bags down to the bedroom, yet again noticing with new eyes how unwelcoming it is for a girl, um, woman. I have to remember that—she's older now, wiser, ready for anything—although she's not acting like it. *I should probably put a towel on the bed.* I unexpectedly find one in the hot press along with, miracle of miracles, an extra pillow. I hope she realizes how fantastic this is.

I'm pretty chuffed with myself because I stopped in at Poppy's and got them to give me some shepherd's pie in one of those tinfoil cooking trays. At least I'll be feeding them tonight with something more than cereal.

I'VE BEEN SITTING out the back for a good bit, making the most of the sunshine and wondering what to do with Una. That feeling like I can just be myself around her isn't there like it used to be. The more she talks, the more separated I feel.

I hear her and Kieran walk up behind me. "I made you both breakfast," I say.

"I know. It was delicious! Tea, porridge with cream

on top? Kieran will be ruined forever after tasting that. Great to see you know how to cook more than sausages. You've come a long way, Cullen Breslin."

I hold my hand up to shield my eyes. "Thanks. And I asked Jimmy, one of the guys, if I could borrow the car, so we can get up to Dublin a bit more easily with having Kieran here and all."

"Brilliant. I'll pack up his nappy bag. Give me about ten minutes." She leaves Kieran on the grass and he turns his head to stare at me and then smiles. I'm still making faces at him when I see Una at the door with a really weird look on her face.

"What?" I say.

"I'm ready," she says, and she swoops in to pick up Kieran.

What's her problem?

# 33

## Ellie

Seeing Cullen help Una out is so good. I was worried about her, but now the lines on her forehead are a bit thinner and she's smiling a little, even though she's worried about the new drip I'm on.

She's stretched out across the end of my bed staring at the patterns on the ceiling tiles. "This is like looking at the clouds, only they never move." She shifts her body on the mattress more. "Janey, this bed is really hard. I don't know how you sleep at all."

I'm only half listening. I've been thinking a lot about life and the things I want to be different. One of them is to stop pretending everything's fine all the time when it matters. The nurses told me this morning I have an infection, so if things are getting dicey, I'd like to start as soon as I can.

"Una," I hear myself say, my nails rattling against the arms of the chair in fear. I flatten my fingers out.

"Hmm?"

"Why do we never talk about stuff? You know— feelings, secrets."

She keeps lying there, but her body stiffens, and the room starts to feel like it's an echo chamber.

"Una?"

She mutters something but won't move.

"Una, what's wrong?" I get off my chair and stand over her at the end of the bed, only to see two lines of tears flowing from her eyes into her ears. "Una!"

She shakes her head, the tears flowing more freely, and rolls onto her tummy. I bend down to force her to keep looking at me, but she turns her head the other way. "I can't talk about it," she says into the cover. "I just can't."

"Well, you're going to have to because I have things I need to say too. The first thing is that I missed you something terrible when you left, and Mam made me do all the cooking instead and it took me ages to learn because you never showed me how, so I still think you're an awful git for letting me let you cook on your own for so long."

She laughs and sits up, wiping at her face while she makes all sorts of weird facial expressions.

"And you always helped me with my maths, and Mam was useless and I would have failed last year without the maths grinds." I swallow. "And Ettie kept crying every time we said your name, and Cullen might as well have." I'm gripping the end of the bed so hard my knuckles turn white. "Because Kieran is Cullen's, isn't he, Una?"

There's a moment of silence. The first sob out of her is more like a banshee wail, and those that follow fill the room, her whole body convulsing with each one. I sit back down on my chair and cover my legs back up with the knobby hospital blanket. I feel cold all over. It's one thing to fear the worst. It's quite another to confirm it.

I'm shaking all over, and my face is as wet as hers.

"Why didn't you tell me the day you left, Una? Why did you let me fall in love with him?"

The sobs intensify again until she starts to breathe more easily, eventually letting out small hiccups. Her face is one big blotchy mess, and I'm pretty sure mine is too. I get back up off the chair and hug her. "No more secrets, Una, okay?" I tuck her wet hair behind her ears.

"Okay," she whispers.

"Does Cullen know? Or have you two been hiding it from me this whole time?"

"No, no, he didn't know either. I swear!" She takes a huge breath in. "I tried. I really tried. I came home after Kieran was born to tell him, but then I saw you together for his debs and got the next bus straight back here." She wipes her eyes on her sleeve. "I was too late, and you looked so happy! I didn't want to end that for you. I didn't want you to be without Cullen like I was when I saw how much he liked you." Her tears start up again.

"I'm such a horrible person. I'm so scared, Ellie. I'm so scared he's going to hate me forever."

I don't ask her if she loves him. There are some things that I just don't want to know. And she's staying at his house.

She splashes cold water on her face from the tap and dabs it dry with a paper towel as hard as my blanket. "I know sorry isn't enough of a word to say how I feel. I don't expect you to forgive me. I can't even forgive myself, but there you have it." She gives a trembly smile. "And as for cooking your dinner all those years, you're welcome."

Her fingers find the handbag strap, and she lifts it

onto her shoulder. "I'd stay and tell you everything, but I have to go. It's half four and I need to get Kieran home." She lifts the shoulder strap up and drops it back down. "I think, Ellie, some secrets are better kept hidden, but there you have it." She bows her head in my direction and walks out to my Cullen and their baby. I should have kept my big mouth shut.

A nurse comes in right after the closing-time bell with a tray of pills and something in an IV bag. She takes the empty bag off the pole and connects the new one to it, setting the pump so it feeds it to me slowly. Then she checks my obs. chart and shakes her head. "We've got to get that temperature down. Dr. Hooper is cutting back some of your immunosuppressants to give your system a chance to fight this, and this bag is full of white blood cells to try and boost the battle against this high temperature." She pumps up the pillows. "Ring the bell if you have any chills or feel any lymph nodes swelling up, okay?"

I lie back against the clean softness and replay what Una just said word for word, over and over in my mind, and with each replay, I can feel every string inside me tighten and tighten until I feel like the inside of a piano, only there are no soft bits on the strings. Not one.

# 34

## Una

Everyone deserves the truth. It's time. Time to grow up. No matter what it does to Ellie, what I've done to Cullen is far worse. God help us all.

He's driving me back to the shop and I have no idea what to say. He's being so kind because he thinks I'm upset about Ellie. I just want to look like I have it together, like I'm not falling apart. Basically the opposite of how I'm feeling right now. My heart's drumming at least two hundred beats a minute. I don't know if I can do this. But I have to now that she's forced my hand, and I have to do this for Kieran anyway. It's not fair to ask Ellie to say nothing.

I unlock the door and ask him to help us upstairs with the buggy. As soon as Kieran's playing with his toys, I seize the day.

"Cullen."

He steps back, staring at the look on my face. "What's wrong?"

"I need to talk to you."

"Okay."

"I need you sitting down."

"Okay." He goes into the kitchen and pulls out a chair while I make us tea.

I pull my mug towards me and sit down too, willing my hands to stop shaking. "I have something to tell you that might make you never speak to me again, and you'd be right to decide to do that. So I'm just going to spit it out and leave it up to you to decide what to do next." I flatten my fingers around the mug. "Kieran is not Dylan's. You're his father."

I'd played this out so many times in my head, but things always end up happening a different way in real life. I link my finger through the handle of the mug, but I have no strength to lift it to my lips. *Go on, say something. Or leave quickly because I can't handle the rejection if you do it slowly.*

I nibble at my nails. Mam always said that if you want to know what a man's really thinking, stare at him and say nothing until he spills his guts. To be fair, I can't think of anything else to say. He stares at the table for a few minutes, lets out a whoosh of air. Then he scratches his head. I'm confused. I suppose I assumed that I'd tell him about Kieran and he'd straightaway react. That's what I'd do. But I'm not him.

"Wow!" He looks at me sideways. "Are you sure?" He holds up a hand and counts. He's staring at me. Silence descends around us.

"So, that's why you ..."

I nod.

"Oh God, Una. Oh God."

He's not doing what I expected at all. I want him to understand. I want to tell him everything, especially now. I want him to get it, to absolve my conscience with a few

253

Hail Marys and a pronouncement of forgiveness, to give me hope. But he doesn't.

I put the mug down and swallow. "Well, okay then. I can see how great the news is."

# 35

## Cullen

I'm in shock, really, and there's a thick mist to swim
through here. I'm a dad, but I'm not a dad? Every
sense has shut down. The clinks of plates on the telly,
the steam from the kettle kinking the air—gone. Until
my heart kicks back to life.

"Well then," I say.

She won't look at me.

"And you're telling me now because?"

"Because you have a right to know. Because I should
have told you as soon as I found out. Because I'm a total
eejit and screwed everything up. Because I'm sorry." She
starts to cry and wipes at the tears.

I can't hack this. There's no guide for saying the right
thing. "What do you want me to do, Una? Just tell me
what you want." I stare at the outline of her face, the
way her hair waves around her ears, her scarf still pushed
up against her chin, and all I can think about is what
could make a woman shut out the father of his own child.
I stand up so quickly the chair falls back, bend down a
bit to look straight into her eyes, clench and unclench

my fists.

I straighten up and lift the chair back up. I'm tired. This is fecked up. "Whatever, Una. You just keep doing your thing. I'm sure it'll all be great for you both." I walk into the hall.

She follows.

"I'll see myself out. Don't you bother yourself any more than you have to."

"No, no! It's not like that!" She's walking behind me, trying to get past me. I keep walking. She runs in front of me. "It's not like that, Cullen. I had no choice. I did what I had to do." Her face is red and tears are starting to appear in sliding globs on her cheeks.

I'm still walking to the door, my thoughts as messed up as an old Rubik's Cube. "'Had' no choice, Una. Past tense. 'Had.' And I doubt even that's true."

She's leaning against the door now, trying to stop me from leaving, her hand over her mouth. I move my hand to the handle and pull the door open.

"You know, Una," I sigh, "I loved you back then. I wish you'd felt the same way about me. It could have been so different."

She stops pushing the door.

She steps back.

And I walk out into the gloom and begin the long drive home.

Round about now, Una is living in a shop with a one-year-old who shares my blood. I wonder what's going through her mind because I can guarantee one thing—her brain is running on fumes right now.

Why didn't she tell me? Why didn't she trust me to at least care about what she was going through? Yeah, I don't know what I would have done, what I would have said, but I loved her then. Even today there were moments when memories of those feelings wafted through. Time doesn't heal all wounds—the minute you're challenged with the face of rejection, it all washes up on the shore again like fractured seashells. And when it all boils down to it, the guts of it all, she discovered a life inside her that was half mine and decided to make sure I was never part of it.

*So, Cullen, what's your next move?* I can't think straight, but I know I'm too pissed at Una to talk to her for a good while.

And now that she's spilled her guts, what was next in the plan? She was happy enough to raise this kid alone for the last year or so. I know there has to be a reason why she's suddenly sprung this on me now. What does she want from this? Does she want a monthly check? Does Kieran want a dad? Did Robbie just leave her stranded? I'd love to be the girly film guy who sweeps her up with shouts of forgiveness and stupid promises, but I'm not. Never will be. Una has a motive here, and I need to know what she expects before I sign up, if that's what she wants. What do fellas do when this happens? Are they at the mercy of the mother?

Why did she dump this on me? To salve her conscience and then leave me hanging? Will I even be allowed to be part of Kieran's life, even though Robbie had such free access to him for so long? Oh God, what do I tell Ellie?

When I get home, there's a note by the phone.

*Una says she told Ellie earlier.*

# 36

## Una

I uncurl my arms and legs from the tangle I turned myself into on the floor. I've been here for a long time and now I hurt all over and inside—deep, deep inside. The shop has turned into this foggy swamp around me, and I can feel myself walking as if without gravity to the back of the shop, up the stairs, and into my bedroom. I take off my shoes, one at a time, and place them at the foot of the bed. It feels as if someone else's fingers undo buttons and clips and hooks and pull off clothes, and within minutes I'm between the sheets and curled up again inside this person I don't like at all. I want to take a spade and shovel everything horrible about her far, far under the ground so I never have to see it again. But what would be left? Nothing. I reach up to turn out the light.

Hello, darkness. Engulf me now.

I MUDDLE MY WAY through Monday, with Catherine driving up and doing almost everything for Kieran when I tell her what's happened, and it's late when I finally wake up on Tuesday. The flat is silent, empty. I put on a dressing gown and shuffle into the kitchen.

Catherine's left me a note.

*Frank's taking care of the shop and Kieran is at the crèche. Enjoy the hours alone.*

*Catherine*

I want to be alone. Shut out all the light. Regurgitate every word Cullen spat at me.

So that's what I do. I go back to bed and I pull it all back up from where I tried to bury it just hours ago, and examine every tiny speck of truth and lies. The saddest part of all, though, is that I can't find any lies at all. He's right. Cullen knows the truth about me. All I really care about is my own heart and no one else's, and in that truth lies another one.

He loved me once.

And I fecked up Kieran's life and my own because I thought I knew better.

"GET OUT OF THAT FECKIN' BED or I'll come over myself and throw you out of it. For God's sakes, woman, pull yourself together. Catherine's way too old and tired to be putting up with your misery."

"I'm already out of the bed on the phone to you! What more do you want?" Gillian's right though. Everybody's right. But all I want to do is sleep. "Fine, fine, you witch. I'll make myself some coffee. Happy now?"

"No. Put your clothes on. I'm coming over."

*Oh shite.* Gillian's the last person I want to see, but

God, how I need her right now.

I fill her in on everything Cullen said, how badly I misjudged him, how racked with guilt I feel, how we could have had it all.

"I knew it! I bloody well knew it!" She slams her bag on the table before walking over to the kettle.

"He said he *did* love me, but he loves Ellie now, Gillian. There's years of difference in that small word. And what difference does it make now anyway?"

All those months I hid from him, from everyone, and now what? What the bloody hell did I expect really? That some stupid fairy godmother would step in and the angels would start singing because I'd finally done the right thing? That Cullen would fall on the ground and beg to make up for lost time with his only son? I'm a bigger eejit than I thought I was if that's the case.

"What are you moping for anyway?" Gilly says as she fills the kettle with water. "Robbie's mad about you."

I lift the sugar spoon out of the bowl and watch the sugar cascade back down. Such little pieces all working together. "Not anymore."

"You didn't!"

I look away. "He told me he'd had enough. Was tired I wasn't putting out for him."

"You're twisting his words. I know it." Gilly grabs the spoon out of my hand and puts it back in the bowl.

"Whatever. He's gone. And I'm not going to call him now and say, 'Oh, Robbie, by the way, Cullen won't talk to me, so come back to me.' And Cullen's right. I'm a loser."

"He never called you that!"

"Yeah. He didn't. But I *am* a selfish cow. I let my own family go through all that stuff with Ellie without me. They didn't get to see Kieran. I cut off everyone I ever loved just so I could be okay, and I kept it that way. And then I used Robbie just so I could feel better about Kieran not having a dad."

"You know that's not true. I've seen the way you look at Robbie. You laugh at all his jokes. If that's not love, then Aislinn was conceived by immaculate conception." She's poking around the kitchen cupboard now trying to find two clean mugs. "So, Miss Selfish Cow, as you're calling yourself, what are you going to do about it? You can't lie around here in your dressing gown feeling sorry for yourself and calling yourself names when you've got things to do, people to see. Go see your mam again. Bring Kieran."

I get up to wash some mugs. "Right." Inside, everything is screaming. I'd rather just go back to bed.

"You're going to call Cullen, right? Tell him to quit bitching about what an evil person you are?"

I smile from one corner of my mouth but let it drop again. "No. But my sister might never talk to me again once she lets herself start thinking about the two of us. I have no boyfriend. I'm about to be homeless." I pull on the belt of my dressing gown.

Gilly tightens up on the chair in front of me, puts her bag on the seat beside her, and clasps her hands together. "Go ahead. I'm all ears on what you're going to do." The phone interrupts her.

I grip the phone with both hands when I hear what the woman on the other end says and slide to the floor.

"Ellie's nurse says the doctor wants to see me tomorrow. She's called Mam and Dad too. Says it's very important and we all need to be there."

I asked the nurse to call Cullen. I don't want to hear

his voice right now, and I'm damn sure he doesn't want to hear mine.

# 37

## Cullen

Mrs. G is sitting down with her handbag on her lap, her grip on it something fierce. If the window of this nurses' office were Timbuktu, that's where Una's sitting. Mr. G is standing behind her, rapping his finger on the windowsill, but all eyes are on Dr. Hooper. He moves some papers around his desk, clears his throat, and begins to tell us all about what his great hopes for Ellie had been, but now she's got something that might undo all the good of the bone marrow.

"I've already talked with Ellie. I'd like you all to work with us here and not visit until she's fought off this infection. She's a delightful young woman, and I have every reason to believe we can pull her through this, but we need to take all the precautions we can."

He answers some questions from Una before she has to run back to the shop. The rest of us file out of the office, still shallow-breathing the now thin air of hope. Mrs. G leans into Mr. G's big chest, face still damp. They tell me goodbye before their long trip home. They weren't even able to see her, but they were able to call through from a phone on the other side of a glass window, thanks to the new room she's in.

I take my turn on the phone after they go. Ellie's hooked up to an extra machine measuring her oxygen levels. There's a second chart on the end of her bed. Neither of us knows where to look. She starts to talk.

"Have you any other secrets for me, Cullen?" Her voice is tight, laced with pain and fervor.

I shake my head and can't seem to swallow the rock in my throat.

"Tell me," she says.

When Ellie's angry, there's absolutely no way around it until you do exactly what she says. And so I do. I can't recall many details because I was so locked that night and it seems so long ago, but I tell her about the weeks that followed it all, about the story Una gave me, about how I should have trusted Ellie with the truth.

Her syringe beeps and she calls the nurse. She says her vein always needs to have something running through it to keep it open. I'm told I need to leave soon. She tells me she loves me, she's always loved me and always will, but that she's hell's bells mad at the same time and hasn't decided how all this will play out when she's this angry. I tell her that when she gets home, I'm going to have ten baby girls with her and they'll all be called after her, Ellie 1 through 10, because I can never get enough of her. She laughs. I manage a smile. I leave, and I can't even kiss her goodbye.

It's when I'm walking to the first bus home that everything inside starts screaming quietly. This dry anger doesn't even begin to describe how I feel when I think about what Una did to me, to us, to our son. As I read in a book once, wet anger means I still care, but dry

anger means I am done.
  So, so done.

# 38

## Una

As I close the front door, Catherine's standing on the stairs, ready for the news. I love this woman, so ready to drop everything to be there for me. We sit on the sofa with the hot chocolate she's made for the occasion. She cries for me. I look at her, really look at her for the first time in weeks. The lines under her eyes are deeper, her skin tired. I think back through the last few weeks of my life and realize that she's been holding me up at a time when she's supposed to be enjoying her retirement. She'd talked about adopting an older dog and going for walks, being with Des every day until the time comes when he has to go into the nursing home, sitting on the beach to watch the water reach for her toes and slink away. Yet again, I'm faced with my own selfishness, but she'll soon be free.

What she says next has me totally focused. "Una," she says solemnly, "we have an offer on the shop." She puts her hand on my back and rubs it. "You have some skills you can put to good use anywhere. I've never really felt like you wanted to be in the leather business for the rest of your life. Am I right?" She peers into my face. I can't look her back in the eye. "I thought so. So here we are, two grown women who need to move on. Instead of you working here until I die, which could be twenty years from now—or more if I eat all my vegetables—you get to live a little."

I finally look up. Her eyes are filled with so much love, so much of something I can't even put my finger on, but it's close to what I'd imagine seeing were I to look into the eyes of Jesus. It washes any protest I have in me away. "The offer is not to buy the shop though; it's to rent it, but the rent is enough to cover our costs down in Ashford each month and the minimum payments on all the loans. He's willing to give us a deposit too, which is enough for three months' rent on a place for you as well."

My whole mouth is wobbling. I don't want this to end. "Thank you, Catherine, but why would you do that? I don't deserve that at all."

She takes my chin between her thumb and forefinger. "Una, dear, it's never been about what you deserve. You came to us when we both needed something from each other. You needed a safe place for you and Kieran. We needed a daughter to love, and you gave us so much more. Neither one of us is perfect, and we've both been annoying at times, but we're connected now forever. That's what family is. We share the good stuff and the bad stuff. We got the better end of the deal as far as I'm concerned."

She pats me on the leg and gets up. "I'm heading back down to Ashford in the morning. We have four weeks to get this place emptied before we hand over the keys. I'll be up and down, as I have been."

I get up with her. "You talked to David about going after Edward Wallace's accounts, right?"

She pauses. "Oh yes, I meant to tell you about that. He said it was a good idea and he'd look into it but not to get our hopes up."

"Okay. Will you call him again about it? I sometimes feel men like that treat any suggestions we have as if we're silly little women and that we should leave it all to them."

Catherine pats my shoulder. "I know *exactly* what you mean! He didn't speak to me like that, but you're right, I should give him a call and keep asking. Thanks for reminding me."

I walk around the shop after she leaves and then sit Frank down and give him the update. He's very gung ho about it all and gets to work writing out a list of all unfinished orders while I work on closing out our accounts, the two of us belting out the chorus of every Queen song playing on Frank's tape recorder as we go. The screaming helps.

I'VE BEEN MOVING AROUND the bed for hours trying different ways to knock out my brain and sleep. The moonlight is bright tonight, and it keeps creeping around the curtains, trying to fool me into thinking dawn is near. I finally resign myself to being awake and plan out my dream house on some paper towel on the kitchen table—a whitewashed cottage with a back garden that's full of flowering bushes and big trees, and a stone wall all around it. It'll have enough space for swings for Kieran, and a brick patio with a table and two chairs for picnics in the summer. I'll have a Mini in the driveway and a job that gives me weekends off. We'll be able to walk to the school, and our neighbors will be the loveliest people on earth, every one of them with a child around the same age as Kieran so he'll never want for friends. And then reality pumps the sludge back into view to ruin it all.

The looks Cullen gave me at the hospital, everyone's scared face, Ellie sealed off from the world, Kieran about to be known by all of Donegal as Cullen's illegitimate baby. I keep trying to put different conversations together that get Cullen and Ellie to talk to me again. Now that he knows, he's going to want to spend time with Kieran right at the time I'd like to forget he exists. Or maybe he wants to pretend we don't exist. And most of all, his venom cuts into my heart in ways I never expected.

I get up and put the kettle on. The *Buy and Sell* is on the table where I left it, and I look again for a two-bedroom flat in town so I can be near Ellie—if she ever talks to me again ... if she makes it through this infection—and have a better chance of finding a new job. I follow my finger down the list of houses and town houses again, all of them too expensive, and move on to the flats, circling three that might work as long as I have a job before the three months of rent money runs out. I'll call tomorrow. And now what do I do with Cullen?

"THE GOOD LORD GIVES and the good Lord takes away. I always thought that was a bit of a copout. If you don't know why things happen, just say so. Don't blame it on the man upstairs."

I'm sitting in John's kitchen and I can't seem to shut up. He's listening and nodding in all the right places, so I suppose that means he cares, not that I should be questioning that, because he found a place for me to live all those years ago. But I'm here because maybe he can help me again, even though I'd like to do it myself, save myself, fix myself. If I could just survive this life without other people, I'd be fine.

Deep inside I know he can't help me become Wonder Woman, which is probably why I'm spouting off every inconsistency I've ever found with faith and religion and church. I want him to save me with his words, to reassure me that even when every solid thing I ever thought I had goes down the toilet, there's still some benevolent God up there watching over me, making sure that things turn out okay.

"Una," he says, when I've run out of questions temporarily, "let me tell you a story. Would that be okay?"

I nod. I've talked the ear off him already anyway.

"I was nineteen years old and studying English literature in Trinity. We had to read all sorts of genres I wasn't remotely interested in, and I started to hang out with a crowd I wouldn't have been seen dead with at secondary school—they knew how to have fun, and I was ready for a bit of that myself." He picks some lint off his jumper before going on.

"We drank a lot, laughed at people, smoked whenever we could afford it, and carried on a bit with the girls, and I got bored with that too. My parents were paying my college fees, and I started to lie to them and pretend I was getting As and Bs when I was really failing most of my classes. It got to where I couldn't even look at myself in the mirror.

"So one day I was alone in my bedsit feeling sorry for myself because life was still all about me, and I felt this peace in the room. Don't ask me how I knew, but I knew it was God. I got scared and started thinking he was going to lay into me about everything, but you know what? I got this thought in my head that might as well have been audible. *You're going to be a blessing.* That was it. That was all I heard, but it changed my life. I told my mum and dad about my lies, stopped hanging out with the others, and changed my degree so I could become a vicar. I felt that of all the ways I could bless other people, helping them know that they have a purpose had to be the biggest."

He smooths out the wrinkles on his trousers. "Maybe God doesn't give and take away. Maybe he does all the giving and taking through *us*. So my question to you, Una, would be 'How are you going to bless other people with your life?' Have you ever thought about that instead of focusing on what you're about to lose and blaming God for it all?"

MY BRAIN IS UPSIDE DOWN. *I've been blessing other people. I've been helping Catherine and Des for years. I've been doing the best job I can raising Kieran.* I move on to my usual methods of justifying stuff I do by attacking John next. *Who does he think he is, telling me what I should be doing? Don't I do enough? Look at him in a dress every week telling other people what to do and probably doing nothing for the rest of his time.* I know that's not true—I've heard so many stories from the old people at church—but I keep going.

*I went for help, not a lecture! So where's the help?*

I get back to the shop and throw my handbag on the table in a huff. Catherine's on one of her days back helping and packing, and she looks up from the books she's been trying to sort for weeks.

"What?"

"That John vicar. He's annoying me."

Catherine gives a knowing smile.

"What? What's that smile about?" I'm ready for a fight now.

"Oh, nothing," she says. "You're just cute when you're trying to be right."

I march past her and make as much noise as I can going up the stairs. This is not funny, not funny at all. I don't want to bless Cullen. I want the A-Team to kidnap him and annoy him forever. But even the A-Team is about family, no matter how weird each person is. Is this what I've been avoiding—everyone who I think is upset with me or doesn't like me much? Do I feel that empty of anything good that I think I'm doing people a favor by avoiding them instead of being okay with being *me* and letting them figure out for themselves if they want to be around me?

I write it out on the notepad by the phone with a marker.

## NO MORE AVOIDING!

I shout down the stairs to Catherine after a few minutes. "Any word from the lawyer?"

"No," she shouts back. "But he's found out where the weasel banks, and I've asked him to speed things up, thanks to our chat the other day. No little women here!"

I turn back into the flat laughing, until I remember that no avoiding means I need to talk to Cullen again and let him make his own choices, no matter how angry I think he is. And by doing that, I bless him and Kieran. It's a twofer.

I'VE PLUCKED UP ENOUGH courage to ask Cullen to meet on Friday before he goes to see Ellie. The doctor said she's out of the woods this time, but they're keeping a close eye on everything to make sure it stays that way. I'm hoping this means Cullen's feeling a bit more civil. He hung up on me two days ago.

My stomach is in bits. People call life a roller coaster sometimes. It's true. One minute my heart is dancing, only for it to be ripped to shreds within hours. Now it's on the slow rattle up the hill, higher, higher, to where you can't even admire the view because you know the fall is going to be too fast, too terrifying, and you can't do anything to stop it and worse, you're the one who climbed into the seat in the first place. So you just squeeze the handle in front of you like you're about to die and scream along with everyone else who was enough of a sucker to join you.

I hope today doesn't leave me screaming.

CULLEN AND I WALK UP to St. Stephen's Green in mutual silence, my last few years of decisions piled up in me like a hoarder's hovel with a few dead cats under it all.

"I'm sorry for what I said," he starts. "It was a horrible thing to say, and now that I've had time to think about it, I understand, I think, why you did what you did." His strides become shorter to match mine. "But this is some massive shite you've dealt me, and it's going to take me a long time to trust you again."

He's always thought things through. This is his valid conclusion.

"I should have told you the day I found out. I let this

big secret clog my soul for much too long. You're
welcome to keep staying over. It would be good for you
to get to know Kieran." I swallow. "If you want to. I
could stay with Gilly those nights so I wouldn't be in
your face."

"God, Una. If I want to?" He shakes his head at me
sadly. "But we have a lot to talk about." He stands there
gracelessly before giving me a limp hug. "I have to go to
Ellie. You tell me what you want me to do and I'll come
back to the shop so we can talk about it later tonight,
okay?" He looks into my eyes, the way he used to when
he knew I was upset, and pats my shoulder. "Want me to
walk a bit of the way back with you?"

I push the handles of my handbag farther up my
shoulder and shake my head. "No thanks—I know a
shortcut, and it'll take you out of your way. But thanks
again. It's a bit of a hike to St. James as it is."

"No worries." He puts a finger on the tip of my nose.
"And you'll let me know what you want me to do, right?
Promise?" He smiles that Cullen smile, the one that turns
up a little more on the right side of his face and reignites
a little part of my heart at the same time.

"Yeah, I will."

I DECIDED TO STAY PUT in Dublin this weekend
rather than go down to Cullen's place, what with
everything being so awkward. I stocked up on Tayto so
I'd have a packet or two waiting for him when he shows
up. A silly peace offering, but I always seem to turn to
food when I want to make someone happy. I can feel
myself moving around him like he's here but not here,
trying to keep quiet but wanting to be available if he
speaks.

"Thanks," he says when he sees the crisps. His eyes follow my hand wiping off the sink. "Are you having some?"

I grab a bag and sit at the end of the table.

"About what you did. Or what you didn't do." His fingers grip a crisp so tightly it cracks onto the table. I wither into the chair.

"I am so bloody feckin' angry, Una. At you, at myself." He cracks his fist on the table and I flinch. "I can't even let myself think about the last two years. I'm so scared of what I'll feel. I'm so angry at myself for believing you, but you gave me Ellie ..."

I can taste the salt from my tears on each side of my mouth, but I don't want to move my hand up to wipe them away in case he sees. But then I see his own tears splashing onto the tablecloth. He moves his finger in and out of a teardrop, finger-painting his pain.

"You took Kieran and destroyed what we had together, but you gave me Ellie," he whispers. More tears splash down. "Dammit, Una. Damn you." His shaky sigh fills the kitchen, and the stiffness leaves his chest and shoulders with it. He lifts his head and looks straight into my eyes. "And how can I take Ellie's pain away?"

I shake my head in reply. He can't. Just like I can't. But two people made Kieran that night, and I think that's part of his tears—his guilt over never telling Ellie we'd been together. "We both need to accept that we were idiots and move on," I say.

"Having sex with you wasn't idiotic," he says gently. "Being drunk and having no condom was idiotic. And what we both did and didn't say after—that was idiotic." He moves his hand around the corner of the table and squeezes mine.

"So," he says, "Ellie."

I start coughing on the crisp that's suddenly stuck in my airway.

"I hate the thought of my mam not being able to meet Kieran 'til Ellie says she's okay with it," he says, "but it is what it is. I've hurt her enough already."

I nod again, knocking back big gulps of tea at the thought of all of them knowing.

"And until then, you two come down every weekend and I can get to know Kieran a bit." His eyes start to fill up, but he wipes them away quickly. "I've a lot to catch up on."

I can feel my own eyes filling up too—for him, for Kieran—my shame rising higher and higher as I tell it to shut the feck up because I have no time for that too. He takes my hand again and bends his head down to look into my eyes. "I'm seriously sorry about what I said last week. I was so upset and confused. I'd trusted you for so long, and you showed another side of yourself I'd never seen before."

I pull my hand out of his and walk to the bin to put the crisp bags in it. "I've seen a lot of myself I've never seen before either. I'm not a fan of it all, to be honest."

He comes up behind me and rubs my shoulder. "Una, like I said, it is what it is. Let's walk forward from here and never run back there. It's not going to help either of us or Kieran or Ellie." We walk back to the table. "So will we leave it at this for now?"

I mark out the lines on the tablecloth. "Yeah." But I tell him about the rental offer on the building so he knows we'll only have a few weeks left of this, whatever it is.

June, 1985

THE MORNING ROLLS AROUND and I'm sort of ready for a completely new kind of Saturday. Cullen walks into the kitchen, all five foot ten of him with perfect hair and a V-neck that clings to his abs. My hands are moving to try to distract myself until I realize that for some reason, his presence does nothing to me. Why was I so afraid of it? I reach up to pull some hair over my ears to try and distract myself from staring though. I'm not a robot.

"Kieran, have you got your shoes on?" I yell. Of course he doesn't.

We eventually walk out together into the cloudy day. "I thought we'd walk down by the Ha'penny Bridge and maybe eat down there first?" He's looking for my permission. "There's a place there called the Bad Ass Café."

"Lead the way," I say to Cullen. Probably the first time I've ever said that.

This is really weird. I don't know where to walk—in front, behind, beside? Cullen's so quiet, but he looks like a natural pushing the buggy.

We walk into the café and I pick out a square table in the middle of the room. It's hard to know what to say, so we eat mostly in silence, Kieran breaking into it occasionally with some hand slaps on the table and some goofy grins at the faces Cullen makes.

We walk up O'Connell Street after, Kieran pointing out things in the windows and on the Floozie in the Jacuzzi monument, which we try to ignore, like good parents would. Every step we take is harder for me. We could have had this from the start. Now we have two years to catch up on and a forced relationship. We were good friends, but how close were we really when I didn't even trust him with something that huge?

At least the cinema leaves me time to sit back and forget about it all for a while, but as soon as it ends, we're back to dancing around each other again. We stop off in Eason's so Cullen can buy Kieran a book and then head back to the shop. Cullen sinks onto the sofa, likely the magnitude of his new life dawning.

I can almost hear his thoughts—how I always started things but let other people finish them so I could stay free and take every adventure. How the last two years have turned me into this functioning person who's lost her heart. I think he sees glimpses of it though. But I've kind of forgotten who that person is.

"We need to talk about going home." He's lying on the sofa, and I thought he had gone asleep. "As long as Ellie's getting better, let's go this weekend and then maybe we can go to your mam's Sunday morning after Mass."

This is what I was dreading, but maybe the fear was always bigger than the reality.

"Ellie's still mad at you, by the way. I'm surprised she's even talking to me, to be honest. She says it's more my fault because you weren't even home to ever tell her."

I agree to call the hospital to make sure Ellie will be okay and not go downhill in the few days we're gone. We plan our trip out over the next thirty minutes, and we're both drained over how it'll affect her, but it has to be done.

# 39

## Cullen

The bus pulls into Donegal Town by lunchtime on Saturday, and a taxi drops Una and Kieran off at her house first for less of a shock to Mam's ticker when he drops me off at my house after. No other cars in the driveway, thank God. Mam comes out to the front doorstep, flowery housecoat flapping in the wind.

"Cullen! Well, isn't this a lovely surprise?"

I give her a long squeeze. "I have a bit of news for you, Mam, and I wanted to tell you myself, so here I am."

"Come on in out of the wind. I'll put the kettle on."

She's asking me all about the job, but I have to tell her now, give her a bit of time to chew on the news. I need a second cup of tea for this. I pour a bit more hot water into the mug and start squeezing the old tea bag into it. She pushes the tin of biscuits in my direction.

"Mam," I say, "I have a bit of news for you. I only just found out about it or I would've told you ages ago, but, well, you see, it's like this. You have a grandson."

"What? What are you saying to me, son?" She looks at my face, puts her glasses down on the table. "Is it

Ellie's? So help me God, if you've knocked her up and her this sick ..."

I grab her hand and suddenly I can't speak. It's like someone has stuck nails all the way through my voice box from the outside in.

"Mam." I'm squeezing her hand so tightly. "His name is Kieran. He's a year old, and Una Gallagher is his mother."

She stands up in shock, her mug on its side making rivers across the table. "Dear God in heaven, Cullen. Jesus, Mary, and Joseph! What have you done?!" She runs to the sink and runs the cloth under the water.

"How old is he? How's all this going to work out with you and Una and little Kieran? Will we be able to see him much? And with you and Ellie after getting together, what happens now?"

I kiss her on the forehead while she's madly wiping up the mess on the table. "Ah, Mam, you're thinking too far ahead. Don't worry so much."

She puts a hand on a hip and waves the cloth at me. "As your mother, it's my job to worry. You come home for an hour and already you have a grandson for me and the mother is someone you never went out with ... or did you?" She looks into my eyes accusingly.

I put up a hand. "Ah, now, hold on to your knickers there. We're only after starting to talk. I'll tell you whatever I know when I know it, but right now, can you just be happy for me?"

"Right enough, but ..." She shakes her head at me but lifts it when she sees Una's mam dropping Una off at the gate.

"And her parents don't know he's mine yet, so don't go calling them until I tell you, okay?" She flaps her hand shut in my direction and hurries to the front door.

"Una! That's a fierce wind out there. Come in, come in. We all wondered what had happened to you, and now here you are on my doorstep." She bends down to pat Kieran's head. "And who's this little fellow?"

"This is Kieran," says Una. He gives her one of his Donny Osmond smiles and wobbles. Una can't look at me, but she gives Mam a shaky smile.

"Well then," Mam says, shutting the door behind them, "come on in to the kitchen. We were just having a cup of tea. Would you like one?" Cheers for Mam, acting like this happens every day.

Una sits at the end of our kitchen table with Kieran on her knee, me at the other end, but he soon hops off and sits on the floor to annoy the cat. The whitewashed version of our story is laid out on the table again, and Mam keeps looking from one face to the other. We don't act like we're mortal enemies because I don't even know what we are anymore. But I'm glad she's here.

"And now here we are," she finishes.

Mam reaches her arms out to Kieran. "Come here, pet. Let me have a look at you." She brushes his hair across the top of his head. "Oh, you're the spit of your dad all right. The spit of him." She turns to me and points. "Would ya look at that cowlick—right where yours is! Kieran," she says, "you can call me Nana."

He gives her a half smile and turns his head back to see where the cat escaped to.

"So you're both here." She looks back in my direction. "And Ellie's in Dublin."

No shit, Mam. Una gets up and puts her cup in the sink. She looks like she needs to get out of here, her face saying she's paid her dues, said her confessions, and now she can finally leave all of these secrets behind her. I give her the slightest of nods, like I get it. She shrugs and moves her eyes to Mam, who's on the floor now with Kieran, talking to him about the cat.

Kieran has missed so much by not knowing everyone. Una must be thinking the same because her eyes fill up with tears yet again. She turns away from the scene in front of her and wipes them away.

We say our goodbyes in the hallway and promise to come up as often as we can, and Una can't get out the door fast enough.

# 40

## Una

It's gorgeous outside, the blue sky carrying racing clouds all the way down to the bay, where the boats wave like tiny specks of dust from the briny waters under them. It revives my soul. Dublin just can't give me this—this kind of natural masterpiece on my doorstep.

"We need to talk." Cullen's snuck up right behind me. My heart rolls over in its box, and I suddenly feel like I'm back in school about to get in trouble. "I'll meet you in the woods at three, okay?"

I nod mutely. Now I have to wait for three hours to see what he has to say to me. After our last conversation, I'm not expecting it to be like a visit from Santa, that's for sure.

KIERAN'S CRAWLING AROUND the house with Ruthie, which is a huge relief—he doesn't mind me leaving.

The wind has died down a bit, and I watch my feet move slowly on the tarmac as I trudge down the road towards the woods. Our woods.

There's a thin trail that meanders uphill from the carpark. I lift my feet over familiar tree roots and smile wistfully at lovers' hearts knifed into trunks, but it makes me wonder why anyone thought bringing a penknife on a date would be a good idea. I come to the fork and turn right, which brings me to our small clearing. He's already there, sitting on a blanket he's brought. I hide for a minute, hoping he hasn't heard me. Seeing him brings up so much inside me. Every. Single. Time. I wanted all of him back then. I wanted to laugh with every joke he told, feel safe simply by his being near me, get his opinion on every random thought that went through my head. He was so patient with me, so kind, so thoughtful. Now I feel fondness, connection of a different sort. Not this craving to be part of him but still wanting to be part of the jigsaw of his life—integral, beautiful in its ups and downs and free of control.

"Una? I know you're here."

I sigh and walk over to where he's patting a spot for me on the blanket. I sit.

He sits there staring into the trees.

I gaze at his boots—the same Doc Martens he's always loved. I'm surprised they haven't fallen apart yet. Older, beaten up, well-worn. Like us.

"Ya know, Una, I get it, the whole running thing." He lifts a twig off the ground and starts twirling it through his fingers. "And I was really pissed about you wanting to stay away from here when family means so much to me. So then I tried to see it from your point of view. I thought about how afraid you were, how you were trying to protect people, trying to protect me. But we're all grown-ups, Una. We don't need you to stand guard."

He leaves his words to land where they may.

These woods, this spot among the leaves and twigs and birdsong, whisper through my being. Cullen is my last obstacle to absorbing this peace of old. My fortress hasn't served me well, and after the last twenty-four hours of stripping away the final pieces of the façade, I'd like to bulldoze it away forever.

"Thanks. I know what you're saying."

He stretches out a hand and grabs my four fingers. "Una, you're as annoying as hell sometimes, but I want my friend back. Ever since we met up and you told me about Kieran, when I ran off without even caring about what you were trying to do …"

I pull my hand out of his. My throat feels so, so tight. "I'm the one who fecked everything up, Cullen, and—"

He rolls his eyeballs. "Una! I just needed a bit of time to think through it all. You know what I'm like."

I crack a smile. "Yup."

"So we're good? We can be friends and we'll work out what me being in Kieran's life looks like long term?"

"Yeah."

"And you're ready to tell your parents now?"

I suck air but say yes. There's that roller coaster again, flying down the hill and heading for the turn.

He stands and starts rolling up the blanket, and then we walk across the field together just like old times.

MAM AND DAD were as shocked as parents could be but delighted at the same time but worried about Ellie too. That's the thing with parents—they think all their worries will somehow save the world. All the same, the rest of the weekend flies by and as we're leaving, Kieran's crying, so are Mam and Dad, and I'm here trying to make it all okay. But it *is* all okay. We've come home. We'll come home again. And all the knots in my life have come undone and I'm holding my kite, wondering if it will catch the wind when I throw it into the sky. Well, almost all of the knots.

Kieran lifts his legs as high as he can to make it up the steps into the bus. I follow him and look out through the window to wave again, only to look down at Kieran after and see him running his arm up and down his dripping nose. I grab his arm and march him to the middle of the bus. I can't give him a lecture, so I just give him the "look," because I have to look like a great mother in public. He gets the message and pushes himself against the window to get one last sighting of Mam and Dad. They're still waving, God love 'em.

WE'RE AFTER STOPPING in Cavan for a loo stop and are back on the road, Cullen giving me part two on what I missed over the last two years. He's just the same Cullen, but being away from him had given him magical powers in my head, which I'm not seeing anymore. He's just a lovely guy who I'm lucky enough to be friends with.

"What?" he says, stopping in the middle of talking about his job.

"I was just thinking about how perfect Ellie is for you."

His face lights up. "Yeah, she really is, isn't she?" Then he reaches out both arms for Kieran. "My turn."

I hand him over and fall gently back into the bus seat, so much peace filling up my insides. I did the right thing.

FOR SOME REASON Gilly is waiting for us at the bus stop, her face empty of its usual glow. I stop the buggy in front of her. "What's wrong? Are you okay?"

She reaches out and puts a hand on each shoulder, facing Cullen at the same time. "It's Ellie."

I can't find a way to let air into my lungs.

"I'll watch Kieran," she says, her words like shadows. "Your parents are on their way there."

We share no words as we make our way across town. What is there to say?

# 41

## Ellie

The doc was right. This could be it. Life was so beautiful, so magical. It's been good. Sitting beside me is my Cullen, smiling his sad smile, Una behind him. "I need to talk to Una," I say.

He clears out, feet shuffling like I'm already gone, like there's no life to be had in here. I disagree. As long as I have breath, there's life. Una's eyes are fixed on me. She's ready to do anything to make things right.

"Una."

She leans in, fingers on mine.

"Yes, I was so angry with both of you. Yes, you're a big eejit. But it's done. Hindsight is foresight with no return. And you came back for Cullen but left again for my sake when you saw us together. You never said another word. You're a good sister, even though that was really dumb."

She gives a choked laugh.

"Life is always changing, Una. Just accept what's been, what is right now, what's coming. Do my living for me, okay? Love Kieran, love Cullen. Feel each moment and live it."

She opens her arms and wraps them around me. "I will," she blubbers into the folds of my gown. "I will."

A nurse comes in. "We're going to try to buck things up with this plasma your sister just donated. I've warmed it up a little."

I give Una a thumbs-up. She holds up crossed fingers. I hold up two praying hands. We smile.

It's still running into my veins when Cullen comes in. I brush his finger with my thumb. It's wet. So are his eyes. "You should sleep," I say. "And have you even eaten yet?"

He laughs halfheartedly.

"It's okay that you didn't tell me about that night with Una. You were afraid." I wipe my sweaty forehead with the back of my hand. "This hot bod was too much for you." I move my fingers to my ring finger and take off the claddagh ring. "I need you to hold on to this for me though. My hand is swelling a bit, and I don't want them to cut it off me for anything."

His hand stiffens, but then he opens it up.

"And don't you dare blame Una for this turn of events. They said this could happen."

He nods, staring at the ring as he twiddles it between his fingers, face morose. Silence for a moment. The chair scrapes back with a violent jerk. He shakes his fist in the air and he slams it back down on his thigh with a quiet scream.

"Ah, Cullen. Don't you be worrying about me. Nothing can hurt me now. I've reached angelic status." He doesn't turn around. "That was a joke, by the way. Me an angel? Ha!"

He lets the air out of his lungs and turns to me.

"Pretty damn close. So don't you bloody well die on me, okay?"

"Got it. No dying."

He sits down again and sketches his finger around every part of my face. "Okay, Ellie Belly. I'm going to hold you to that." He drops his lips onto my hot forehead and he keeps them there until I tell him he needs to stop hogging the visiting hours.

Mam and Dad come in last. Dad kisses me on the forehead and strokes my head fuzz, Mam gives me a long, wet hug. They sit with me until the night nurse comes in to do my vitals.

"I think we're good for tonight. Go home and get a good sleep. We'll call if we think you should come in."

Mam shifts in the chair. Dad looks at her.

I agree. Who can sleep? But they slowly push themselves to their feet and keep looking at me as they back out the door.

# 42

## Una

We're all at the flat above the shop in different rooms, trying to sleep but listening for the phone. Cullen's on the floor beside me.

I stay there on my side staring at his outline in the dingy night, his chest rising and falling on its way into another world where people don't die and those you love don't lie. I think about Ellie in her hospital bed, hoping, praying my plasma will somehow override her own system and tell it to get its act together—something I've been telling myself all my life, but it hasn't worked too well. Do my living for me, she said. How can I even begin to match her life of making everyone around her smile?

WE'RE ALL BLEARY EYED, sitting around the table eating toast and marmalade, drinking tea, silent in happiness after calling the hospital and hearing that she's hanging on. They want me to donate more blood and give it to her as soon as possible, so I'll do that and hope to God it makes a difference. Gilly's got Kieran, so we

291

all get the bus down, and apart from my brief hour giving blood, sit in the waiting room for the morning. Plastic floor, plastic chairs, even plastic flowers. No life in any of it, but it serves its purpose.

Dad's about to get us all sandwiches from the machine in the canteen when Dr. Hooper walks in. Cullen jumps up. I sit forward on my chair.

"Una, is it?" He reaches out a hand to shake mine. "It looks like your plasma helped overnight. Her bloodwork is looking a small bit better. Here's hoping your next donation will keep her on the mend." He puts his hand back in his pocket and addresses all of us. "Things are still up-and-down here, but we're watching her carefully. Go on home, and we'll call if we need to."

For some reason my mind travels back to history class with Mr. Matthews. Mount Vesuvius gave so many warnings before the eruption, and when she blew, she covered Europe in ash. That's what my heart was ready for—death and ashes, with a huge helping of shame. But why did I preemptively choose this position as the scapegoat, the receiver of blame for Ellie's death? I can change what's in my head.

*Ellie will live and not die.*

*I will live and not die of shame.*

I look around the room at all our bodies standing up and getting ready to get back to the shop—Mam, Dad, Cullen—and I want us all to stay together as one cohesive unit in this. I want our combined hope to somehow reach heaven and will Ellie to get through this because if I've learned anything these days, it's that family is stronger than everything. But the face I need most of all isn't among them. *Feel each moment and live it.* It's like her words are breathing life into my tainted heart.

*Live it. Live it. Live it.*

My fingertips run over the cover of the romance novel she gave me. She said she loved it because it was full of so much hope, so much possibility.

*Live it. Live it. Live it.*

I jump up, frantic. Here I am, sitting, waiting, ready to do anything I can to help Ellie fight for her life, but I've been passive about letting others dictate what happens in my own. Mam said I had to give up the baby; I let her words take precedence and ran rather than fight. And I didn't fight for love. I avoided the crash, let all the bricks fall, and waited for people to hand me new ones rather than forge my own. But now my hands, my mouth, my brain are all fighting each other when they need to run *to* life. *Get in line, body. This one's for me.*

"Here's the key to the flat, Mam. Help yourselves to the food and everything. There's something I have to do." I don't even wait to see their reaction and pelt out the waiting room door.

A phone call later and I'm on my way into town, pulling bits of my hair ends with both hands every time the bus stops and starts. I jump off at the Bank of Ireland and nearly lose a shoe on the turn into the arch at Trinity. The cafeteria is a long run over timeworn cobblestones to the back buildings of the college, and the sweat has collected in what feels like a thick film under my clothes as I head for its double doors.

"UNA!" a voice behind me shouts.

Cullen runs up, panting. "I had to get a taxi to follow the bus and then leg it after you, but Ellie and I can't lose you, Una. Don't run. Don't leave us. We can't go through that again."

He stops. "No, no, no, not like that! Feck. I'm not saying this very well." He rubs a hand through his hair. "I need you, Una.

"Feck. I'm really making a shagging mess of this." He takes a deep breath. "I love Ellie with my life, but you're my best friend. I want 'us' back—you and now our boy. I want your support, your presence." He bends forward, fighting for breath. "God, Una. Please say you won't run again!"

I put both hands around his neck and stare into his eyes. "Cullen. My friend. I'll tell you why I'm here in a few minutes, but right now I need you to stand at that statue over there and wait for me, okay?"

He frowns but makes his way to the base of it, and I walk through the doors into the smell of roasted coffee beans and intellectualism.

He's easy to find—his blond hair and familiar height pop out between the heads leaning over book pages and coffee cups. I slow down walking towards him. What do I say now? But the second I stop in front of him and his eyes lift up to mine, my salty tears pour out.

He stands up.

I wrap my arms around him, cling to his chest, baptize his T-shirt in wet love.

He lifts hair away from my face and strokes my cheek with his forefinger. "You came back," he says. "But I always told myself that if you ever did, I'd tell you I was a big eejit to make you choose between me and Cullen. He's family. Nothing's more important than that." He hesitates.

I look back at him with a big smile on my face, eyes wide, and in response he leans forward for my lips. *Finally* we kiss in one of the many ways I've dreamed of for months, all softness and excitement and need, but a tamed-down version thanks to all the onlookers.

I tell him briefly about Ellie and how I need to go back ASAP, and he immediately puts his books in his bag and walks out with me. We're walking back to the entrance, his arm tight around me, but he stops when he sees what's ahead.

"I see Cullen followed you here. Does he feel the same way about me?"

I can't help but respond with a loud laugh, but I give Cullen a wave and point at Robbie.

He gets it.

I get it too. I've finally set Cullen free.

# 43

## Una

Catherine shows up on Monday. We celebrated Ellie's breakthrough on the phone and how it looks like she'll be okay, but Catherine's studying my face now like it's a comedy trailer.

"Is there something else you're not telling me?"

My smile almost reaches my ears. "Robbie."

She shrieks and claps her hands together. "Oh, Una, that's the second-best thing I've heard in the last few days!"

I fill her in, Kieran more than me in single words and gobbledygook. Once he's out of words, Catherine scratches his little back until he finally looks sleepy enough to have a nap. Then we move into the kitchen. Catherine gets out the Tupperware of lemon slices Mam made before she left, and we nibble on them as she talks.

"So, Una, about the building."

Now I can feel my insides squirming. "Is something wrong?"

"The opposite!" she says happily. "We left things to where we had to rent out the building to slowly pay off the debt, but things have changed now. It turns out that your Robbie has been helping David this whole time without telling us and was able to do a whole load of stuff that really impressed David. SO!" She lets out a massive laugh.

I'm jointly melting at hearing about Robbie's help and surprised at Catherine laughing so loudly. I don't often see her this free with herself.

"I'm suddenly loaded!" she shrieks. "We got the assets from that shyster and they include *six houses. Six!* Can you believe it?"

My eyes feel like they've left their sockets. "You what? They got everything? Six frigging houses!"

"Lucky for us," she says, "he bought them a long time ago, so even though their value is low now, the loans on them are much lower. He thought he'd hidden them well enough away, but he was no match for our fella and Robbie. *They were brilliant.*

"So here's where it gets fantastic." She starts almost bouncing but puts the lemon slice down first before clapping her hands together again. "Two of them are huge cottages in Enniskerry sitting together on about three acres! They're the most gorgeous cottages you've ever seen off one of those windy roads near the Powerscourt Waterfall, and they're not too far of a drive from us. And we're giving you, our adopted daughter and grandson, the offer to live in one of them rent free for life; and you can rent out the other one for us, and two more in Kilmacud, and live off their income until their value picks up again and this awful recession is over. We need you to be the property manager.

"I'll sell the last two houses now to pay off the loans, and the rent on the building in town will be more than enough to cover Des's care. I'll have a dazzling retirement while you can do whatever you want. It all makes so much sense."

I gasp. "I can't. I can't take that much from you and Des."

She squeezes my chin tightly. "You can and you will, Una, dear. I know I said it was an offer, but I lied. This is not negotiable.

"Again, I'm delighted for all your great news. It's a fabulous time to be alive, now isn't it?" She giggles like a little schoolgirl and rubs her hands together before skipping off to the bathroom.

I'm flabbergasted. I'll never be worthy of anything she's done for me, but that's the thing with family—it doesn't matter what you think of your own value; if they see it in you and want to give, you have to let them have their happiness and bury your own pride.

# 44

## Una

Gillian and I took a break from it all, and we're sitting in her classroom while Kieran and Ashlinn scrape chalk on the blackboard. "God, you're a property manager about to live in posh Enniskerry with a gorgeous view. And to think I knew you when." She reaches back to slap Ashlinn's leg so she'll stop dragging her nails down the board. "I don't think I'm ever going to know someone as posh as you."

"I haven't a clue what to do, but I'm delighted."

"You're so boring. Here I was thinking you'd be off to Ibiza on the rent deposits for the next three weeks with your best friend. I'm disappointed in you, Una Gallagher. Really."

"The other two haven't even rented yet! So, much as I'd love that, I have to at least wait until those deposits are in my hands."

"So what's Robbie got to say about all this then? Aul' lover boy." She smirks and jabs me with her elbow.

"Pretty much the same as you—that he's gentry now and he'll never live it down."

She hits my arm. "You're the lucky one. He's a great fella."

A smile blasts across my face. "Yeah."

She blinks a few times and clears her throat. "Listen, Una, I'm going to say something, but you need to hear me out. All this beating yourself up isn't healthy for anyone, especially you, and I don't think you're going to be able to enjoy all this good stuff unless you deal with it." She leans over to pick up a piece of chalk but keeps talking.

"You didn't wake up that morning in your bed at home and think to yourself, Hey, today will be a great day to destroy everyone's life. You did what felt right in the moment. You did what you did to protect people."

She looks me in the eye. "You have a good heart, Una. You care about people a lot. And you need to accept that you're a normal person who sometimes messes up and that's okay."

My eyes feel a bit wet.

"I can see you think I'm full of shite, but, Una, if I had done the same thing, you wouldn't destroy me with the words I know go around your head. So why should you treat yourself any differently when you have just as much value as I do? You wouldn't rip me to shreds every day; don't do it to yourself."

I can feel a catch in my throat and nod. "Okay," I whisper. "Okay."

She grabs my hand. "Good girl. Now go rent out those two houses, and I'll be keeping an eye on the postman for my tickets to Ibiza."

# 45

## Cullen

Kieran's been waiting for me. I can see his little face squished in the front window glass. He gives me a big wave and runs to the door.

"Fwree houses!" he yells through the crack before I can even make it in.

"What?" I look over at Una by the till.

"Yes. It's so exciting. I'll tell you all about it on the way." We walk out and wait while she locks the door before following the curve of the streets out to Grafton Street and straight into McD's queue, her excited hands and words all dancing together in the sunlight.

"So there you have it—by next month we'll be in Enniskerry."

We order our food and I sit Kieran on a booster seat at a table.

"I've been thinking a lot," she says, as she puts each person's food on the table from the tray, "and I'd love your opinion on some of my ideas. I want to do what's best for Kieran, you know, but this is a once-in-a-lifetime kind of thing, so I can't banjax it all. I haven't told any of them at home, but ..." She pauses and looks up at me. "... I've been thinking of how lovely it is to have you near Kieran, and I was wondering if—" Her eyes are so hopeful.

"You want me to move next door? After all these years of trying to stay away?"

"Yeah, I know, but I have a lot of time to make up for with that one. And after Gilly telling me off about all my regrets, I really want to look ahead more instead of back, and look at all the possibilities in myself instead of my failures."

She looks over at Kieran. "Here's the thing, Cullen, I was thinking of forming a sort of community where artisans and craftsmen could come together and make stuff and then sell it on-site, and teach about it too. Like a teaching craft village with a shop. And we'd have local competitions and workshops and call it something like Ennis Village. Ellie could even have a place to do hair and makeup for short film scenes there.

"I know you might think this is an Ellie kind of harebrained idea that's come out of nowhere, but I've always had this idea of teaching people how to work with different materials and design their own stuff. I got the idea from all those kids we've had at the shop over the last year or so. I always felt so happy doing those little school trips, and I think we could age it up and expand it so we can help creative people get their work seen and appreciated too.

"Gillian loves the idea. She says as soon as she gets her teaching degree, she's going to bring a class every year, and get every other teacher in the school to bring their classes too."

"Wait. We?"

"Well, yeah. Would you be interested at all in helping me with it? You wouldn't have to if you didn't want to," she says, the words rushing out of her mouth quickly, "but I'd love to do it with you—have a forge there, work with the schools and all that. And Kieran would love having you next door." Her whole body is getting more animated, her smile is bigger, her words are flowing. "And it would make being his parents so bloody easy!"

I push my cold chips away from me. "Sounds great. Where do I sign?"

"Oh God, really? You'd really do that for me?"

"Well, I'd be doing it for me too. Una, I don't want you to move somewhere with Kieran where it's really hard for me to spend time with him or have him for the weekend. We're only after finding each other, and to be honest, I can't waste more time. And me with my own forge? That'd be brilliant."

She's all chuffed. "Ah, but you're a lovely dad, Cullen Breslin. A lovely, talented man. My sister's lucky to have you."

Kieran's already pointing at the ice cream machine. He runs to it and looks around to see if we're watching. I give him a wink. He's an easy kid to love. So's his aunty, and so worth it.

# 1986

# Epilogue

## Una

## July

It's been a long day, what with the business workshop this morning and the art by the glass sessions this afternoon that Ellie's friend Nathalie teaches, but my heart is so full. I walk from building to building on this hill and look up at the Sugar Loaf lying on his back like a man with a cold, while at the same time trying to hold down the wind slapping my hair around my face. I've long since grown it out—have to keep up with this Celtic look for the tourists.

A silver car creaks and rattles up the lane towards me, and when it pulls to a stop, out jumps Kieran. Mam climbs out of the driver's seat a bit more slowly. "That boy of yours'll be the death of me someday. But not today, love." She pulls her cardigan down over her skirt to get rid of its rumpled state from the drive over. "So how did it go?"

"It was a great class, but I probably shouldn't have

had that last bit of wine. Hated to see it go to waste; you know how it is." I giggle.

"Should have called me. I would have had no problem 'helping' you." We cackle like two hens.

Cullen walks over to Kieran and rubs his back. I still love looking at the two of them together. Kieran catches me staring at him and sticks his tongue out at me before they disappear into our office together.

"Una," says Mam, "Cullen and I've done our best getting the house ready for Ellie, but he's too much bachelor stuff in the house still. Can you not take one thing?"

"Sorry, Mam." I feel sorry for Ellie trying to persuade him to get rid of his knickknacks. They have so many wedding presents already.

She sighs, muttering to herself. "They just grow up too fast."

"Let's go on up to the house. Get out of the wind," I say.

We climb into the Rattler, as we lovingly call Mam's car, and let it climb up the lane a bit farther before we park by the line of trees at the edge of the garden. We walk past all the wildflowers Kieran, Ellie, and I planted last year, and on into the cottage I'm still renovating.

Mam heads to the sink with the kettle while I get a knife to the envelope that was on the mat when we walked in. It's not long.

Una,

I got Ellie's wedding invitation today. Isn't life so wonderful that we get to look back at the past differently and see how much love we've let fill our *lives? I'm delighted you're so happy and that we were able to help in our own small way before Des passed on. It's given my life a purpose I never expected, and I'm all the more grateful for Des and me being on this earth in the right place at the right time for you. Worth every minute, I'd say.*

*Anyway, I'll stop my rambling. Looking forward to your next visit with Kieran.*

*Love you,*

*Catherine*

It doesn't take much to make me cry. Robbie did it just the other day when he put this gorgeous engagement ring on my finger that one of our artisans helped him make from his rough drawing. I reach out for a tissue and hand the letter to Mam, who adds her sniffles to mine. "Such a lovely woman. You're so lucky to have her."

I kiss her cheek. "I'm lucky to have you, Mam."

She presses the crumbs on the table with her finger. "Ah, get away with you."

"It's true, Mam, you've done your best with all of us, and now look at you—about to have a life full of nappies and baby smells again, if Robbie has his way, and who knows with Ellie? The doctors could be wrong about that too."

She laughs loudly. "The whole brood has me set for babysitting! They're going to have to build a better road from Donegal to Dublin."

"Ah, no one better." I pull the chair in tighter and

put my arm around her back. We sit there until the kettle boils.

Who knew three years ago I'd be in my own place with an adorable boy and the man who keeps me laughing signing up for life with me? I thought my life was over, yet it had barely begun.

Family is a strange thing, but I always had the choice to flow with it and embrace the messiness or act like I knew better. At sixteen, I wasn't quite used to letting my heart be so connected to everyone who loves me, but now it's older, wiser. Yes, my heart went walking. *But now it's come back home.*

> *You are the road of love and at the end, my*
> *home.*
> *—Rumi*

If you enjoyed this book, please review it on your favorite book review sites! It would mean a LOT to the author.

# ACKNOWLEDGMENTS

I set this book in Donegal after visiting it many times with my husband, who spent some of his teenage years there. Its extravagant beauty of beaches, mountains, history, and people is unparalleled. My father-in-law's (George Hanan) legacy lives on there in the Donegal Railway Heritage Centre, where visitors can see his incredible scale model railway and paintings.

Una's story is a fictional one, but I grew up in Ireland and placed Una and Cullen in some of my favorite spots as I wrote. I studied nursing at the Adelaide Hospital in Dublin, and this is where I placed Ellie for one of her many doctor's appointments. I also worked in St. Luke's Hospital for a while, a real place with great cancer treatments and nursing care for adults of any age.

So many people have helped me bring this book from the first idea of the plot to the day it went live, so there is no one editor, beta reader, or author I can primarily thank. It truly is the result of a lot of wonderful people. My sad brain is terrible at remembering names, so while I can remember many, I'm terrified of leaving someone important out. That said, thank you so much:

FaithWriters writing friends, who I had so much fun with once I started writing for real and who gave such excellent feedback on my Writing Challenge entries every week.

Pitch Wars mentors Jessica Calla and Leonie Kelsall, for your kind words about my writing. You encouraged me by saying this novel was worthy of publication.

Editing team, you added so much sense and depth to my story and turned it into what it is today. Steph Morgan, your input at the end helped everything make sense. Rebecca Alexander, you're a genius.

Fellow Facebook #pitchwarriors writers, going through this writing journey with your help is amazing. Morgan Hazelwood, you're doing such a great job in running it.

Wattpad fellow writers, thank you for your comments on my stories and the great chats about Irish weather and whiskey.

Beta readers, there are so many of you to thank, and every one of you made this book stronger, funnier, and better.

Literary agents who made the time to say nice things about the book, thank you, even though you felt you couldn't sell it.

Facebook friends who cheered me on—so, so many of you!

And Gerry, my one and only. Thank you for your fantastic support of my writing and for patiently listening to everything I read aloud for your opinion, even though you don't like reading.

# ABOUT THE AUTHOR

Sally Hanan grew up in Ireland and became a nurse, but she left all the big family dinners, rain, and cups of tea when she and her husband won a green card lottery and moved to Texas. Her family now raised, she works as a book editor and occasional lay counselor and life coach. Sally lives near Austin, Texas, in a gorgeous 1930's home with her "hunk of burning love" husband and their spoiled-rotten doggie.

Also a writer of flash fiction, nonfiction, and poetry, Sally has won numerous awards for her writing in smaller competitions. *My Heart Went Walking* is Sally Hanan's debut novel, and she is grateful it's a good one because, as she puts it, the four novels that came before it turned out to be practice runs.

Readers can visit her website at www.sallyhanan.com for more information about her books and writing life, and to subscribe to her mailing list.

# Reader's Discussion Points

1. Una often takes too much responsibility for other people's reactions or potential reactions (her mom's and Cullen's) and that makes her behave in ways that inadvertently make things worse and hurt herself and others. She feels the need to make her decisions primarily to manage other people's feelings. Have you ever enabled others to not take responsibility for their own mistakes?

2. Do you think Una was right to not tell Cullen about his child? How do you think she could have handled it better?

3. Cullen accepted Una's story as the truth only to wonder later if he'd been right. How have you refined your radar for truth over the years?

4. Des and Catherine welcomed Una. Have you ever welcomed "strangers" into your home? How did it turn out?

5. Cullen felt bad about liking Ellie. Did he owe Una anything based on their long friendship and what she had told him? Do you ever do things out of obligation only to later realize it was a mistake?

6. Una could have remained silent once she left home, but she called twice and sent a note. How important is connection to you, even when someone disappoints you greatly? How hard do you try to keep connections open?

7. Cullen went to a lot of trouble to find Una. How hard has it been for you to find old friends and others who mattered a great deal to you in the past?

8. Una forgives her mother for forcing her hand. Ellie forgives Cullen and Una. What does forgiveness mean to you?

9. Ellie got very sick, almost to the point of death. In that situation, what would you have done to help each person emotionally and mentally, should they have asked for help? Has your help ever been rejected? Have you ever rejected someone else's help?

10. Ellie talks about living life fully alive. If you were to live your life this way, what would change?

11. As time passes, Una starts to speak up for herself and lead the way (with the lawyer, with Robbie) rather than go with the flow. What do you think made her find her voice? Has there been any time in your life when you had to speak up? How did it go?

12. Gilly is a very honest but practical friend. What do you appreciate about friends who say exactly what they think, or do you avoid those kinds of people?

13. What do you think of the final choice Una made in love?

14. Una is very hard on herself and can't seem to get over her mistakes and past decisions. What have you done to be kind to yourself lately?

15. Things worked out for Una in the end, but many times in life, they do not. Do you think having Ellie's overall positive attitude could ever change your own circumstances?

# OTHER BOOKS BY SALLY

## Flash Fiction

## Nonfiction

## Children's Books

*No Cat on My Back* (forthcoming)

CPSIA information can be obtained
at www.ICGtesting.com
Printed in the USA
LVHW032028280122
709649LV00004B/109/J